CW00927143

The EARLY HOURS

A novel by

MARMADUKE PICKTHALL

with a new foreword by
Abdal Hakim Murad

First published 1921 by W. Collins Sons & Co. Ltd.
Reprinted 2010 by
The Muslim Academic Trust
32 London Road
Cambridge CB22 7QH
United Kingdom

Distributed by
Central Books Ltd
www.centralbooks.co.uk

ISBN 978-1-902350-10-3

Foreword and glossary to this edition © 2010 Abdal Hakim Murad
Designed by Abdallateef Whiteman
Printed by: Mega Basım Yayın San. ve Tic. A.Ş. Istanbul, Turkey

Foreword

Marmaduke Pickthall: a biographical sketch

MARMADUKE PICKTHALL (1875-1936), one of the most popular novelists of his generation, was also among the most unusual and original. Defying conventional wisdom on almost every subject, he used his deceptively conservative prose to present views on politics, gender, and religion which conformed neither to the Edwardian mainstream nor to any contemporary strand of dissident culture. Of course, an attraction to the Orient was hardly new, and was even a recognized convention, but unlike Byron, Burton, Doughty and others fascinated by 'the splendour and havoc of the East' he took the view that the best of Ottoman culture derived from religion. His Turcophilia was rooted in religious faith of a kind which eluded most serious writers of his age. For him, a culture's most precious possession was trust in God, and this the East had preserved, while the West was throwing it away in the name of Progress.

Pickthall's devout humility did not prevent him from taking pride in his ancestry, which he could trace back to a knight of William the Conqueror's day, Sir Roger de Poictu, from whom his odd surname derives. The family, long settled in Cumberland, came south during the reign of William III, and Pickthall's father Charles, an Anglican parson, held a living near Woodbridge in

Suffolk. Charles's wife, whom he married late in life, was Mary O'Brien, a staunch Nonconformist despite her Irish name. She took pride in being the daughter of Admiral Donat Henry O'Brien, a hero of the same Napoleonic war which (though the story is disputed) brought Sheikh Abdullah Quilliam's grandfather fame as first lieutenant of *Victory* at Trafalgar. O'Brien, immortalised by Marryat in *Masterman Ready*, seems to have passed on some of his heroic impulses to his grandson Marmaduke, who throughout his life cherished a rather Shavian ideal of the righteous warrior. It is interesting that Pickthall, Quilliam and, before them, Lord Byron, who all found their vocations as rebellious lovers of the East, were the grandsons of naval heroes.

Marmaduke was born in 1875, and when his father died five years later the family sold the Suffolk rectory and moved to the capital. For the little boy the trauma of the exodus from a country idyll to a cold and cheerless house in London felt like a deep blow to the soul, and his later delight in the outdoors, which runs through all his novels, may have owed much to that early formative transition. The claustrophobia intensified when he entered Harrow, whose arcane rituals and fagging system he was later to send up in his novel *Sir Limpidus*. Friends were his only consolation: perhaps his closest was Winston Churchill.

Once the sloth and bullying of Harrow were behind him he was able to indulge a growing range of youthful passions. In the Jura he acquired his lifelong love of mountaineering, and in Wales and Ireland he learned Welsh and Gaelic. His remarkable gift for languages moved his teachers to put him forward for a Foreign Office vacancy; yet he failed the exam. Undismayed, he proposed to Muriel Smith, the girl who was to become his wife. She accepted, only to lose her betrothed for several years thanks to one of the sudden picaresque changes of direction which were to mark his later career. Hoping to learn enough Arabic to land a consular job in Palestine, and with introductions in Jerusalem, Pickthall had sailed for Port Said. He was not yet eighteen years old.

The Orient came as a revelation. Later in life he wrote: 'When I read *The Arabian Nights* I see the daily life of Damascus, Jerusalem, Aleppo, Cairo, and the other cities as I found it in the early nineties of the last century. What struck me, even in its decay and poverty, was the joyousness of that life compared with anything that I had seen in Europe. The people seemed quite independent of our cares of life, our anxious clutching after wealth, our fear of death.' He found a khoja to teach him more Arabic, and armed with a rapidly increasing fluency took ship for Jaffa, where, to the horror of European residents and missionaries, he donned native garb and disappeared into the Palestinian hinterland.

Some of his experiences in the twilight of Ottoman Asia may be glimpsed in his travelogue, *Oriental Encounters*. He had found, as he explains, a world of freedom unimaginable to a public schoolboy raised on an almost idolatrous passion for the State. Most Palestinians never set eyes on a policeman, and lived for decades without engaging with government in any way. Islamic law was administered in its time-honoured fashion by qadis who, with the exception of the Istanbul graduates in the great cities, were local men. Villages chose (or inherited) their own headmen, and the same was true for the wild Bedouin clans. The population revered and loved the Sultan-Caliph in faraway Istanbul, but understood that it was not his place to interfere with their lives.

It was this freedom, as much as intellectual assent, which set Marmaduke on the long pilgrimage which was to lead him to Islam. He saw the Muslim world before Westernisation had reshaped the lives of the masses, and long before it had infected Muslim political thought to produce the modern vision of the 'Islamic State', with its ideology and centralised bureaucracy. That totalitarian nightmare he would not have recognised as Muslim. The deep faith of the Levantine peasantry which so amazed him was sustained by the sincerity that can only come when men are free, not forced, in the practice of religion. For the state to compel compliance is to spread vice and disbelief; as the Arab proverb which he well-knew says: 'If camel-dung were to be prohibited, people would seek it out.'

Throughout his life Pickthall appears to have seen Islam as a radical freedom, a freedom from the encroachments of the State as much as from the claws of the ego. But he also believed that it offered freedom from narrow fanaticism and sectarian bigotry. Late Ottoman Palestine was teeming with missionaries of every Christian sect, each convinced, in those pre-ecumenical days, of its own solitary rightness. He was appalled by the hate-filled rivalry of the sects, which, he thought, should at least be united in the land holy to their faith. But Christian Jerusalem was a maze of rival shrines and liturgies, where punches were frequently thrown in churches, while the Jerusalem of Islam was gloriously united under the Dome, which seemed like the physical crown of the city and of her complex history.

1897 found him in Damascus, then a quiet city of lanes, hidden rose-bowers, and walnut trees. It was in this deep peacefulness, resting from his adventures, that he worked methodically through the mysteries of Arabic grammar. He read poetry and history; but seemed drawn, irresistibly, to the Koran. Initially led to it by curiosity, he soon came to suspect that he had unearthed the end of the Englishman's eternal religious quest. The link seems to have been Thomas Traherne and Gerrard Winstanley, who, with their nature mysticism and insistence on personal freedom from an intrusive state or priesthood, had been his inspiration since his early teens. Now their words seemed to be bearing fruit.

Winstanley is an important key to understanding Pickthall's writings. His 1652 masterpiece, *Law of Freedom on a Platform*, had been the manifesto of the Digger movement, the most radical offshoot of Leveller Protestantism. In this book, which deeply shaped the soul of the young Pickthall, Winstanley outlined what was to become the essence of Christian Socialism. The Diggers believed in the holiness of labour, coming by their name when, in 1649, they took over a plot of waste land at Walton-on-Thames, planting corn, beans and parsnips. This gesture was, Pickthall realised in Damascus, illegal in Christendom, but was precisely the Shari'a principle of *ihya al-mawat*, gaining entitlement to land by reviving it after its 'death by neglect'. The Diggers were held together, not by cowed obedience to a religious state, but by love among themselves, fired and purified by the dignity of labour.

It soon became clear to Pickthall that their Dissenting theology, which moved far beyond Calvin in its rejection of original sin and orthodox Trinitarian doctrine, and in its emphasis on knowing God through closeness to nature, was precisely the message of Islam. This was a religion for autonomous communities, self-governing under a single God, each free to elect its own minister. *The Early Hours*, while not disrespectful of the imperial past, seeks to combine Pickthall's love of rural life with an enthusiasm for the levelling and apparently liberating programme of the Young Turks.

Another Digger theme which attracted Pickthall was a communitarian optimism. The brotherhood of Muslims which Pickthall observed in Syria, the respect between Sunnis and Shi'is, and their indifference to class distinctions in their places of worship, seemed to be the living realisation of the dreams of English radicals at the time of Cromwell's Commonwealth. This theme of Muslim brotherhood was to be fundamental in Pickthall's later writing and preaching. No less important was the Digger rejection of traditional Church exclusivism. Irrespective of creed, they thought, all men were candidates for salvation. Christ's sacrifice indicated, in its orthodox understanding, a meanness unworthy of a loving God, Who can surely accept the repentance of any faithful monotheist, whether or not he had been bathed in the blood of His son.

In an odd way, then, Pickthall came home in Damascus. The picaresque adventures of his days in Palestine had given way to a serious spiritual and intellectual quest. He seems to have identified in Islam the fulfilment of the English dream of a reasonable and just religion, free of superstition and metaphysical mumbo-jumbo, and bearing fruit in a wonderful and joyful fellowship. Hence, perhaps, his relaxed attitude to his own religious transformation. As the *New Statesman* put it in 1930: 'Mr

Marmaduke Pickthall was always a great lover of Islam. When he became a Muslim it was regarded less as conversion than as self-discovery.'

If such was his Road to Damascus, why, then, did the teenage Pickthall hold back? Some have thought that the reason was his concern for the feelings of his aged mother, with her own Christian certainties. But here is his later explanation:

> The man who did not become a Muslim when he was nineteen years old because he was afraid that it would break his mother's heart does not exist, I am sorry to say. The sad fact is that he was anxious to become a Muslim, forgetting all about his mother. It was his Muslim teacher—the Sheykh-ul-Ulema of the great mosque at Damascus—a noble and benign old man, to whom he one day mentioned his desire to become a Muslim, who reminded him of his duty to his mother and forbade him to profess Islam until he had consulted her. 'No, my son,' were his words, 'wait until you are older, and have seen again your native land. You are alone among us as our boys are alone among the Christians. God knows how I should feel if any Christian teacher dealt with a son of mine otherwise than as I now deal with you.' […] If he had become a Muslim at that time he would pretty certainly have repented it—quite apart from the unhappiness he would have caused his mother, which would have made him unhappy—because he had not thought and learnt enough about religion to be certain of his faith. It was only the romance and pageant of the East which then attracted him. He became a Muslim in real earnest twenty years after.

He left Damascus, then, without Islam. But jobs were beckoning. The British Museum offered him a post on the basis of his knowledge of ancient Welsh and Irish, but he declined. He was offered the vice-consulship at the British consulate in Haifa, but this offer was withdrawn when officialdom discovered how young he was. His family, and his patient Muriel, summoned him home, and, penniless, he obeyed.

He travelled back slowly, considering the meaning of his steps. As he left the sun behind him, he seemed to leave courtesy and contentment as well. The Muslims were the happiest people on earth, never complaining even when faced with dire threats. The Christians among them were protected and privileged by the Capitulations. Yet as Europe approached, the picture was altered. The Ottoman Balkans had been cruelly diminished by crusade and insurrection, prompted, as he believed, from outside. He saw the Morea, the first land of Greek independence, in which a third of a million Muslims had been slaughtered. The remaining corners of Ottoman Europe seemed threatened by a similar fate; but still the people smiled. It was the grace of *rıza*: contentment with God's decree.

Back in London, Pickthall proved faithful to his earlier promise. He paced the pavement outside Muriel's home in the time-honoured way, and battered down her parents' resistance. He married her in September 1896, the groom having fasted the previous day as a mark of respect for what he still considered a sacrament of the Church. Then he bore her swiftly away to Geneva, partly for the skiing, and partly, too, to associate with the literary circles which he admired.

During his sojourn in the dour Calvinist capital,

Pickthall honed the skills which would make him a widely-known exponent both of novel-writing, and of the still underdeveloped sport of skiing. He began a novel, and kept a diary, in which, despite his youth, his mature descriptive gift is already emerging. He wrote of

> a pearly mist delicately flushed from the sunset, on lake and mountains. The twin sails of a barque and the hull itself seemed motionless, yet were surely slipping past the piers. There was something remote about the whole scene, or so it appeared to me. I was able to separate myself from the landscape: to stand back, as it were, and admire it as one admires a fine painting. I crossed a bridge: starless night on the one hand: dying day on the other. There was a mist about the city: a mist that glowed with a blue spirit light which burned everywhere or nowhere, out of which the yellow lights looked over their dancing semblance in the water watchfully, as from a citadel. The distance of the streets was inundated with stagnant grey light, from which the last warmth of light had just faded. As I penetrated the city it had no other light than that which the street lamps gave it, and the glow from a lamp-lit window here and there. But the sky was still pale and green, with a softness as of velvet. The great round globules of electric light, rising up on the bridge against illimitable space, and their lengthened reflections, caught the eye and blinded it.

But this landscape concealed a *tristesse*, the local mood that Byron had dubbed 'Lemancholy.' By morning, a thick fog hung over the city, like a veil on the face of a plain woman, hiding blemishes and defects, softening all hardness of outline, soothing with the suggestion of a non-existent beauty. It is a law of nature, as it is of art, that half-revelation is more attractive than naked-ness. Unhappily there is another law which forbids a man to rest content until he has stripped his ideal and beheld it naked. Hence the end of most men's dreams is disappointment. And this disappointment is pro-portionate to what the world calls success.

By the shores of Lake Leman, the novelist-in-waiting acquired his love of light, which later became one of the strengths and hallmarks of his mature prose. Here, too, he developed that sense of the fragility, even the unreal-ity, of observed nature, and the superficial nature of man's passage upon it, attitudes which enriched his novels, and increased the readiness of his heart for Islam. In all these ways, his writing mirrored the sensitivity of the paintings of his contemporaries and fellow-converts, Ivan Aguéli in Sweden, and Étienne Dinet in French Algeria. Aguéli's paintings have a Sibelian sense of dreamy timelessness; while Dinet's exuberant Algerian and Meccan scenes re-call the Muslim sense that God is present in our daily joys: that, as the Koran says, 'Wherever you turn, there is the face of God'. Pickthall's novels, at their best, can resemble a marriage of the two styles: northern restraint and south-ern joy. That combination was key to the temper of much Western Muslim novel-writing in the twentieth century: Isabelle Eberhardt and Eric Winkel furnish particularly good examples.

On the surface, however, his religious needs were sat-isfied by an increasingly high Anglicanism. He frequent-

ly fasted and took communion, and insisted (to the an-
noyance of his chapelbound in-laws) on the truth of the
Apostolic Succession. Behind this, however, his note-
books indicate a robust willingness to accept and face
doubts, and even a solid cynicism about the ultimate
truth of God; he wrestled with these difficulties, seeking
help in the secular philosophy of the day, eventually to
emerge, as al-Ghazali had done, a stronger man.

True literature either reflects faith, or obsesses over
its absence; and Pickthall's youthful doubts energised
the first of his writings to see print: his short stories
'Monsieur le Président' and 'The Word of an Englishman',
both published in 1898. The novel which he had begun in
Switzerland was never published: it is simple juvenilia,
a laboratory experiment that in print would have done
him no good at all. Sadly, his first published novel, *All
Fools*, was little better, and contained, in the eyes of that
now unimaginable England, morally problematic pas-
sages which were to saddle him in later years with the
reputation of a libertine. Even his mother was disturbed
by the most offending passage in the book, which used
the word 'stays', an unmentionable item of Victorian un-
derwear. The Anglican Bishop of Jerusalem, to whom
Pickthall unwisely sent a copy, was similarly agitated, and
the young novelist lost many friends. Soon he bought up
the unsold copies, and had them destroyed.

But by then he had already written much of the novel
that was to catapult him to fame as one of the major
British novelists of the day: *Saïd the Fisherman*. This
was published by Methuen in 1903, to spectacularly favourable reviews. A blizzard of fan-mail settled on his
doormat. One especially pleasant letter came from H.G.
Wells, who wrote, 'I wish that I could feel as certain

about my own work as I do of yours, that it will be alive and interesting people fifty years from now.' Academics such as the Cambridge orientalist Granville Browne heaped praises upon it for what they took to be its accurate portrayal of Arab life. In later years, Pickthall acknowledged that the novel's focus on the less attractive aspects of the 'Arab personality' which he had encountered in Palestine could never make the book popular among Arabs themselves; but even after his conversion, he insisted that the novelist's mission was not to propagandize, but to tease out every aspect of the human personality, whether good or bad. As with his *Early Hours*, he was concerned to be true to his perceptions: he would document English and Oriental life as he found it, not as he or others would wish it to be. The greatness of the Oriental vision would in this way shine through all the brighter.

His next novel returned him to England. *Enid* is the first of his Suffolk tales, reminiscent in some respects of the writings of the Powys brothers. It was followed by *The House of Islam*, which he wrote while nursing his mother in her final illness, and at a time when his life was saddened by the growing realisation that he would never have children. The novel is unsteady and immature: still only in his twenties, Pickthall could manage the comic scenes of *Saïd the Fisherman*, but could not fully sustain the grave, tragic theme which he chose for *The House*, which describes the anguish of a Muslim compelled to take his sick daughter to a supercilious European doctor when traditional remedies had failed.

This productive but sober period of his life ended in 1907. An invitation to St James's Palace to meet the wife of Captain Machell, advisor to the Egyptian Prime Minister

Mustafa Fehmi Pasha, began with a discussion of his books, and ended with an invitation to Alexandria.

Pickthall accepted with alacrity, and soon was back in his beloved East. In native dress again, he travelled through the countryside, marvelling at the religious festival (*mawlid*) of al-Sayyid al-Badawi in Tanta, and immersing himself in Arab ways. The result was a series of short stories and his novel *Children of the Nile*. It also offered an opportunity to help his friend James Hanauer, the Anglican chaplain at Damascus, edit his anthology of Muslim, Christian and Jewish tales, *Folklore of the Holy Land*, a small classic which is still in print today.

1908 brought intimations of the collapse of the old world. At first, the Young Turk revolution seemed to presage a renewed time of hope for the Empire. As shown in *The Early Hours*, Pickthall welcomed the idealistic revolutionaries, imagining that they would hold the empire together better than the old Sultan, with his secretive ways. While other novelists, most recently Barry Unsworth, have typically seen them as secular Jacobins determined to destroy Ottoman culture, Pickthall took a more complex view.

He knew the Turkish ulema well enough to know that the Committee of Union and Progress, whose revolution forms the backdrop to the *Early Hours*, was a broad coalition which included many religious scholars, and was close to the *Cemiyet-i Ilmiyye*, the main ulema's association. In fact, when the revolution took place, all the leading religious figures welcomed this feat of the 'sacred committee' which had restored constitutional rule and parliamentary representation. Many Sufis, too, were deeply involved. Shaykh Erbilli Mehmet Es'ad, the best-known leader of the Naqshbandi Order, who had been exiled for criticizing the autocracy of Abdul Hamid, lauded the Young Turks. So did the Istanbul lodges of the Mevlevi Order which had served as secret dissemination points for Committee literature arriving from abroad. And in Macedonia, heart of the Young Turk movement, the Committee received the wholehearted support of orders such as the Melamiyye.

Here, perhaps, is the essence of Pickthall's apparent remoteness towards Sheikh Abdullah Quilliam, then the leader of Britain's small Muslim community. Quilliam had been a confidant of Abdul Hamid, 'the Sultan's Englishman', his private advisor and his emissary on sensitive missions to the Balkans. Quilliam knew the Sultan as Pickthall never did, and must have felt that his opposition to the Young Turk movement was fully vindicated by the disasters of the Balkan War of 1912, when the Empire lost almost all her remaining European territories to vengeful Christians. More calamitous still was the Unionist decision to cast in its lot with Prussian militarism during the First World War. Pickthall, too, became anxious for Turkey, seeing that the old British policy of upholding the integrity of the Ottoman Empire, which had begun even before Britain intervened on Turkey's side in the Crimean War, and had been reinforced by Disraeli's anti-Russian strategy, was steadily disintegrating in the face of Young Turk enthusiasm for Germany.

Coup and counter-coup let much gifted Osmanli blood. The Arabs and the Balkan Muslims, who had previously looked up to the Turks for political and religious leadership, began to wonder whether they should not heed the siren calls of the European Powers, and press for autonomy or outright independence from the Porte. Behind the agitation was, on the one hand, the traditional British fear that, in the words of Sir Mark Sykes, 'the collapse of the Ottoman Empire would be a frightful disaster to us.' On the other were ranged the powers of predatory French banks, Gladstonian Christian Islamophobia, and a militant pan-Slavism bankrolled from the darker recesses of Moscow's bureaucracy.

Sheikh Abdullah Quilliam, that undying Empire loyalist, fired off a hot broadside of polemic:

> List, ye Czar of "Russias all,"
> Hark! The sound of Freedom's call,
> Chanting in triumphant staves,
> "Perish tyrants! Perish knaves!"

Like Pickthall, he knew that the integrity of the traditional lands of Islam was threatened not by internal weakness so much as by the Russian system of government, which, as Pickthall saw, 'must have war. War is a necessity of its existence, for an era of peace would inevitably bring to pass the revolution which has long been brewing.' The collapse of the Ottoman Empire, Pickthall was sure, would plunge the region into disorder for an age. He seems to have had little confidence in the ability of Arab or Balkan peoples to recreate the diverse and stable space which the Ottomans, at their best, had supplied, and he lamented the Foreign Office's change of heart. 'An independent Turkey,' he opined, 'was regarded by our older, better-educated statesmen as just as necessary […] as a safety-valve is to a steam-engine: do away with it—the thing explodes.' Lawrence and his Arab allies would soon demonstrate the truth of his predictions. Balkan history was to be no less tragic.

Despite his eulogies in *The Early Hours*, and his almost Cromwellian dislike for Hamidian centralism and absolutism, Pickthall was never fully at ease with the Unionists. In later years, he must frequently have wondered whether Quilliam's insistent conservatism, now to be manifested in support for the Liberal party of Old Turks, was not the course of a wiser head. Quilliam had moved behind the scenes at Yıldız Palace, and knew Abdul Hamid as few others had done; and he had trusted, even loved the man. The Young Turks promised a new dawn for Islam, the Caliphate and the entire Muslim world; but as Pickthall suggests, the religious vision was blunted amongst some, who, despairing of the ideal of a multinational empire, evolved nationalistic and Turanian preoccupations which were liable to alienate the very minorities that they claimed to emancipate. Quilliam had urged the Sultan to allow the Balkan Muslims to retain their arms; the Unionists had disarmed them; and the results were to be seen in the tragic refugee columns that fled the ethnic cleansing of 1912 and 1913.

As the dismal news rolled in, it seemed as though Heaven had finally abandoned the Empire to its fate. In England, Pickthall campaigned vigorously on Turkey's behalf, establishing an Anglo-Ottoman Society, but could do nothing against the new Foreign Secretary, Sir Edward Grey, who was, as Granville Browne commented, 'russophile, germanophobe, and anti-Islamic.' He wrote to a Foreign Office official demanding to know whether the new arrangements in the Balkans could be considered to further the cause of peace, and received the following reply: 'Yes, and I'll tell you why. It is not generally known. But the Muslim population has been practically wiped out —240,000 killed in Western Thrace alone—that clears the ground.'

While campaigning for the dying Empire, Pickthall found time for more novels. *Larkmeadow*, another Suffolk tale, appeared in 1911, and in 1913 he produced one of his masterpieces, *Veiled Women*. This follows *Saïd* in its gritty, often Zola-like depiction of Middle Eastern life, but now there is an undercurrent of polemic. Edwardian imperial convictions about the evils of slavery stood little chance against the charming reality of a Cairo harem, where concubinage was a career desired earnestly by many Circassian girls, whose slave-guardians thanked God for the ease of their lot. Lord Cromer, although generally contemptuous of Egyptian ways, made an exception in the case of slavery, an institution whose Islamic expression he was able grudgingly to respect:

> It may be doubted [Cromer wrote] whether in the majority of cases the lot of slaves in Egypt is, in its material aspects, harder than, or even as hard as that of many domestic servants in Europe. Indeed, from one point of view, the Eastern slave is in a better position than the Western servant. The latter can be thrown out of employment at any moment. […] Cases are frequent of masters who would be glad to get rid of their slaves, but who are unable to do so because the latter will not accept the gift of liberty. A moral obligation, which is universally recognised, rests on all masters to support aged and infirm slaves till they die; this obligation is often onerous in the case of those who have inherited slaves from their parents or other relatives. (Lord Cromer, *Modern Egypt*, New York, 1908, II, 496-7.)

In its portrayal of what he saw as the positive aspects of polygamy and slavery, *Veiled Women* was a daring, even an extraordinary book, calculated to shock those nurtured on familiar fantasies and prejudices about Oriental life and the natural superiority of monogamy. It was, perhaps for this reason, one of his least popular works.

During the same period Pickthall contributed to the *New Age*, the fashionable literary magazine supported by Bernard Shaw, sharing its pages, almost weekly, with Ezra Pound, D.H. Lawrence, and G.K. Chesterton. As a political advocate he was failing miserably; but as a literary figure he had arrived.

Veiled Women gave him the fare to Istanbul. Lodged with a German lady (Miss Kate, Turkicised to 'Misket Hanum') in a house in the quiet suburb of Erenköy, he learned Turkish with a khoja from nearby Göztepe, and made the acquaintance of a full range of the city's inhabitants. *The Early Hours* shows his powers of human observation nicely. Everyone seems to be caught between two worlds, as is marvelously shown in the scene at Zekki Pasha's reception, where Turkish and European musicians are playing simultaneously, at opposite ends of a hall, in the middle of which Turkish ladies, to their great discomfort, are encouraged to unveil to please the Christian guests. Pickthall admirably diagnoses the new Istanbul elite's abject longing for Western approval, a frailty which has much more recently been brilliantly described by Orhan Pamuk. On the great stage where the Empire's closing scene is being enacted, Pickthall gives us cameos of particular types he has known. One is Deyli Ferid, half-Westernised and cynical, who is able to take both sides in almost any dispute. Arif Hikmet is a lover of conspiracy for conspiracy's sake, and cannot stop intriguing even after the revolution has succeeded. Basri

Bey is the type of the patriotic young CUP activist whose company Pickthall had already sought out in Damascus and Cairo. And the chief protagonist, Camruddin, is an icon of Balkan Muslim sincerity, almost a symbol of the whole Turkish people, whose faith in God allows him to carry the tragedies which Fate decrees for him. His Gulraaneh is his female equivalent: of humble origin, yet pure-hearted and proud.

At Erenköy, Pickthall watched the capital's political tumult, which he recorded in his dramatic but sad memoir *With the Turk in Wartime* and a set of passionate essays, *The Black Crusade*. He wrote that during this time, despite the Balkan massacres, Christians went unmolested in the great city. He recorded a familiar scene at an Orthodox church in Pera one Easter Friday: 'four different factions fighting which was to carry the big Cross, and the Bishop hitting out right and left upon their craniums with his crozier; many people wounded, women in fits. The Turkish mounted police had to come in force to stop further bloodshed.' It was a perfect image of the classical Ottoman self-understanding: without the Sultan-Caliph, the minorities would murder each other. The Second Balkan War, which saw the victorious Orthodox powers squabbling over the amputated limbs of Turkey, looked like a full vindication of this.

Pickthall returned to an England full of glee at the Christian victories. As a lover of Turkey, he was shattered by the mood of triumph. The Bishop of London held a service of intercession to pray for the victory of the Bulgarian army as it marched on Istanbul. Where, in all this, was Pickthall's high Anglicanism?

It was the English mood of holy war which finally drove him from the faith of his fathers. He had always felt uncomfortable with those English hymns that curse the infidel. One particular source of irritation was Bishop Cleveland Coxe's furious paean to a latter-day imperial Christianity:

> Trump of the Lord! I hear it blow!
> Forward the Cross; the world shall know
> Jehovah's arms against the foe;
> Down shall the cursed Crescent go!
> To arms! To arms!
> God wills it so.

And now, in a small Sussex village church where he sought refuge against a London in the grip of xenophobic rage, Pickthall heard a vicar hurling imprecations against the devilish Turk. The last straw was Charles Wesley's hymn 'For the Mahometans':

> O, may thy blood once sprinkled cry
> For those who spurn Thy sprinkled blood:
> Assert thy glorious Deity
> Stretch out thine arm thou triune God
> The Unitarian fiend expel
> And chase his doctrines back to Hell.

Pickthall thought of the Carnegie Report, which declared, of the Greek attack on Valona, that 'in a century of repentance they could not expiate it.' He thought of the forced conversions of the Pomaks in Bulgaria. He remembered the refugees in Istanbul, their lips removed as trophies by Christian soldiers. He remembered that no Muslim would ever sing a hymn against Jesus. He could stand no more. He walked out of the church before the end of the service, and never again considered himself a Christian.

The political situation continued to worsen. Horrified by the new British policy, which seemed hell-bent on plunging the Balkans and the Middle East into chaos, the Young Turks strengthened their ties with Berlin. Meanwhile the British government, driven by the same men who had allowed the destruction of Macedonia and Thrace, marched headlong towards war with the Central Powers. In August 1914, Winston Churchill seized two Turkish dreadnoughts, the *Sultan Osman* and the *Reshadiye*, which were under construction in a British yard. The outrage in Turkey was intense. Millions of pounds had been subscribed by ordinary Turks: women had even sold their hair for a few coppers and schoolboys made do with dry bread in order to add to the fund. But the ships were gone, and with them went Pickthall's last hopes for a peaceful settlement. The hubris of nationalistic Europe, the tribal vanity which she pressed on the rest of the world as the sole path to human progress, was about to send millions of young men to their deaths. The final trigger was the murder of Archduke Franz Ferdinand by a Serbian nationalist, on the streets of Sarajevo.

The war had broken Europe's ideals, and the machines of Krupp lent new efficiency to her patriotic hatreds. The Hun reached the Marne, and English dowagers strangled their dachshunds with their own hands. Asquith proclaimed that 'the cross will replace the crescent on the minaret of St Sophia.' It was no time to be a Turcophile. But Pickthall had found a new source of strength. The hubris of human autonomy had been shown as a lethal fantasy; and only God could provide succour. But where could He be found?

In 1913, Lady Evelyn Cobbold, the Sutherland heiress and traveller, tried to convert him during a dinner at Claridges, explaining that the waiters would do perfectly well as witnesses. He politely demurred; but he could marshal no argument against hers. What he had seen and described, she had lived. As an English Muslim woman familiar with the heart of Asia, she knew that his love for Islam was grounded in much more than a Pierre Loti-style enjoyment of exotica. And so, on 29 November 1914, in the middle of a lecture he was giving on 'Islam and Progress', he took the plunge. From now on, his life would be lived in the light of the One God of Islam. Muriel followed him soon afterwards.

The war ground on, and Pickthall watched as the Turks trounced the assembled British and colonial troops at Gallipoli, only to be betrayed by the Arab uprising under Lawrence. Like Evelyn Cobbold, Pickthall despised Lawrence as a shallow romantic, given to unnatural passions and wild misjudgements about British intentions. As he later wrote, reviewing the *Seven Pillars of Wisdom*:

> He really thought the Arabs a more virile people than the Turks. He really thought them better qualified to govern. He really believed that the British Government would fulfil punctually all the promises made on its behalf. He really thought that it was love of freedom and his personal effort and example rather than the huge sums paid by the British authorities and the idea of looting Damascus, which made the Arabs zealous in rebellion.

While Europeans bloodied each others' noses, and encouraged the same behaviour in others, Pickthall began to define his position in the British Muslim community. The Liverpool congregation had lost its mosque in 1908, and Sheikh Abdullah had gone to ground in the Turkish town of Bostancık, to return as the mysterious Dr Henri Marcel Leon, translator of Sufi poetry and author of a work on influenza. There was a prayer-room in Notting Hill, an Islam Society, a Muslim Literary Society, and also the eccentric Anglo-Moghul mosque in Woking. In all these institutions Pickthall, whose novels had already made him a celebrity among British Muslims, assumed the role of a leader. He began to preach the Friday sermons in London and at the mosque in Woking. 'If there is one thing that turns your hair grey, it is preaching in Arabic', he later remarked. In due course some of his sermons found their way into print, drawing the attention of others in the Muslim world. In addition, he spent a year running an Islamic Information Bureau in Palace Street, London, which issued a weekly paper, *The Muslim Outlook*.

The *Outlook* was funded by Indian Muslims loyal to the Caliphate. Their 'Khilafatist' movement represented a serious threat to British rule in India, which had previously found the Muslims to be less inclined to the independence party than the Hindus. But the government's Turkey policy was too much to bear. On January 18, 1918, Lloyd George had promised Istanbul and the Turkish-speaking areas of Thrace to post-war Turkey; but the reality turned out rather differently. Istanbul was placed under Allied occupation, and the bulk of Muslim Thrace was awarded to Greece. This latest case of Albion's perfidy intensified Indian Muslim mistrust of British rule. Gandhi, too, encouraged many Hindus to support the Khilafat movement, and few Indians participated in the

Raj's official celebration of the end of the First World War. Instead, a million telegrams of complaint arrived at the Viceroy's residence.

Pickthall was now at his most passionate:

> Objectivity is much more common in the East than in the West; nations, like individuals, are there judged by their words, not by their own idea of their intentions or beliefs; and these inconsistencies, which no doubt look very trifling to a British politician, impress the Oriental as a foul injustice and the outcome of fanaticism. The East preserves our record, and reviews it as a whole. There is no end visible to the absurdities into which this mental deficiency of our rulers may lead us. […] Nothing is too extravagant to be believed in this connection, when flustered mediocrities are in the place of genius.

This bitter alienation from British policy, which now placed him at the opposite pole from his erstwhile friend Churchill, opened the next chapter in Pickthall's life. Passionate Khilafatists invited him to become editor of a major Indian newspaper, the *Bombay Chronicle*, and he accepted. In September 1919 he reached the Apollo Bunder, and immediately found himself carried away in the maelstrom of Indian life and politics. When he arrived, most of the *Chronicle*'s staff were on strike and the paper was foundering; but within six months he had turned it around and doubled its circulation, through a judicious but firm editorial line in favour of Indian independence. The Government was incandescent, but could do little. However Pickthall, who became a close associate of Gandhi, supported the ulema's rejection of violent resistance to British rule, and their opposition to the migration of Indian Muslims to independent Afghanistan. Non-violence and non-co-operation seemed the most promising means by which India would emerge as a strong and free nation. When the Muslim League made its appearance under the very secular figure of Jinnah, Pickthall joined the great bulk of India's ulema in rejecting the idea of partition. India's Muslim millions were one family, and must never be divided. Only together could they complete the millennial work of converting the whole country to Islam.

So the English novelist whose imagination had been fired by the Young Turks became an Indian nationalist leader, fluent in Urdu, and attending dawn prayers in the mosque, dressed in Gandhian homespun adorned with the purple crescent of the Khilafatists. He wrote to a friend: 'They expect me to be a sort of political leader as well as a newspaper editor. I have grown quite used to haranguing multitudes of anything from 5 to 30,000 people in the open air, although I hate it still as much as ever and inwardly am just as miserably shy.' He also continued his Friday sermons, preaching at the great mosque of Bijapur and elsewhere.

In 1924, the Raj authorities found the *Chronicle* guilty of misreporting an incident in which Indian protesters had been killed. Crushing fines were imposed on the newspaper, and Pickthall resigned. His beloved Khilafatist movement folded in the same year, following Atatürk's abolition of the ancient title. Although he effectively left political life, he was always remembered gratefully by Gandhi, who was later to write these words to his widow:

Your husband and I met often enough to grow to love each other and I found Mr. Pickthall a most amiable and deeply religious man. And although he was a convert he had nothing of the fanatic in him that most converts, no matter to what faith they are converted, betray in their speech and act. Mr. Pickthall seemed to me to live his faith unobtrusively.

His job was gone, but Pickthall's desire to serve Islam burned brighter than ever. He accepted the headmastership of a boy's school in the domains of the Nizam of Hyderabad, outside the authority of British India. This princely state boasted a long association with British Muslims, and had been many years earlier the home of one of the most colourful characters in India: William Linnaeus Gardner (1770-1835), a convert who fought in the Nizam's forces against the French in 1798 before setting up his own regiment of irregulars, Gardner's Horse, and marrying his son to a niece of the Moghul emperor Akbar Shah.

In the 1920s, Hyderabad resembled a surviving fragment of Moghul brilliance, and the Nizam, the richest man in the world, was busy turning his capital into an oasis of culture and art. The appointment of the celebrated Pickthall would add a further jewel to his crown. Pickthall's sympathies were aroused by the Nizam, who had made his lands the pride of India. 'He lives like a dervish', Pickthall reported, 'and devotes his time to every detail of the Government.' It was his enthusiasm and generosity that enabled Pickthall to launch the journal *Islamic Culture*, which he edited for ten years, and which continues to be published in the city as one of the Muslim world's leading academic journals.

Under his editorship, a wide range of Muslim and non-Muslim scholars published on a huge variety of topics. A regular contributor was Josef Horowitz, the great German orientalist. Another was Quilliam, now writing as Harun Mustafa Leon, who contributed learned articles on early Arabic poetry and rhetoric, on Abbasid medical institutions, and a piece on 'The Languages of Afghanistan.'

Pickthall also directed the school for Hyderabadi civil servants, encouraging their attendance at prayer, and teaching them the protocols to observe when moving among the burra sahibs of British India. Prayer featured largely in all his activities: as he wrote to a friend, after attending a conference on education:

> I attended prayers at Tellycherry. The masjids are all built like Hindu temples. There are no minarets, and the azan is called from the ground, as the Wahhabis call it. When I mentioned this fact, the reforming party were much amused because the maulvis of Malabar are very far from being Wahhabis. I stopped the Conference proceedings at each hour of prayer, and everyone went to the adjacent mosque. I impressed upon the young leaders the necessity of being particularly strict in observance of the essential discipline of Islam.

In the midst of this educational activity, he managed to find time to write. He wrote a (never to be published) Moghul novel, *Dust and the Peacock Throne*, in 1926, and the following year he composed his Madras lectures, published as *The Cultural Side of Islam*, which are still widely read and reprinted in the Subcontinent. But from 1929 until 1931 the Nizam gave him leave-of-absence to enable him to complete his most precious project: a new translation of the Koran. As he noted: 'All Muslim India seems to be possessed with the idea that I ought to translate the Qur'an into real English.' He was anxious that this should be the most accurate, as well as the most literate, version of the Scripture. As well as mastering the classical Islamic sources, he travelled to Germany to consult with leading Orientalists, and studied the groundbreaking work of Nöldeke and Schwally, the *Geschichte des Qorans*, to which his notes frequently refer.

When the work was completed, Pickthall realised that it was unlikely to gain wide acceptance among Muslims unless approved by Al-Azhar, which, with the abolition of the Ottoman post of Shaykh al-Islam, had become the leading religious authority in the Muslim world. So to Egypt he went, only to discover that powerful sections of the ulema considered unlawful any attempt to render 'the meanings of the Book' into a language other than Arabic. The controversy soon broke, as Shaykh Muhammad Shakir wrote in the newspaper *Al-Ahram* that all who aided such a project would burn in Hell for evermore. The Shaykh recommended that Pickthall translate Tabari's commentary instead, a work that would amount to at least one hundred volumes in English. Other ulema demanded that his translation be retranslated into Arabic, to see if it differed from the original in any respect, however small.

Pickthall published, in *Islamic Culture*, a long account of his battle with the Shaykh and the mentality which he represented. He included this reflection:

Many Egyptian Muslims were as surprised as I was at the extraordinary ignorance of present world conditions of men who claimed to be the thinking heads of the Islamic world—men who think that the Arabs are still 'the patrons,' and the non-Arabs their 'freedmen'; who cannot see that the positions have become reversed, that the Arabs are no longer the fighters and the non-Arabs the stay-at-homes but it is the non-Arabs who at present bear the brunt of the Jihâd; that the problems of the non-Arabs are not identical with those of the Arabs; that translation of the Qur'ân is for the non-Arabs a necessity, which, of course, it is not for Arabs; men who cannot conceive that there are Muslims in India as learned and devout, as capable as judgment and as careful for the safety of Islam, as any to be found in Egypt.

The battle was won when Pickthall addressed, in Arabic, a large gathering of the ulema, including Rashid Rida, explaining the current situation of Islam in the world, and the enormous possibilities for the spread of Islam among the English-speaking people. He won the argument entirely. The wiser heads of al-Azhar, recognising their inability to understand the situation of English speakers and the subtle urgencies of Islamic mission, accepted his translation. The former Shaykh al-Azhar, al-Maraghi, who could see his sincerity and his erudition, offered him these parting words: 'If you feel so strongly convinced that you are right, go on in God's name in the way that is clear to you, and pay no heed to what any of us say.'

The translation duly appeared, in 1930, and was hailed by the *Times Literary Supplement* as 'a great literary achievement.' Avoiding both the Jacobean archaisms of Sale, and the daring flourishes and expansions of Yusuf

Ali (whose translation Pickthall regarded as too free), it was widely recognised as the best translation ever of the Book, and, indeed, as a monument in the history of translation. It has been reprinted hundreds of times, and, unusually for a translation, has been further translated into several other languages, including Tagalog, Turkish and Portuguese.

Pickthall, now a revered religious leader in his own right, was often asked for rulings on difficult issues of divorce and inheritance, and continued to preach. In this capacity, he was asked by the Nizam to arrange the marriage of the heir to his throne to the daughter of the last Ottoman caliph, Princess Dürrüşehvar. The Ottoman exiles lived in France as pensioners of the Nizam, and thither Pickthall and the Hyderabad suite travelled. His knowledge of Ottoman and Moghul protocol allowed Pickthall to bring off this brilliant match, which was to be followed by a Mecca pilgrimage, his private hope being that the Caliphate, which he regarded as still by right vested in the House of Osman, might now pass to a Hyderabadi prince yet to be born, who would use the wealth of India and the prestige and holiness of the Caliphate to initiate a new dawn of independence and success for Islam. Delhi's decision to forcibly absorb the Nizam's domains into independent India made that impossible; but the princess, a true survivor of the world depicted in *The Early Hours*, devoted her life to works of charity, whose benefits continued even after her death in 2006.

In 1935 Pickthall left Hyderabad. His school was flourishing, and he had forever to deny that he was the Fielding of E.M. Forster's novel *A Passage to India*. (He knew Forster well, and the claim may not be without foundation.) He handed over *Islamic Culture* to the new editor, the Austrian convert Muhammad Asad. He then returned to England, where he set up a new society for Islamic work, and delivered a series of lectures.

Despite this new activity, however, his health was failing, and he must have felt as Winstanley felt:

And here I end, having put my arm as far as my strength will go to advance righteousness. I have writ, I have acted, I have peace: and now I must wait to see the Spirit do his own work in the hearts of others and whether England shall be the first land, or some other, wherein truth shall sit down in triumph. (Gerrard Winstanley, *A New Year's Gift for the Parliament and Army*, 1650.)

He died in a cottage in the West Country on May 19 1936, of coronary thrombosis, and was laid to rest in the Muslim cemetery at Brookwood, near Woking. After his death, his wife cleared his desk, where he had been revising his Madras lectures the night before he died, and she found that the last lines he had written were from the Koran:

Whosoever surrendereth his purpose to Allah, while doing good, his reward is with his Lord, and there shall no fear come upon them, neither shall they grieve.

'By the early hours and by the night when it is darkest
Thy Lord has not forsaken thee, nor does he hate thee.
And verily the latter portion shall be better for thee than the former,
And verily thy Lord shall give to thee and thou shalt know his favour.'

THE CORAN

Chapter I

CAMRUDDIN SAT on his heels beneath the blossomed fruit-trees in the orchard, watching the black-and-white cow tear the herbage, and giving praise to Allah. The grass between the trunks was not a sward. It grew as separate tufts amid rank weeds and starry flowers. The little tethered cow soon browsed up all within her reach; as often as that happened Camruddin must move the peg; and that was all he had to do that afternoon.

'Praise be to Allah!' he kept saying in his soul. The sunlight, captured by the mass of blossom overhead, came to him only as a touch of colour in the shade. The hum of bees and other insects was so loud and so incessant as to seem the stress of silence rather than an actual sound. There was no breath of wind. A village visible between the tree-trunks, across a down-and-up of terraced vineyards, with two red roofs conspicuous amid its housetops, on the border of a forest-clad ravine, was too far off for noise to travel thence; and the house close by, beside the orchard, was deserted. It stood agape with door and shutters open, all its inmates having gone to market except Camruddin, whom his mother, smiling, had called lazy, when she started out.

He was not lazy. Nothing called him, that was all; and nothing needed doing round the homestead save this small attention to the cow, which he paid regularly, patting the gentle beast between the horns with words of blessing. He recalled a saying of the Holy Prophet, how the happiness of man is as a halt for rest beneath a tree beside the way. It was as that and nothing else that he beheld his present idleness. And Camruddin had earned the right to rest awhile.

He was twenty-five years old, had served in the army, and had seen hard fighting both in Kurdistan and in the Yemen. He had attained the rank of chaûsh or sergeant by the mercy of Allah; and then, no less by Allah's mercy, had been discharged because of illness. That happened one fine morning at Hodeydah. He had only three mejidis in his purse. By the kindness of a Muslim merchant he was shipped to Suez, where he recovered health enough to undertake the pilgrimage in the train of an Egyptian bey, who took a fancy to him. From Mecca, the slow journey homeward filled two years, for it was often broken by the need of earning money. He worked as a night-watchman in Damascus, a gardener in Aleppo, a shepherd in a village of the Taurus Mountains; and at Konia he was proud to be the servant of a mosque, and take the alms of pious persons who frequented it. In all conditions he gave praise to Allah for the miracles of day and night, of life and death and all the wonderful arrangement of the world; and as he looked back on his army service and his travels, he thought that he had been exceptionally fortunate.

Once, indeed, he had attained the height of fame. In a straggling palm-grove on the outskirts of an Arab village, his own General had embraced him before all the troops, and had sworn that if they both survived the war, he would provide for him. Sâdik Pasha had survived the war, and so had Camruddin. The former held a high command at Saloniki, and Camruddin's mother, ever since she heard the story, had been urging him to go there and remind him of his promise. And Camruddin agreed that he would go there some day. But having found his way, by Allah's grace, back to the house and orchard on the mountain-side, to find his father dead, his brothers men, his sister grown to marriageable age, he had no wish to turn his back on it again without some call more sacred than ambitious hopes. Lefteri, their Christian neighbour, blamed his indolence in this respect, seeming to regard the generous outburst of the Pasha as something in the nature of a mortgage on the latter's property. Lefteri's delight was money and its acquisition. His talk was of the price of things, the weight of taxes, the extortions of the Government. The Christians were exempt from military service. Their religion did not make them, at least once in life, confront a long and dangerous journey for no earthly gain. Being thus free to cultivate a selfish purpose, they gave their whole devotion to that kind of wealth which fails men altogether when they come to die. The loss of money was for them a crime; and far from praising Allah for his gifts to all mankind, they prayed for special favours for themselves. They seemed to Camruddin like blind men in a pageant, who think of nothing but themselves because they cannot see.

At this point in his musing it behoved him once again to move the peg to which the cow was tethered. As he did so, he caught sight of Lefteri, in person, on the path below the orchard, leading a mule half-hidden in a load of brushwood. The Christian calling out 'Good-day,' in friendly fashion, Camruddin strolled down to chat with him.

Just at that moment a sharp noise of firing shattered the stillness of the sunlit valley, and reverberated from the heights. Lefteri jumped as if the shots had all found lodging in his carcass. He crossed himself and with a cry of 'Holy George!' hustled his mule up a steep bank, from which he afterwards had much ado to get it down again, succeeding only with strong help from Camruddin. By that time all was still.

'What was it?' Lefteri inquired, still tremulous.

'You know as much as I do of the matter. Perhaps a battle of the Christian bands.'

'Allah forbid! They are not in our neighbourhood. It must be work of vengeance or sheer murder. Rifle shots!'

'No, pistol shots,' corrected Camruddin with an indulgent smile. 'As for the matter, neighbour, let us go and see!'

Lefteri crossed himself again. 'Go thou! he answered. I meddle not in business which does not concern me … In Allah's keeping!' And he strode away, dragging the bridle of the mule which plodded after him.

The sound of firing had appeared to come from the direction of a wood of walnuts, at no great distance, as the bird flies, from the spot where the two men were talking. Beyond those trees, and hidden by them, ran the main road through the valley. Camruddin set off at once across the intervening vineyards, taking in his stride the drop from terrace walls. He reached the shade. Doves murmured overhead. Stray beams of sunlight strewed gold pieces on the darkened ground. Nothing could have been more peaceful than the outward aspect of the grove.

He came to the road, a causeway of great stones, still in the shade of trees, without adventure. Proceeding up that road a little way, he saw a saddled horse among the trees, and went towards it. In so doing, he came suddenly upon a human form which sprawled half-hidden in a growth of flowering nettles. A Turkish officer in uniform lay there, face downward.

'There is neither power nor might save in Allah the High, the Tremendous! Allah have mercy on him!' murmured Camruddin.

Turning the body over he beheld a boyish face as white as plum-bloom, the pencilling of a moustache upon its upper lip. The eyes were closed. On close inspection it appeared that life was not extinct.

Camruddin ran to a spring of which he knew the whereabouts, bringing back sufficient water in his fez to bathe the young man's brow and wet his lips. A faint moan and a flutter of the eyelids thanked him. Then, having listened to make sure that there was no one coming on the road, he went up to the grazing horse, which proved obedient, climbed to the saddle, and was riding off when he descried another body lying on its back behind a bush—the body of a trooper, who had had his brains blown out. The ground about the place was thick with hoof-prints.

'The servant of the officer,' he guessed. 'His horse was of a baser breed—it fled. Allah have mercy on him!'

With which reflection he pressed his heels against the charger's flanks, and went careering up the terraced slope not without pleasure, the horse negotiating the low walls without a slip. His people, by good fortune, had returned from market. Amid their din of exclamation at the sight of such a horse, he told them briefly what had happened, and his plan of action. His mother raised objections, but he, supported by his sister Melek, overcame them. In the end she grumbled: 'Be it as thou wilt. My fear is of disaster and suspicion for our house. Allah forbid that we should turn away from the unfortunate.'

His brothers, meanwhile, had produced an ancient litter, which they had in readiness when he returned from stabling the horse. And then they three, with Melek as a scout, went down and fetched the wounded man, leaving the dead man where he lay, with prayers to Allah. For days the young bey flickered between life and death, the members of the household taking turns in nursing him.

At last one morning he awoke and spoke to Camruddin, who chanced to be on duty at the moment, in a feeble voice. He wished to see his uniform. Camruddin produced the garments from the press in which they lay, and spread them on the bed for his inspection. With feverish anxiety the young bey felt the tunic. 'Empty!' he wailed and seemed to swoon away, but presently his eyes reopened and he asked,—

'Did Ahmed take them?'

'Which Ahmed?' inquired Camruddin.

'Ahmed, my orderly, I mean, of course.'

'He was shot dead.'

'Allah have mercy on him!' The patient paid no other tribute to poor Ahmed's fate, but went on to exclaim,—

'Then they have got them!'

By dint of patient questioning the listener gleaned that there had been dispatches of importance in the tunic.

'How long ago?' was asked, and 'Five days' answered.

'Then all is lost,' declared the wounded man.

He closed his eyes, and lay awhile as if unconscious. Then suddenly he spoke in stronger tones,—

'Behold me penniless and near to death. My promise is worth nothing. But if you seek the good reward hereafter, go to Saloniki to my captain, Arif Hikmet Bey, and tell him what has happened to me, Basri Bey. The welfare of Islâm is in the message. It must be delivered in ten days from now or all is lost.' He added in a weaker tone: 'Unless the Lord of Right vouchsafes a miracle.'

'Be easy. I will go at once,' said Camruddin.

'Allah reward you!' The young man closed his eyes and fell asleep.

Camruddin went out to seek his mother, who was washing at the spring. She cried aloud against his going on so long a journey. The danger and the need of haste were all imaginary. Men near to death had often evil dreams; Camruddin had done well to humour their sick guest, but as for really setting out on such an errand—and so forth.

It was Melek, her daughter, who reminded her that Saloniki was the present home of Sâdik Pasha, Camruddin's benefactor, and of her repeated wish that he would go there to salute His Excellency.

'I did but wait for an occasion,' put in Camruddin.

'Ay, go to Sâdik Pasha, that is different,' she conceded, 'and treat this other matter by the way. It is a sick man's fancy, or if it is not that, it must be dangerous. Hire Lefteri's old mule. He will not need it for a week or two. To-morrow or the next day will be time enough for thee to start.'

But Camruddin was on the road within an hour, on foot. He had not said a word of any kind to Lefteri. The agonised entreaty of the wounded Bey had touched his heart. The call had come. His time of rest beneath the wayside tree was at an end. He started clean from head to foot, in clothing lately washed, and unencumbered with another's property; for he had a feeling that he was engaged in sacred work.

Chapter II

CAMRUDDIN REPOSED at noon beside a stream which fell from pool to pool beneath a group of flowering trees. The banks were clothed in deep, sweet-scented brushwood, the usual garment of the mountain slopes. The water, mirroring the blossom overhead, appeared quite pink among the reeds and water-plants. The hum of insects was ecstatic in the air, and silent insects flitted on the surface of the pools. A partridge cried upon the heights above. He marvelled at such beauty in so wild a place, arranged, it seemed, with art for man's enjoyment, and praised God for the growth of flowers, the voice of streams, the life of insects.

It was the third day of his journey. He had lost regret for home, and with it something of the earnest mood which had been his at starting. The joy of walking in the flowery hills made him forget his purpose while pursuing it.

He said the noon-day prayer beside the stream, and ate some food which he had brought with him. Then he resumed his way along a path by no means easy to discern, for it kept winding in and out amid a tangled growth of cistus, myrtle, broom, and aromatic plants which sometimes reached the level of his shoulder. Towards the middle of the afternoon he reached a summit from which blue distant mountains could be seen with flashes of the sea between them; whence, dipping down again through forest he came to a paved mule-track, which was in fact the road which he had all along been seeking but had never felt quite sure of finding till he set his foot upon it. After a while, descending by that road, which doubled like a snake upon the mountainside, he heard the tinkle of approaching bells, and presently a laden mule appeared in sight, led by a bare-legged man with turban half-unwound. Another followed; there were four in all. The barrel of a gun appeared above their guardian's shoulder.

'Peace be upon thee!' cried that person, meeting Camruddin. He stopped, the four mules halted, their bells jangling.

'Upon thee be peace! To Saloniki. Whither thou?'

'To Monastir. Would God I saw the place! A weary way!'

'Allah will make it easy for thee!'

'Allah reward thee; but mistake me not. It is not the fatigue I fear. That is my portion. I was born for that. I fear disturbance in the country. There are ugly rumours.'

'Fear nothing,' answered Camruddin. 'The Christian bands have had a lesson which they will not soon forget. Praise be to Allah!'

'Praise be to Allah! But it is not them I fear, though Allah knows they are a torment. May they all go blind!'

The muleteer assumed an air of the profoundest mystery, looking around him with extreme precaution, as if he feared eavesdropping on the open hill.

'I do not know thee, nor dost thou know me; if Allah wills it, we shall never meet again, and no one hears our talk save the cicadas; so I will tell thee what I would not tell another man: The army plots against the Padishah. I fear an earthquake.'

'Ma sha'llah! Never!' answered Camruddin, flatly incredulous. 'That fear is not worth five paras … The

Muslim army plot against the Padishah—and for no reason?'

'There may be reasons though I know them not. Men talk in whispers, only two together; and part as if in terror when a third approaches. My brother is mixed up in the affair, on one side or the other, foolish man. Because a spy once gave him ten piastres for a hint, he thinks himself a mighty politician. He tells me nothing when I question him, but grins and hums. But I have a relative employed in the police office. He told me plainly there is trouble brewing, and asked me to look out for symptoms on my journey. The horror of it makes my chest diminish and my head expand! Take my advice: go not to Saloniki. Turn back with me. What takes thee to the city?'

'I go to pay a visit to the Commandant, who was my General in the Yemen war.'

'He has forgotten thee: the great are so. Most likely he will have thee beaten for such reappearance. Better turn back with me!' advised the muleteer.

Camruddin laughed outright, exclaiming: 'The Lord of Right console thee, O despondent man!'

'And thee, O rash one!' said the other, laughing also, though less gaily.

With that they parted. For a long time after Camruddin could hear the ding-dong of the mule-bells as he trudged along the stony track between the brushwood, while the sun sank slowly down towards the western heights. He passed two villages with shady orchards, and several groups of travellers upon the road. The colours of the landscape became richer as its shadows lengthened. The air had grown perceptibly cooler, the scent of the brushwood perceptibly more pungent when suddenly, upon a rising ground, he heard a shout which stirred his blood.

'Padi-shah-im-iz-chôk-yasha!' (Long live our Padishah!).

Below him, on a well-made carriage road, a squad of Turkish troops which had been resting, raised the heartening shout as they resumed the march.

Camruddin lay down upon the hill and watched their going. He had no wish to overtake them, having seen men pressed into the ranks, and papers of discharge derided in his day. But the sight of them evoked no bitter memories. There was comradeship and unexpected kindness as well as hardship in that marching life. Again his heart leapt as the shout came on the breeze:—

'Long live our Padishah!'

Rebel against the Padishah? His soldiers? Never! Injustice and neglect there might be: what were they compared with the religious duty, to protect Islâm against bad Muslims and the hordes of Christendom? That man who talked about rebellion of the Muslim troops was mad, or else the victim of some evil joke. There was much that needed mending in the army and the empire, but the Padishah and no one else could mend it; and, please God, he would ere long, when he had time to think about it. The vision of the army plotting made him laugh. He cast the stupid thought out of his brain as he stepped out again.

It was twilight when he reached a village bowered in foliage, and turned into the courtyard of an inn. Threading his way among the beasts of burden in the yard, he shouted for the master of the house. A grumbling voice replied: 'Well, here I am!' and a stout man with a face of grievance came out of the doorway.

'Give me to eat!'

'No, that I cannot—may the Lord of Right forgive

me!—because my house is taken altogether by a mighty prince, for whom a son of Adam, such as you or me, has no existence. Sleep in the yard and welcome, but the house is taken and everything to eat is ordered by that potentate.'

'Cuckold!' A petulant though not unpleasant voice came from within. 'Dost take me for a ghoul? I am a lover of mankind. Whoever the man is, let him come in at once, or I will shoot thee, pimp, procrastinator!'

The landlord turned to Camruddin again, and, with a shrug, observed : 'Well, deign to enter, since it is his pleasure!'

Camruddin obeyed, taking off his shoes at the threshold.

He found himself in a large room, furnished not only with the usual divan round the walls but also with a table and chairs round it in the Frankish manner. The divan was already occupied by several men whom Camruddin could not distinguish in his first abashment. The same peculiar voice which had abused the landlord, ordered him to take a seat and then again cried 'Kerata!' (Cuckold) rather as a comprehensive expletive, it seemed, than as a personality. When Camruddin had been at rest a little while, he was able to take stock of the strange company in which he found himself. Next to him sat a tall black eunuch of enormous girth, and on his other side a hunchbacked dwarf, and then a Bektashi dervish telling his beads devoutly, a Greek merchant in smart Frankish clothes, a swart, down-looking man attendant on this latter, two Albanian cavasses in full war-trim, and in a corner of the divan, lounging on a heap of cushions, with one hand through the open window stroking some hanging tassels of wisteria, sat the personage to whom they all deferred—a man still young, arrayed in the official dress of black frock-coat and trousers and red fez, the latter worn at an audacious angle.

'Kerata!' he cried. 'Take this and bring the other!' And he began to divest himself of the frock-coat. One of the Albanians brought a flowered dressing gown and helped him on with it; the eunuch brought a pair of yellow slippers. When the change had been completed he put his feet up comfortably on the divan, once more ejaculating 'Cuckold!' in a tone of thankfulness. Every time that he let fly his favourite expletive, the Greek merchant started—for the word was a Greek insult—and his attendant checked him by a gesture, as it seemed, of fear.

The landlord came in with a deprecating air and set light to two hanging lamps above the table. The illumination roused the members of the party, who all sat up and stared at one another. Camruddin then saw the visage of his host for the first time distinctly. It was a jolly, oval face, bisected by a nose just like a beak. The large and prominent dark eyes, the smiling mouth contributed to the resemblance, which struck Camruddin at once, of this unknown believer to a waggish owl.

'Kerata! Where is the food? Where are the others?' cried the great one. The landlord answered: 'Waiting your good pleasure.' And, presently, in trooped a group of village worthies headed by the local khoja, whom the great one welcomed with much courtesy, letting it be known in the course of conversation that it was his custom thus to commandeer the inn wherever fate ordained that he should spend a night upon the road, in order to perform an act of charity.

'These innkeepers are scoundrels. May they burst!' he said. 'They fleece poor wayfarers habitually. I, while I keep the inn, make all men welcome without payment.'

'Allah reward Your Excellency!' came from all sides; and the Greek merchant thought it necessary to complain of the extreme embarrassment he felt, under a benefit which he could not repay.

'Thou canst repay it,' said the great one bluntly. And when the Greek, assuming ecstacy, asked in what manner, he replied: 'Forgive the debtor you are going to the town to prosecute!' at which the Greek looked down his nose and smiled awry.

The food was set upon the table, and they all fell to. It was a feast of thirteen courses, making conversation desultory. When everyone had finished eating, the great man made the eunuch and the two Albanians carry out all that remained, bidding them summon the whole village so that not a morsel might be wasted. Then he stretched his length on the divan and asked: 'What news?'

The Greek told of a fight between two robber bands upon the mountains, and also of the fluctuations of the money-market. The dervish told the story of an accident which he had that day witnessed, the village worthies spoke of quarrels with the tax-farmer. And then the owl-like nobleman, who had been listening to them with indifference, stretched out his hand towards Camruddin and said: 'Now thou, O silent man! It is thy turn.'

'Spare me, efendim. I have nothing to relate, excepting that I met a madman on the road to-day, which, after all, is nothing to cry out about.'

'It all depends upon the kind and measure of his madness. Deign to describe it to us.'

'The man I speak of was a prey to needless fear. His mind foreboded trouble soon to come upon our country. He warned me not to go to Saloniki, and wanted me to go with him to Monastir, although, to judge from his alarm, that way was just as dangerous. The army, he declared, was in a plot against our Padishah. I, who have been a soldier, laughed at him, but he would not be comforted.'

Every one kept silence, save the Greek, who argued eagerly: 'But it is true. All men desire improvement and reform; the soldiers more than others for they suffer most.' And he proceeded to detail the soldiers' grievances with 'You, who have been a soldier, tell me: is that true or false?' and Camruddin was forced to answer 'True' in each case, yet stuck to his original contention that to think of Muslim soldiers plotting to rebel was madness.

'Why not, if by so doing they can get redress?' inquired the Greek, with fervent gestures beseeming one who pleads the cause of the oppressed.

Camruddin could not tell him that the soldiers and their Padishah were bound together by a sacred duty to defend the territory of Islâm from wicked and usurious Christians such as he. He merely said that nothing was impossible, but he for one could not conceive of Turkish troops at war against the Padishah.

The Greek then shrugged and clicked his tongue against his teeth, impatient of such dense stupidity. It seemed to Camruddin a little odd that no one else seemed conscious of the altercation, except the nondescript attendant of the Greek, who watched it closely. All the others appeared wrapt in private meditation. Recovering from his disgust, the Greek smiled upon Camruddin and condescendingly inquired,—

'What business takes you to the city?'

'I go to pay a visit long deferred, to one who is to

some extent my patron, and I have an errand also to a bimbashi of the garrison, one Arif Hikmet Bey.'

One of the Albanian bravoes, who was sitting next to Camruddin, here turned in his seat in such a manner as to bring the handle of his scimitar in painful contact with the latter's ribs. The move could not have been quite accidental. Camruddin looked round, prepared for vengeance. The face of his assailant was averted, but the face of the great man was full upon him, and its aspect was portentous, with inflated cheeks and eyes which seemed about to bolt out of their sockets. Even as he noticed it, the strange appearance vanished and the features of the nobleman resumed their usual calm. The hump-backed dwarf was wriggling in his seat. When Camruddin looked at him, he put up a finger to his lip and cast his eyes in the direction of the Greek, so swiftly that Camruddin could not be sure the movements were deliberate. But he was sure that the Albanian who had struck him whispered 'Fool' repeatedly.

All this took much less time in fact than in description, so that there was no long interval between the Greek's remark,—

'He is my friend. What is your business with him?' and Camruddin's answer, 'He is quite unknown to me. A relative of his, who is my neighbour, hearing that I was going to the city asked me to salute him.'

The private signals which he had received suggested caution, though for what reason he could not divine, being unconscious of the slightest indiscretion. It would have been another matter had he told the story of the battle in the walnut-grove. He parried all the further questions of the Greek, who soon grew weary of assailing him. And then the great man gave the word: 'To bed.'

Some two hours later, as Camruddin lay on the floor of a room in which the Greek, the dervish, and the two Albanians also lay, some of them snoring, he felt a light touch on his brow, and by the flicker of the night-light saw the hunchback dwarf kneeling beside him.

'A message from my master: Art thou mad, or what, to speak of secret things in such a company? That Greek who tempted thee to argue is a spy. The man with shifty eyes who sat beside him and said nothing is his blood-hound.'

'Merciful Allah! But I do not understand.'

'Think over what I say and thou wilt come to understanding.'

'Tell me only one thing: thy good master's name?'

'Ferid Bey, called Deyli Ferid for his eccentricity; the best of men. Good-night!' whispered the dwarf, as he withdrew.

Camruddin lay awake and listened to the others snoring. Though he pondered Deyli Ferid's message, he could make no sense of it; rather he had the feelings of a man bewitched. But the presence of the Greek and his attendant, though asleep, in the same room with him, was now unwholesome to his senses, and in the middle of the night he rose and left the place.

Chapter III

CAMRUDDIN HAD been walking in the mountain shadow and, when he suddenly beheld a world in sunlight, it was for him as if the sun had that minute risen, though it had been shining on the sea for near two hours. Pleased with the sight, he sat down on a wayside bank to contemplate it. On the one hand, in the distance, were blue, snow-capped heights in shadow; on the other, heights illumined for the most part. Before him, filling all the space between them, was the sea—a sea of cornflower blue, with here and there a flake of foam the sunlight gilded. The two horns of the gulf were edged with yellow sand, but in the centre, the part nearest to him, all the beach was hidden by some rising ground on which appeared red roofs of houses, with minarets and domes and cypress-trees—the outskirts of a city, the main part of which was hidden by those very hills from where he sat.

'Paradise!' thought Camruddin, as he surveyed the scene. 'Praise be to Allah!' And then, as he recalled that city's name for wickedness, and the number of indecent infidels which it contained, he humbly prayed to be preserved from its temptations and delivered from the dangers which its streets possessed for countrymen.

Some two hours later he was in the suburbs, trudging along a dusty road between high garden walls, as dusty as the road, with here and there a tress of mauve wistaria or branch of white acacia hanging over them. The heat by then was great, so, coming to a shady tavern, he went in, sat down upon a wooden stool, and called for sherbet. The place was a mere wooden frame supporting an immense tree of wistaria, which at that season was a mass of bloom. Then, for the first time since he set out from his mountain home, he brought his mind to bear completely on the objects of his journey.

There was no one in that spacious bower except the owner and his little son, both of them busy in a corner where was set a brazier, a rack for cups and glasses, and some earthen vessels. A ray of sunshine filtering through the flowery roof illumined now the face of one of them and now his clothing. The boy came presently to Camruddin, bringing a glass of sherbet, placed for reverence upon a saucer, which he set down upon a table near the customer, who then inquired,—'Dost know the residence of Sâdik Pasha?'

'What Sâdik Pasha?' asked the youngster dubiously, pushing aside his fez to scratch his head.

'Arab Sâdik Pasha, so named from his victories over the wild rebellious Arab tribes,' said Camruddin a little highly, for that Sâdik Pasha was his General and the Arabian expedition was his own campaign. 'All men must know him, surely, for he is the Commandant.'

'I know not,' said the boy.

He went and fetched his father who, taking stock of the appearance of the wayfarer, inquired,—

'What is it?'

'I seek direction to the residence of Sâdik Pasha, the provincial Commandant.'

'Allah kerim!' was the cool reply. 'And then?'

'I have an errand to His Excellency.'

'May Allah prosper it!' rejoined the other. 'But is it thy

own errand or His Excellency's, may I ask?' The taverner, despite his cynicism, spoke agreeably; so Camruddin requested him to take a seat while he explained the matter.

It was this: He, Camruddin, had been for years a soldier in the Pasha's army, and had risen to the rank of chaûsh or sergeant. For some time he had been attached to the person of the General, therefore in daily contact with His Excellency. Once, when the army, being on the march, had narrowly escaped an ambuscade, the Pasha had embraced him, Camruddin, in the most public manner, praising his conduct upon that occasion and promising, if they should both survive the war, to wed him to a damsel of his noble house. After that the duties of the chaûsh had taken him away from his beloved General, and when he happened to be invalided six months later, there was no way for him to let the Pasha know his plight. 'Or all would have been different,' Camruddin concluded. 'With the help of Allah I returned to my own village, and lo! I heard by chance that Sâdik Pasha, my own General, is now in high command in this country. That instant I resolved to come and see him; but I have put it off and put it off till now.'

The tavern-keeper eyed him with compassion.

'And thou wouldst know his place of residence?'

'I would.'

'Well, I will make inquiry since thy wish is firm, though much I fear a disappointment for thee.'

'His Excellency loves me, that is sure.'

The tavern-keeper shook his head. 'Who knows?' he murmured. 'Great personages lose remembrance of small folk like you and me, as one ascending a high mountain loses sight of things below. And they are guarded by a crowd of sycophants who wish to keep the source of bounty to themselves. If thou hadst asked me for advice there, in thy village, I had told thee: Never start upon a quest so doubtful unless thou hast some other cause to go that way.'

'I have another errand, as it happens,' put in Camruddin. But the tavern-keeper took no notice of the interjection.

'But since thy mind is set upon a visit to His Excellency —well, is it my affair?—I will consult the neighbours. Some of them are sure to know the dwelling of a man so famous. … Why, there goes Mikhaîl Efendi, who knows everything.' A man was passing on the road, beneath a white umbrella. The tavern-keeper called: 'Efendim, deign to enter. Here is a stranger from the country need-ing sage advice.'

The parasol was lowered and its owner—a dark-faced, white-haired Christian in frock-coat, dark trousers and a crimson fez, wearing upon his nose a pair of gold-rimmed spectacles—parted the hanging curtain of wistaria.

'May your Honour's day be good!' he murmured ami-ably. 'What is the difficulty? Deign to state it that I may resolve it for you.'

'Where is the dwelling-place of Sâdik Pasha?'

'What Sâdik Pasha?' asked the new arrival.

Camruddin renewed his explanations, and Mikhaîl Efendi commented upon them wisely. And so it was with every new arrival; for, as it drew towards noon, the bower began to fill with customers who all, from the mo-ment of entrance, became occupied with Camruddin's affair. The shade within was tinted mauve or green ac-cording as the light fell through the blossoms or the leaves of the wistaria, which gave a curious effect to all

those eager faces. One thought that Sâdik Pasha lived at
Eski-keuy, another had a strong suspicion that he dwelt
at Kizil-baghcheh, and yet another swore his house was
by the sea. At length, when Camruddin, having arrived
at nothing useful through their conversation, rose to go,
remarking that he had another errand in the city, which
must take him to the barracks, all exclaimed:

'That is the place to hear true tidings of His Excellency.
Ask at the barracks. Is he not the Commandant?'

And Camruddin was grateful for advice so kindly prof-
fered, though it was a thing he could himself have found
without consulting them.

The garden walls gave place to rows of lofty wooden
houses, with painted shutters and projecting balconies,
and these in turn to narrow, dim bazaars full of imprisoned smells and of the hum of voices, resort of all the
nations of the world. Then, from an open space before a
mosque, Camruddin saw the sea a-crawl with coloured
boats; and then, by a broad street lined with buildings of
a foreign aspect, he came to lofty iron railings on a yellow wall, within which, in a broad parade ground, stood
the barracks. The sentry at the gate, on learning that
his errand was to Arif Hikmet Bey, admitted him, and
pointed to a group of idle soldiers squatting in a doorway, saying:

'My soul, you see that Arab? It is His Honour's servant. Speak to him.'

That Arab was a negro, black as coal. His answer, when
addressed by Camruddin, was that his master was not in
the city. He had gone upon an expedition in the country. He might return that evening or to-morrow morning
or—Allah knew!—it might not be for days.

The soldiers were polite, they brought him food and

water, and in return he gave them cigarettes. They sat and gossiped in the doorway till the call to prayer from an adjacent mosque informed him that it was the middle of the afternoon.

'Where is the house of the Commandant?' he then inquired; and another twenty minutes were consumed by their precise instructions.

After leaving them he went into the mosque for prayer, and then obeyed their indications to the best of his remembrance, until obliged to seek the help of other wayfarers. At last, among the western suburbs of the town, some loungers in a baker's shop beneath a fine acacia-tree jumped up with one accord at his demand, and, all together, pointed at a door in a high wall, which was, it seemed, the entrance to the house he wanted.

Down the wall, beside the door, there hung the handle of a bell; Camruddin pulled it, rousing a great din. The door was opened cautiously, and a man in an Albanian cap looked out.

'Is the Pasha Efendi in the house?' asked Camruddin.

'Who knows? Hast thou a letter? Give it here.'

'I bear no letter. I am well known to His Excellency.' The door was shut again. Camruddin sat down before it, waiting patiently, chaffed by the idlers in the baker's shop across the road, who laughingly proposed to fetch a bed for him. At length, perceiving that he was forgotten, he got up and rang again. The Albanian cap appeared exactly as before. Its owner, seeing him still there, began abusing him. But in the chaff at him, thrown by the idlers in the baker's shop, there had been grains of good advice, which Camruddin had picked out and digested. He thrust his hand into the opening of the door, and on the palm there was a silver coin which quickly vanished. The door then opened wide enough for him to enter, which he straightway did.

He found himself in a place half courtyard and half garden, containing trees and flowering shrubs, yet three parts paved. Before him at the end of a little avenue of orange-trees growing in tubs was a kiosk consisting more of glass than woodwork, which he recognised as the selamlik of the mansion. A crowd of men in uniform sat out before it upon chairs or on the pavement. The porter pointing to them, Camruddin advanced. He felt sure that the Pasha was in that kiosk, and, if he heard about his coming, would receive him. But, meanwhile, the stare of all those seated men was like a wall against him. Experience having taught him that the higher a man's rank the more benevolent he is, in general, to a modest suitor, he stopped before the nearest officer—a colonel of dragoons—saluted and inquired again for Sâdik Pasha.

'He is in there, my son,' was the reply. 'But much I fear he cannot see thee since he is engaged in public business. I will ask, however.'

The colonel called an orderly, who sprang to the salute and ran off instantly to do his bidding, returning in a minute with a person of imposing mien, who proved to be the major-domo of the house. 'Veli,' said the colonel to this dignitary, 'here is a person who desires an audience of His Excellency— an old acquaintance, as I understand. Is he at leisure yet?'

'I think not, Bey efendim, but if the person deigns to follow me, I will make sure.'

'Go with Veli,' said the Colonel, with a smile to Camruddin.

The major-domo led the way towards the selamlik, but when quite close to it turned off into a shrubbery.

When they were out of sight and hearing of the Colonel, he looked at Camruddin, and asked in outraged tones:

'What brings thee here?'

Camruddin began to tell his story. The major-domo interrupted rudely: 'Pshaw! Has every soldier who has served with Sâdik Pasha the right to thrust his way into this house? Am I to dance attendance upon dogs?' and so on, working himself into a fury, strange to witness in a man so ponderous.

'His Excellency knows me well,' protested Camruddin.

'Too well, I wager! If thou hast a claim, write out that claim on paper and take it to the clerks at the Serai.'

If Camruddin had had a Turkish pound about him, this would have been the proper moment to present it: that he knew. A promise even might have mollified the servant's rage. But, being angered by the other's insults, he could think of no such thing, but answered warmly, with the result that, other servants drawing near, he found himself ere long surrounded by Albanian bravoes, who hustled him discreetly to a postern gate and pitched him out.

Chapter IV

BY THAT time it was dusk; so, seeing he had failed in both his errands, he gave up the adventure for that day, and walked into the city to a tavern, where he supped. When he had rested and refreshed himself he started out again to seek some sleeping-place. Misliking the more crowded quarters near the sea, he strolled uphill again into the suburbs, and had half resolved to go into the open country when, amid the gloom of garden walls beneath a starry sky, he came upon that very bower of wistaria in which at noon he had inquired his way to Sâdik Pasha's house. Two lanterns hanging from a cross-beam lighted up the place, showing the colour of the hanging blossoms and green leaves. Despite the lateness of the hour there were some customers. Camruddin entered with a sense of homecoming, and, sitting down beside a table, called for coffee.

'What luck?' inquired the tavern keeper, with a grin of recognition.

Camruddin shrugged and spread out both his hands.

'No matter, I will try again to-morrow.'

'Have you a lodging?'

'No, I shall sleep out.'

'Sleep here and welcome, in the name of Allah. My son and I have often slept here undisturbed. The sentry at the corner keeps an eye upon the place to see that nothing happens to my stock-in-trade. I will tell him you are here when I go by.'

'I offer many thanks,' said Camruddin.

His host then brought the coffee he had ordered, and asked to hear the story of his day's pursuit.

An hour was spent in pleasant conversation, interrupted by the necessary business as one after another of the customers took leave and paid his score. When all was done, the landlord and his son, with help from Camruddin, piled up the stools and tables and prepared a bed beside the brazier. The landlord then put out one lantern, saying,—

'The other I will leave alight to keep you company.'

He said good-night and went out with his son.

Before the pair had passed the hanging curtain of wistaria, Camruddin was fast asleep. He woke to find it daylight and to see the tavern-keeper, on his stomach, blowing at the charcoal in the brazier. The friends embraced each other and then made ablutions, each pouring water for the other, for the morning prayer which they performed together, side by side. The tavern-keeper then made coffee, and brought bread and olives for his guest who, thus refreshed, set out again upon his errands. His first recourse was to the barracks as upon the day before. After squatting for a long time in the yard, he saw the negro servant of the bimbashi, who shrugged, regretting that his master had not yet returned.

Going away again resignedly, Camruddin was greeted just outside the gate by a man of very rascally appearance, who seemed pleased to see him, and reminded him that they had met two nights before at Deyli Ferid Bey's reception at the wayside inn. It was, in fact, the mute attendant of the Greek, who, as the hunchback dwarf had warned him, was a spy.

Now, Camruddin was feeling lonely in the city, and the tone of cordiality appealed to him. The man might be a spy; he was no less a human being who showed a disposition to be friendly. And Camruddin, an honest man and loyal subject of the Padishah, was conscious of no reason to fight shy of him. Indeed, he thought of dissipating by a friendly confidence any suspicions which the other might have gathered from his conversation at the inn. So when the man invited him to take refreshment at his lodging he accepted gratefully, and went with him through dirty alleys, across a courtyard strewn with garbage, up a creaking stairway to an upper room in which five other worthies were assembled. Then Camruddin felt sorry he had come, for all the men were of most villainous appearance, and their language foul, which was the more offensive since they wore the costume of efendis and affected fashionable airs.

'I saw you at the barracks yesterday and then to-day. What are you after?' asked his host, by name Khalîl. If the question had been put to him in private, Camruddin would probably have answered frankly; but in presence of that group of dunghill beys he said,—'I have a message for an officer.'

'For Arif Hikmet Bey, the bimbashi—I heard you say it at the inn,' put in Khalîl. 'A message of what nature?'

'From a friend of his.'

'Ah, he has many friends, we know—a perfect army! And I, though in a small way, may be counted one of them. No need for caution here, You can speak openly.'

'I do not understand your meaning,' answered Camruddin.

'Well, I will tell you! There are men you know—a few— who get the word from men you do not know, and pass it on to you. Tell us the name of one of those you know and we will tell you what the first word was which you received. That will show you we are in the secret.'

'I do not understand at all,' said Camruddin. 'I bring a message to the yuzbashi from one who loves him—a sick relation, to be more particular—who longs for tidings of his health.'

'Your caution is all wasted, for we know your errand perfectly,' observed another of the swaggerers. 'And yet it would be better for you to be frank with us, who offer friendship. We can place you in the way to wealth and honour, or destroy you. So beware!'

'I do not understand,' repeated Camruddin. 'The hour grows late. I must depart, with your permission.'

Khalîl at that assured him it was all a joke, and begged him not to take offence, but stay and talk with them. Yet still he kept returning to the matter of the errand, striving by every means to worm it out of him. And Camruddin, as he looked round on that ill-favoured crew, longed for the open street as for the breath of Paradise.

'Well, tell us but the name of him who sent you,'— said Khalîl at length—'the bimbashi's relation. We will be content. Your telling us can do no harm to any one, and to refuse us, who have offered friendship, every information, even the most trifling, is mere churlish insult. Come, his name!'

'Nasruddin Khoja,' answered Camruddin defiantly.

At that they rose against him with terrific oaths. Expecting an attack, he thrust his hands into his girdle and grasped the handles of a knife and pistol there concealed. But Khalîl, who seemed to be their chief, restrained their violence, speaking to them sharply in a foreign language. He turned then to the visitor and said,—

'Thou hast refused our friendship and defied us. So beware!' And Camruddin was suffered to depart uninjured, a boon for which he rendered heartfelt thanks to Allah. In that room, with those rascals round him, he had known the taste of death.

When, escaping from the cut-throat alleys, he came out upon the quay in blazing sunlight, the muezzins were just calling to the prayer of noon. Camruddin obeyed the call. Emerging from the mosque half an hour later with his fortitude restored, he once more climbed the street which leads up to the barracks. As he sat waiting for the orderly of Arif Hikmet Bey, he saw his late tormentors grinning at him through the railings. The negro came to him at length, smiling regret. His master had not yet returned, it seemed, nor sent a word.

'Is there another way out of this yard?' asked Camruddin, desirous to avoid a fresh encounter with the dunghill beys.

The negro showed him a small gate which led on to a piece of waste land at the back of houses. Camruddin took that way. But his pursuers must have watched him through the railings, for when he issued from the gate he saw them coming round the corner of the barracks-wall. They gave a view-halloa. He ran for the first opening in the houses opposite, which proved to be a narrow street, turned to the right at the first opportunity, then to the left beneath a stinking tunnel; and continued dodging thus at random until he felt that he had baffled all pursuit. That done, he set to work to ascertain his whereabouts, meaning to go to Sâdik Pasha's house. On his way thither, in a broad and crowded thoroughfare, he suddenly caught

sight of Sâdik Pasha seated in a carriage. He was darting out into the road to claim his notice, when another
carriage from the opposite direction came between. He
narrowly escaped destruction, and was locked in heated
altercation with the driver when he saw the rogue Khalîl
upon the further pavement. Without waiting to consider
whether he himself had been espied or no, he plunged
once more into a maze of by-streets, and again it took
him time to find the right direction, so that the afternoon was well advanced before he reached the General's
house.

The same group of men—or one exactly similar—
was lounging in the baker's shop beneath the great acacia
tree. They recognised him and threw out polite remarks.
He rang the bell, prepared for the Albanian's arrogance,
but the door was opened by another servant, who let
him in before inquiring of his errand.

'Is the Pasha Efendi in the house?' asked Camruddin.
'No, I regret,' was the reply. 'He did return an hour ago,
but he has gone again. It is like that.'

'When is the time to find him at his leisure for one
who needs to speak to him in private?'

'The first hour after noon or in the evening.'

'Many thanks.'

As Camruddin went out again into the road he saw
a person, with his back towards him, talking to the gos-
sips in the baker's shop. That person turned. It was the
rogue Khalîl. Camruddin could have screamed. He felt
bewitched. The ruffian ran to him and seized his arm, exclaiming: 'What is this? I see you come out of the dwelling of the Commandant—you, the confidential messenger of some one else?'

'I have told you that I do not know the yuzbashi. But

His Excellency Sâdik Pasha I know well, for I was with him in Arabia.'

'Ma sha'llah! Well, be not churlish any longer. Come and sup with me. Then after supper we will go together to the cinema.'

'I offer thanks, but I am weary. I would seek my lodging.'

'Where?'

'That is my affair.'

'Merciful Allah! Are these manners? Be more sociable! Come, let us feast together and then take our pleasure. This city has its secret joys which I will show thee.' Khalîl kept pleading in an injured tone, till, finding Camruddin immovable, he cried,—

'May you go blind!' and flung away. Before he had gone many paces he called out 'Beware!' and then began to hum an air as if to close the incident. Camruddin strolled back to the bower of wistaria, where, having appeased his hunger with a dish of eggs and sour milk, he told the story of the day's adventures to the host; who looked exceeding wise.

'Who are these men?' he questioned irritably. 'Why do they follow me? What have I ever done that they should plague me with suspicion? I am bewitched. The Lord of Justice is my refuge!'

The host was going to reply, but just then he was called to serve another customer. On his return he said: 'Some evil threatens you. Take my advice. Rest here to-night, and in the morning go straight home.'

'In truth I have a mind to do so,' answered Camruddin.

The lantern hanging from the leafy roof had just been lighted, bringing back the colour of the hanging blossom, and turning the surrounding twilight from dim gray to blue, when a horseman stopped before the bower and shouted,—

'Ey, Huseyn Agha!'

'Hâzir, efendim!' came the answer, as the tavern-keeper bustled out. Another minute and the horseman went his way. The host returned to his position facing Camruddin, but with a new expression of dismay. He told him,—

'News! … Somebody fired upon your friend, the Com-mandant, an hour ago as he was driving to his house, just before sunset. Some say the bullets missed him altogether, others that he is wounded in the arm.'

'Praise be to Allah, he escaped!' said Camruddin.

'That man on horseback had the tidings from his cousin, a lieutenant of police. Suppose that the assas-sin had to do with those same rogues who followed you about to-day! … Who knows? They might attempt to throw the blame on you, though you were sitting here with me at sunset when the shots were fired. In truth, I like not the appearance of your business in this city. Go straight home!'

But Camruddin, though he accepted that good friend's advice, felt far too much concern for Sâdik Pasha's welfare to think of going without some assurance of his patron's health. Accordingly, next morning when the sun appeared, he turned his steps once more towards the dwelling of the Commandant. All his disquiet of the night before had passed away. This morning he was in serene religious mood, uplifted high above the cares of this low world, in contemplation of the splendid tragedy of life and death, with Allah's mercy like sunlight over all. The road which wound between the high, gray walls was cool and shady, the sky above was flawless sapphire infinite.

The distaff cypress trees, the tapering minarets seemed pointing upward to that wondrous purity. Every one he met upon the road was friendly. Mankind were brothers under one blue sky, with one inexorable fate awaiting them. Without the thought of Allah's mercy he might well have grieved for them. But, as it was, he felt exultant in subjection, a willing bondman to the Lord of Heaven and Earth, who 'knows the weight of the black ant on the hard stone in the dark night.'

Reciting in his mind a verse of the Coran, he came into the quiet road before the Pasha's house. It was no longer quiet. Soldiers were sitting out on chairs before the garden door, and round the baker's shop beneath the great acacia-tree there was a considerable crowd of loiterers and buzz of gossip. Camruddin approached that crowd in search of tidings. Calling down peace upon them all, he put his question to those nearest;

What happened then he never knew exactly, except that he espied the rogue Khalîl and then was tripped up from behind, while some one near him shouted 'Praise to Allah!'

Chapter V

WHEN CAMRUDDIN regained his senses he was being half-carried and half-dragged along amid a throng of men. His first assailants had now given place to soldiers, who were much more gentle in their handling of him and inspired more confidence. A voice exclaimed: 'The crowd impedes us. Call a carriage!' In another minute he was being hoisted up into a hackney vehicle, his warders taking seat, two opposite and one beside him, while another climbed upon the box beside the driver and yet another perched upon the step and clung on desperately as the whole agglomeration was transported at full gallop through the streets to the Serai. There they all got out and Camruddin was led into a whitewashed entrance-hall, where he stood a long while with his escort, waiting further orders.

'Brother, for the love of Allah say: of what am I accused?' he asked the corporal.

'Brother, you ought to know,' replied the other kindly. 'You tried to kill the Commandant. It will be bad for you.'

'But I am innocent, by Allah the Tremendous. I would not hurt a hair of him. He is my patron.'

'Hush!' said the other, with a sudden sternness.

Some persons of importance had just come into the vestibule, talking and laughing as if life were gay. The voice of one of them was known to Camruddin. He knew its owner to be Deyli Ferid Bey even before he heard the well-known expletive and saw the face of that eccentric notable. The group of careless ones came up the hall. As they were passing near the soldiers and their prisoner, Camruddin cried: 'Efendim, help, for I am innocent!'

The other fashionables took no notice of the bitter cry, but Ferid Bey stood still and faced the prisoner.

'Kerata!' he exclaimed. 'It is my simple countryman! Of what, pray, do men venture to accuse this lump of guilelessness? ... Answer me, you—the corporal only! I would not be deafened.'

To give still further emphasis to this command, Ferid Bey prodded the corporal gently in the stomach with his walking-stick.

'Efendim, he is charged with the attempt to murder Sâdik Pasha yesterday evening, as His Excellency was returning homeward in his carriage.'

'Ma sha'llah! A crime indeed! A good fat crime!' Ferid Bey turned and prodded Camruddin, inquiring,—

'And what is your defence, my child?'

'I have not seen His Excellency for the last three years. He is my patron, and my life is his ransom. He promised to befriend me when the war was ended. I sought to see him but they kept me back. Having heard how he escaped death yesterday, I went to-day to offer my congratulations. As I drew near the gate I was assaulted and made prisoner. Efendim, that is all I know about the matter.'

'Good,' replied Ferid Bey. 'Thou speakest truth, no doubt, but by misfortune I am not the judge, and there are some formalities to be fulfilled. Say, have you any witnesses?'

'Allah is my witness, and the Commandant himself, efendim. He knows me well, and has great love for me.'

'Ay, that is something,' answered Ferid Bey, 'but unless you have a friend to speak for you, it seems improbable that you will see the Commandant.'

Again the great one turned his point against the corporal, asking abruptly 'Who are the accusers?'

'Agents of the police, efendim. I heard them say they have no end of witnesses.'

'They always have,' said Ferid Bey; 'may they all burst! … In that case everything is possible. May Allah help you!'

The pious wish was thrown aside to Camruddin as the young bey hastened to rejoin his gay companions. The hope which had leapt up in the prisoner's breast at sight of a face known to him was now extinguished.

'He can do something for you, brother,' said the corporal; 'for he is a near relation of the Commandant. If he will take the trouble,' was appended with a shrug.

Camruddin remembered the contented state of mind in which he had set out that morning from the arbour of wistaria, which now appeared remote as paradise. He could not but contrast that happy freedom with his present plight. His thoughts retraced the whole road he had travelled from his native village; and fain would he have been transported to the wildest part of it far from this hell of madness and iniquity. His soul longed for the scent of myrtle on the mountainside, the song of mule-bells on the valley road. Instead there came a harsh word of command, and he was led into a room where many persons were assembled. In a dream, he heard the story of his crime recited circumstantially and then confirmed by witnesses. Some of the circumstances were true, and after listening to so much evidence, he himself was half persuaded that the other circumstances which were new to him were also true; that he had done all that they related in a fit of madness or beneath some evil spell. Dazed and discouraged by the flood of eloquence, he was trying to collect his wits to meet the questions which he knew were coming, when every one stood up. The door had opened. His Excellency Sâdik Pasha came into the room, attended by an aide-de-camp and Deyli Ferid Bey.

'There stands the man who claims old friendship with your Excellency,' said Ferid when the salutations were concluded and the door was shut.

Sâdik Pasha looked at Camruddin, whose heart stood still. Then he replied 'He speaks the truth,' and, traversing the room with quiet dignity, laid his right hand upon the shoulder of the prisoner. 'It is my chaûsh, Camruddin Agha, a brave, true man,' he said distinctly so that all might hear. 'Of what is he accused? I am his surety.'

'He tried to kill your Excellency.' 'He is involved in the New Turk conspiracy.' 'He was heard by many witnesses, efendim, inquiring at the barracks for a certain officer, who is only too well known, and he was followed from the barracks to your Excellency's house. When questioned by an agent he could give no proper reason for his presence in the town. He was seen, lurking near your Excellency's house, by several first-rate witnesses yesterday evening but an hour before the crime, and several first-rate witnesses identify him as the criminal ...'

'Enough!' exclaimed the Commandant impatiently. 'He wished to see me, it is only natural. He is an old friend, one of my chief supports in the campaign of Yemen. He saved my life on more than one occasion.'

'Efendim, all is as you say,' answered a voice in accents of despair, 'but in that case the charge against a certain officer, who is but too well known, falls through for lack of evidence; and that would be a disappointment to the Government. I entreat your Excellency to let things take their course.'

Camruddin had courage now to look about him. With his General's hand upon his shoulder, he felt equal to his persecutors.

He saw the faces round the table individually, and recognised among them the same Greek who had so feelingly expounded the abuses of the Government in the conversation after Deyli Ferid's banquet at the wayside inn. Those faces brightened for a moment at the strong entreaty; but when the Pasha answered: 'What is that to me?' relapsed once more to gloom of disappointment.

'The man is innocent. I am his surety. If any one has claims against him, let him come to me.'

The members of the court threw up their hands and rose with sighs, as men who see that things have passed beyond their power; and Camruddin was free. He went out with the Commandant, who, in the corridor looked at his watch and said,—

'Praise be to Allah, I have got you safe and sound! Now I must leave you. Go with the Bey Efendi. He will take care of you until this evening, when I expect to see you at my house. Till then, in Allah's keeping!'

And he walked off with his aide-de-camp. 'Now come and laugh with me, my soul,' said Ferid Bey. 'I owe you twenty pounds bakhshish for this day's work. Those cuckolds are for once defeated. May they all go blind!'

Chapter VI

THE SUNLIGHT and clamour of the city appeared strange to Camruddin as he came out of the Serai, feeling as one arising from the dead. A carriage with fine champing horses was in waiting. Ferid Bey said: 'Up!' and Camruddin climbed hurriedly on to the box-seat indicated by the great man's golden-headed walking-stick. Thus high exalted he was carried through the town, the coachman shouting constantly to clear a way.

The carriage stopped at last among the suburbs, before a garden gate which opened instantly. Servants came running out. Camruddin climbed down and stood aside respectfully, hoping to be dismissed. The arbour of wistaria was in his mind as a desirable resort. But Ferid Bey, alighting, pointed at him with that awful walking-stick, commanding: 'Go indoors!'

'Istaghfaru'llah!' exclaimed Camruddin. 'After your Honour.'

'Kerata!' snarled the Bey with sudden rage, making as if to hurl the stick at him. 'Indoors, I say! And quick! You are my prisoner. Seek to escape and I will have you flayed alive.'

When Camruddin obeyed, he thrust the point of the stick into the middle of his back, and thus propelled him up the path to the selamlik. The victim of this rage, however, observing that the faces of the servants showed no consternation at this outburst, but rather pleasure and a fond indulgence, judged that the rich bey's temper was not dangerous.

Having shepherded his captive up some marble steps into a great reception-room, Ferid Bey flopped down on the divan and ordered sherbet. Through open windows came the scent of roses, with the coo of doves among the branches of the garden-trees. The softly modulated voices of the company did not disturb the atmosphere of peace. But Camruddin remembered it was Friday, and as the hour for noon-day prayer drew near, grew restive. At last he mustered up the courage necessary to ask leave to go.

'What ails you? Does our company displease you or are you tired of life?' asked Deyli Ferid with a formidable frown. 'Do you suppose the agents love you for this morning's work? Or do you think that they are not afoot to do you injury? … No, you cannot depart. But we can lock you up!'

'Efendim, it is not for pastime that I ask. It is the day of congregation, and I would fain perform my prayer and hear the sermon. It was from respect that I desired permission to depart. I now ask leave to go together with your Excellency.'

Ferid Bey stared in pure amazement at the speaker, while a look of smothered mirth appeared on the attendant faces. He looked as if he would explode, but then thought better of it. 'Good,' was the one word that he uttered after many gasps. But thenceforth he was restless, seeming irritable; and when the chant of the muezzin quivered in the still, warm air, he rose and stretched himself, exclaiming: 'Hie to prayer!' Seeing dismay upon the faces of his followers, he added 'Cuckolds! Am I not a Muslim?' and cursed them for a set of rotten atheists. Yet no one showed the least alarm, which seemed to Camruddin remarkable.

Having perfected their ablutions, the whole party crossed the garden where a fountain chuckled, and went out by a postern to a quiet road in which the mosque was situated. The small white building was already three-parts full of worshippers. Ferid Bey sat down on the left of the last row and beckoned Camruddin to take his place beside him. He fidgeted a little during the long sermon; but, when the ranks stood up for prayer, Camruddin forgot his presence and all earthly things, remaining absorbed in his devotions some time after the remainder of the congregation had dispersed. When he arose, at last, he found the bey and his attendants waiting for him at the door. No word was spoken until they were again in the selamlik, when one of the companions chanced to sigh as if relieved. The great man turned on him, inquiring: 'What has wearied thee?'

The hunchbacked dwarf replied with a broad grin:

'Efendim, we are all heart-weary with suspense and grave anxiety, of which, praise be to Allah, we are now relieved.'

'Kerata, rogue! Explain thy meaning instantly!'

'My meaning is that through the whole length of the khutbeh we feared to hear your Excellency cry out "Kerata!" or "May he burst."'

At that the bey laughed heartily, and Camruddin began to feel affection for him. In the army he had come across such characters and found them good.

The bey insisted on his captive's sitting with him at the midday meal, which was set forth in the Frankish manner on a table raised so high above the ground that everybody had to sit on chairs to get at it; and when the meal was over and the bey retired, the dwarf took charge of Camruddin, and in the garden told him of the bey's mad pranks: how, hearing of the way in which the tax-farmer of a certain district, in which he had estates, defrauded husbandmen, he asked the rogue to dinner, and defrauded him in precisely the same manner, of his food, in the presence of the Vali, the Naïb, the Mufti and a host of notables, to whom he afterwards explained the meaning of the play; and how, when the agents of the Government arrived to seize a learned man, his neighbour in Stamboul, by night, he, being warned of what was happening by the little daughter of the learned man aforesaid, armed his servants and repelled the agents in a way so comical that they had never dared to breathe a word of the affair; and many other merry doings which the dwarf retailed with fits of laughter at the mere remembrance.

Then Camruddin received a summons to the private chamber of the bey, who, when they were alone together, thus addressed him,—

'O son of Adam, at our first encounter, when you spoke of discontent among the soldiers and said you had an errand to a certain yuzbashi, and when I found you under guard at the Serai this morning, I judged you nothing less than a conspirator. But now, having observed you somewhat closely, I see you are no schemer, but the sport of circumstance. ... Kerata! Let me finish! This is my advice: Forget the faces of the men who dogged you and the witnesses. Forget whatever you have heard or seen to cause bewilderment. By that I do not mean, forget completely that would be impossible—but ask no questions on the subject and, above all, never speak of it in any company … Now, what have you to say? I see you bursting.'

'Efendim, it is in my mind to ask a question.'

'Ask in safety!'

'Why did your Excellency choose to help me if you thought me guilty? If I had been guilty I should have deserved to die.'

'Aha! you do not lack intelligence, my friend. Well, now, suppose two parties in dispute: on one side rottenness, ennobled by a few good men, and on the other, health, with the exception of a few bad individuals, all this within the body of Islâm'. Which party would you choose?'

'The second surely.'

'Then make a further supposition: Suppose that from the side of health a good man or a bad man—God knows which!—assailed one of the good men who contend for rottenness, not aiming at the man but at the evil he defends; suppose the said assault to fail—no harm is done—and the assailant to be captured. Suppose that the bad faction can, through him, bring harm to other persons more important. Tell me, as a Muslim, would you seek to punish that assailant? Would you not rather seek to rescue him?'

'Efendim, I should seek to rescue him,' said Camruddin. 'Your Excellency speaks in allegory; that is understood. But how can my lord, Sâdik Pasha, be compared to one upon the side of evil, seeing that he is a loyal servant of the Padishah?'

'Ah, there we come to facts and personalities. I cannot say. But think upon the matter, without ever speaking of it; take notice of the things around you, reconsider your past life, and you will solve the riddle for yourself. You have been a sergeant in the army—that means some-thing—and in these last days have suffered at the hands of spies. The faces of the persons who denounced you and their witnesses are known to you. Say: are they good or evil?'

'Evil, efendim.'

'Yet to-day such men are numbered by the hundred thousand in the House of Islâm—the country which was once the realm of happiness, the region of the Sacred Law. For any man who has intelligence or learning, for any man desiring progress or reform, for any man who cherishes the right of every Muslim to free opinion and free speech accorded by the Sacred Law, they blight exis-tence. They are the slaves of all abuses, all corruption, and they are the darlings of our men of power. Is all that good or bad, I ask you?'

'Bad, efendim.'

'I have said enough.'

'It grieves me that your Excellency should dislike my patron.'

'I dislike him? He is my maternal uncle and has been a father to me since I was a child so high! By Allah, there is no man dearer to me in the world. Sâdik Pasha himself, were he to speak his mind, would say the same to you that I have said. He is not blind to their good purpose, though they try to kill him.'

Camruddin flung up both his hands and murmured: 'Ma sha'llah!'

'And now, since it is clear that you are not what I at first supposed, I ask you with most lively curiosity: What do you know of Arif Hikmet Bey?'

Camruddin gave an outline of the story while Ferid's face assumed a curious, gloating look. 'I still must see him,' he insisted, in conclusion.

'Be easy, you shall see him here to-morrow. And now I wager that you think I am a plotter, a man of earnest purpose under all my madness. That is not the case. I love the men too well to love the causes which set them by the ears. If for a time I side with either party, it is in a jesting way, for caprice or the love of mischief as to-day, in your case. My mind is indolent and cynical. I hate decisions which are not my own. Now go, while thou hast still some senses left, before my madness has bewildered you completely.'

Camruddin then went back into the garden. It was not till after sunset prayers that Ferid Bey appeared again, inquiring if the carriage was in waiting. Hearing 'Yes,' he ordered Camruddin to go with him to Sâdik Pasha's house. This time his guest sat in the carriage, facing him. For a long while they both were silent; then the bey exclaimed,—

'I am a wretch! My being was polluted before I could think. I had a foreign tutor who made fun of all our ways; and then they sent me to a school of Frankish missionaries, whose teaching, though I scorned it, fouled my brain and muddles everything which should be clear for true believers. Rottenness and health seem much alike to me. I tolerate all kinds of men, but scoff at causes as no Muslim should. I feel ashamed in the presence of a man like you.'

'Istaghfaru'llah! I was frightened of your Excellency, but now I know you for the best of men,' said Camruddin, and bending down he kissed the young bey's hand.

Chapter VII

IN SÂDIK PASHA'S house, Ferid Bey gave Camruddin into the care of the now obsequious major-domo, while he himself repaired to the haramlik. The major-domo led his charge upstairs to a small sitting-room with window looking on a cypress grove, and left him there with the remark that he would tell the Pasha. The room was nearly dark though the remains of sunset still tinged the western sky—a streak of orange shading into apple-green beneath the blue of night. The cypress trees stood up like shrouded watchers. An owl was hooting, and, from farther off, by caprice of the wind, came now the city's restless murmur, now the sighing of the sea.

Full of the new ideas he had received that day, Camruddin fell into a reverie. It was a fact that much was wrong with the Islâmic empire. The thought that men were striving for improvement, even to the death, now thrilled him like an inspiration. It gave him hope for the revival of Islâm, for which all Muslims prayed. The sad and shameful things which happened daily in the empire were all against the teaching of the Sacred Law, they were the product of ambition, lust of power and man's oppression in the realm where God alone was rightful King. All this appeared to him as he recalled the guarded words of Ferid Bey, though at the time those words were uttered he had failed to grasp their meaning. As he looked across the dusky garden to the western glow, he had the vision of new life for all mankind. The voice of Sâdik Pasha saying 'Bring a light!' recalled him. A negro servant in white raiment came, bearing a lamp. The Pasha followed in the servant's shadow.

'Peace be upon thee. Pray, sit down, my soul!'

Camruddin tried to kiss his patron's hand, but could not, for that hand was laid upon his shoulder firmly. 'Now, tell me all that has befallen thee since last we met. I sought for thee in every corner of Arabia.'

Efendim, I was invalided at Hodeydah. Thence, by the kindness of a merchant I was sent to Suez, where, feeling better, I became attached to an Egyptian bey, with whom I had the honour to perform the pilgrimage. And then'— he shrugged—'I journeyed home "on Allah's mercy," as the saying goes.'

The Pasha sat upon a sofa with one foot tucked under him, his elbow on his knee, his chin supported on his hand. He was a man of sixty, but without infirmity, his figure still elastic and his eye alert. A close-clipped beard and massive curled moustache gave dignity to his demeanour under the severe red fez.

'A pity thou didst leave the army,' he observed reflectively. 'Thou wouldst have made a useful officer, with some instruction.'

He frowned a little, keeping silence for some time—a silence which his visitor did not presume to break. A servant, bringing in refreshments—coffee, water, and a pile of sweetmeats, on a finely-wrought brass tray, inlaid with silver—made diversion. A little girl of nine or ten years old appeared behind him in the doorway.

'Come hither, Sâmieh!' the General cried. 'It is my youngest daughter,' he explained to Camruddin. 'She always comes exactly at this hour to say good-night to father. Come hither, sugar-lips, and make obeisance to Camruddin Agha. Kiss his hand. And now a curtsey in the Frankish manner! Aferîn, efendim!'

He put the pretty child between them on the sofa, and held her there while she devoured three sweets which he picked out for her; then kissed her fondly on the brow and bade her run to nurse, a smiling negress who appeared that moment in the doorway.

Alone with Camruddin once more, the Pasha said,—

'I am distressed and much ashamed to hear the story of thy sufferings, though Allah knows they were not of my willing. After my promise given on that morning I ought not to have let thee go away from me. The words of gratitude I spoke in that abominable sandy wilderness made me thy guardian.'

'Efendim, it is not to be remembered. Allah knows, the words were far beyond my merit. The public honour was reward enough.'

'I promised before Allah and all men there present that, if we both returned alive into the Guarded Realms, I would care for thee as for a child of my own house, and would give to thee a child of my own house in marriage. That vow has been incumbent on me ever since. A girl attendant upon Leylah Hânum, by name Gulraaneh, is of marriageable age. I have already spoken to her mistress upon thy behalf, that she may ascertain the disposition of the girl herself. If she consents, then I, as thy adopted father, provide a dowry of one thousand pounds—one half of which I pay in cash to thee, to give her a position some degree above the common. Is this acceptable?'

'Efendim, may the Lord of Right reward your goodness! … I make thanksgiving … What is man to say? …'

'Then come again to-morrow evening, and, if all goes well, we will then execute the marriage contract before witnesses.'

'Efendim,' began Camruddin, and hesitated.

'Efendim?' questioned Sâdik playfully.

'Efendim, this young lady will be my superior in education and refinement. She is used to luxury. I cannot in a day prepare a dwelling worthy of her, nor can I in a day improve my manners and behaviour.'

'Claim thy bride when it pleases thee. All that I demand is that the marriage be secured by law as soon as possible. If that bullet had not missed me yesterday, I should have gone to my account with this debt undischarged. That is the third attempt to kill me which has failed by Allah's mercy. It will not be the last, for they must kill me; I myself perceive it. My death is necessary for the purpose which they have in view. I myself make it so by standing forth against that purpose, when it would be easy for me to play double and avoid offending them. On both sides it is an affair of conscience. I blame nobody. To die is easy when the mind has rest. And I would sooner perish at the hands of noble-minded dreamers than at the hands of vulgar rogues.' He seemed for a moment to be talking to himself, forgetful of the presence of his visitor. Remembering that presence suddenly, he smiled and said: 'To every man his kismet—Allah is greater!'

'The man who could take aim deliberately at your Excellency is far from noble-minded,' exclaimed Camruddin.

'Who knows?' replied the General with a shrug. 'Thou knowest how in war brave, honest men, who if they met in peace would be sworn brothers, kill each other of necessity, without malevolence. It is like that in the secret strife at present raging in this province. Some are for change and some for the existing order, yet both are for Islâm, and both—I do believe it—for the Padishah. Both recognise that there is something wrong, and both are heart-sick at the fallen state of this great empire, beleaguered by the Christian powers as by a pack of wolves. They lie around us with their tongues out, waiting for us to die. The only chance, as it appears to some of us, of prolonging our existence is to feign decrepitude, to cultivate the symptoms of approaching dissolution in much the same way that a beggar trades on his infirmities. I think reform would be the signal for the final onslaught; but others—good men, too— believe that it would change the enmity which now surrounds us to sincere goodwill. … But here I talk to thee of things uninteresting.'—Camruddin made a gesture of denial—'All that I truly wished to say was this: There is a chance that they are right, and I am wrong. Allah is greater! Time alone will show. I cannot call the men who seek to kill me scoundrels, because my own son holds the same opinions, and I have talked with him and know that there is nothing base in his ideas. But men in power, even the worst of them, are not perhaps such malefactors as they think them. So-and-so is governor of somewhere; he takes gifts from every comer, a most wicked man! But does he take the money for himself? Is it not rather for a retinue of relatives and poor retainers for whom he is, by custom, called upon to make provision? These—and there may be hundreds of them—praise his name. The custom rose in days of great prosperity, and now, in leaner days, it still prevails. How can one human being break away from it, and earn reproach from those dependent on him? It is very hard. And there are other cases—but I weary thee.'

'No, by Allah,' replied Camruddin enthusiastically. 'It is the best instruction that I ever had.'

'Thy marriage then is for to-morrow night, if all goes well. When that is settled, my debt paid thee, I shall be clear of earthly obligations and prepared to die. Here comes my nephew, Ferid Bey, to take thee from me. A good lad though a lazy. Thou art safe with him. Praise be to Allah, who restored thee to me!'

As Camruddin sat in the carriage facing Ferid Bey during the homeward drive, he felt as if he had emerged from some religious ordeal. His mind was opening to new and wonderful ideas of life, without an effort, as buds open to the sunlight when their hour has come, the hour known only to Allah; and he was hushed in contemplation of the miracle. As luck would have it, Ferid Bey was silent too.

Chapter VIII

NEXT MORNING Camruddin was lying in the shade of a great mulberry tree conversing with the hunchback dwarf and other members of the household, when a eunuch, coming from the women's quarters, called to him by name. He was slow to move, for it was pleasant in that isle of shadow amid blazing sunlight, screened from the sun's blue fire by layer on layer of leaves and snowy bloom. But as the summons was repeated and the eunuch drew no nearer, he rose at length, exclaiming 'Bismillah!'

'A veiled one asks a favour of thee,' said the eunuch for his private ear.

'Mercy!' And what is her demand?' said Camruddin.

'Merely that thou wilt follow her a certain distance as far as to a lane which runs beside the mansion of the Commandant Pasha, in order that a maiden may behold thy likeness and take note of it. Come now into the house —it is my master's order—that we may make of thee a sight provocative of love's disease.'

Half an hour later Camruddin came out again, elegantly clad in clothes provided by the bey, washed, brushed, and perfumed, but exceedingly self-conscious, with the sense of being some one new, as yet untried. The household, taking pride in his appearance, wished him well. Outside the gate a figure shrouded in black charshaf waited. It moved as he appeared, then stopped to see if he was coming, beck-oned, and moved again with shuffling gait. He followed with a wildly beating heart. The road, with country carts drawn by gray oxen, and people in all kinds of raiment in them, appeared now a blur, and now appallingly distinct before his eyes. Never in his life before had he experienced such shyness.

Not until his guide had led him past the gate of Sâdik Pasha's house and reached the turning next beyond it did she let him overtake her. A narrow alley ran between high garden walls down towards the cypress trees of a great cemetery. A latticed window of the Pasha's man-sion overhung it, and a little farther down the lane a fig-tree grew against the wall. The shrouded figure pointed to the tree, while from behind the veils there came the voice of a self-satisfied old woman, saying: 'Now, my lamb, be good enough to walk down past that lattice on the farther side until thou comest to that fig-tree, then return. Step out with ease, and yet not hurriedly; with dignity, and yet with sprightliness. Look up when pass-ing by the window, that one who hides behind the lat-tice may behold your face: and in so doing smile in such a manner as to show your teeth completely. Praise be to Allah they are white and small and none is missing. Return in the same manner. I will meet you.'

Camruddin began to do as he was told, feeling in-tensely solitary, shy, and foolish.

'Very pretty!' the old woman shouted after him.

He looked up at the window with the exhibition of his teeth. It occurred to him as more than possible that there was no one there, that the old woman was a joker who was making fun of him. But when, having gone up to the fig-tree, he returned, he heard soft voices and even fancied he could catch a glimpse of girlish forms within the lattice. The hag was standing underneath it listening. At his approach the talk was hushed. The crone said,—

'Good. And now, my lamb, my pretty ruffler, it is the lady's will to see you run. Run to the corner and back again. Run as you would run to save your love from danger.'

Camruddin hesitated for a moment. Then he ran. On his return there was a cry of 'Bravo' from the lattice.

'Now jump as high into the air as may be.'

Camruddin waited to recover his breath, then made the leap demanded.

'Now, hop upon your right foot as far as to that stone and back, preserving balance.'

Camruddin obeyed, now grinning broadly. He heard giggles.

'Now on the left foot likewise.' His instructress seemed but to repeat the orders which she heard from one concealed within the lattice.

'Now, stand on one leg, stretch out one arm sideways, the other upwards, and see how long you can preserve your body's balance.'

Camruddin assumed the posture, but at once relinquished it. The giggles had become a silvery peal of laughter. To the old woman's cry of 'What is this?' and 'Persevere, my lamb!' he answered: 'It is finished. I have shown enough,' in tones a little gruff with indignation.

At that a voice within the lattice cried: 'Behold his anger! The anger of my lord! That is the best of all! Tell him, Kalfa, that I shall do just what I like with him, that if I tell him always to stand on his head, he must obey me.'

'You hear, ravisher of spirits,' said the crone to Camruddin. 'What do you say in answer to the Spring of

Life, the Food of Hearts?'

'I say it is no bargain. She examined me for half an hour; but I have not seen her. The bargain would be all one-sided. I reject it.'

'Believe in the Unseen. It is a Muslim's duty.'

With the words a wicket in the lattice opened showing him a roguish face, which made a quaint grimace at him, then disappeared.

'Oh, fie! What boldness!' chided the old woman.

Camruddin stood entranced, deprived of thought and movement. All the blood in his body seemed to have rushed to his head, and yet his lips were parched, his throat was dry. He breathed with difficulty.

As he stood there panting, feeling fit to swoon away, the wicket in the lattice once more opened and a hand and arm like ivory peeped out, to be at once withdrawn. The wicket closed again. A flower of no uncommon sort but sweetly scented—a yellow gillyflower—lay at his feet. He picked it up and pressed it to his lips.

'Thou art in luck, my lamb,' croaked the old servant, who, as if to show the farce was at an end, had thrown the veil back from her shrivelled face and twinkling eyes. 'Laughing, laughing, go, and laughing, laughing, come again. Be sure that there is some one here whose eyes will brighten at thy coming.'

She led the lover back to the main road, where at the corner he gave her with kind words a present, as the eunuch had instructed him to do; and, sped by her blessings, found his own way back to Ferid Bey's kiosk. The solemnising of the marriage contract in the evening was, by comparison, a dull affair, and tantalising to the bridegroom, who desired his bride, because he knew it might be months ere he could claim her honourably.

Chapter IX

THAT MORNING Ferid Bey, when riding through the town, had called at a coffee-house—an open shed built out on piers over the sea—and there inquired of the proprietor for news of Arif Hikmet Bey. The man scooped up imaginary dust with his right hand, and, laying it to lips and brow, replied,—

'Efendim, he was here last evening, and I expect him here again at noon to-day.'

Ferid produced his memorandum-book, tore out a leaf, and laying it upon the cover, stood for a moment gazing meditatively at the gnat-like dance of sunbeams on the sea, the pencil point between his lips, before he wrote:-

'A messenger has come from Basri. Says the horse is not worth buying. As it was you, not I, who thought of buying him, I suggest that you interrogate the messenger, efendim —Ferid.'

He read the message over carefully. The first sentence only was of meaning; the others he had added merely to mislead unlicensed persons who might chance to read them. There were many professional inquisitors about, who took an almost proprietary interest in anything to do with Arif Hikmet Bey. The passers-by upon the sunny quay looked innocent and careless, but any one of them might, that minute, in his heart, be wondering what Deyli

Ferid could be writing on his notebook, and whether some one might not be prepared to pay for knowledge of that writing. The words which he had written seemed enough. He folded up the slip of paper and presented it to the taverner, with strict command to place it in the bimbashi's own hand.

The bimbashi received it an hour later, when he came into the tavern with some friends of his. Having read the words he held it crumpled in his hand, keeping up conversation with his brother-officers for several minutes till suddenly he recollected something that he had forgotten at the barracks. There was a row of empty carriages near the corner of the quay, of which the drivers offered him their service loudly; but he passed them by, turning another corner ere he thought it wise to hail a passing araba. And then his first instruction to the araba-ji was to drive in a direction opposite to that of Deyli Ferid's kiosk, at which, however, he arrived, eventually, with less delay than might appear from this account of his proceedings.

This Major Arif Hikmet was a great conspirator. Having espoused conspiracy, in the first place only as a means to an end, he had come in time to love it for its own sake, just as some men who enter commerce in the hope of fortune become enamoured of the work of money-making. Like all the educated young men of his day, he had come under the influence of European literature, and had been impressed by its humanity. Six months of service under an English Inspector at Monastir had strengthened this impression, and convinced him of the sincerity of England's wish for Turkish progress. Imbued, like all his Muslim countrymen, with passionate devotion to his country and his faith, which in his mind could not be separated, he felt a burning shame in the perception that Christians now controlled the world upon a plan which Christianity could neither claim nor comprehend, since it was based on reason; but which Islâm could have reclaimed and elevated by giving it religious purpose and a soul. The Christians of the West had thrown off superstition and adopted the religion of humanity, a godless faith without coherence or stability. What prevented them from turning to Islâm? Simply the lethargy, the lack of progress, which they saw among the Muslim peoples of the earth. A great example of Islâmic progress was required, and where could it be shown if not in Turkey? But Turkey was made helpless in the grip of tyranny. In the name of Allah, therefore, for the good of all mankind, that tyranny must be destroyed.

It was astonishing how many of his comrades held the same ideas; astonishing how eagerly the same ideas were welcomed by the people everywhere. They appealed to every ardent Muslim as the truth from God. They gave the vigour of new hope to men who had long fought despairingly. The so-called fatalism of the people was mere hopelessness, a product of the despotism; it was fast dispersing. The Muslim people deemed it wrong to strive for selfish ends. The only way of public effort open to them had been service of the tyranny, which seemed the sole defence of the Islâmic world against the hordes of Christendom, whose strength and overwhelming multitude had brought despair! But now another way of public effort was discernible, and it was true Jehâd. When that was realised, the losses of the realm, the people's sufferings appeared the just reward of men who, having the Coran for guidance, had let bad customs enervate the Muslim realm. And the punishment from God for their wrongdoing appeared a promise of God's help if they did right. The Western Powers were justified in hatred of the despotism; they were not really hostile to Islâm. When the despotism was abolished and they saw the people bent on progress, they would give up their displeasure and befriend the Turks.

The bimbashi, Arif Hikmet, held these views religiously, and was prepared to give his life for them at any moment, aware that life which is not risked for Allah's service is not the kind of life which can survive the grave. A merciful and genial soul originally, he was relentless in pursuit of his ideal aim, and, if in that pursuit he met with treachery or cowardice or any kind of meanness, he was cruel. For a sword-thrust or pistol-shot he bore no malice, nor did he blame an adversary for employing guile. But personal ambitions, private spite or calculation, and mere venality revolted him. He gave his deadly enemy the choice of weapons, but killed the hireling spy as one would crush an earwig. He was a man of pleasant manners and polite address, and bore the reputation of a zealous officer. His chief fault was that he was very proud.

When he sauntered into Ferid Bey's selamlik, and sitting down on the divan undid his sword-belt, there happened to be several persons in the room. Within two minutes they had all departed except Camruddin. The master of the house, who went out last, informed him: 'I leave the messenger with you alone. He will not tell me all the story, having promised Basri to convey it to you only.'

'Well, my friend, and what hast thou to tell me?' inquired Arif Hikmet loftily, when he and Camruddin were left alone in the great airy room.

He listened to the story, frowning heavily, and sighing 'Allah! Allah!' under his breath.

'And now, my soul, go out and ask the bey efendi to return and speak with me. Thy story gives me much to think about. I offer thanks for thy devotion, which shall be rewarded,' was his only comment.

'Istaghfaru'llah!' answered Camruddin as he obeyed. 'I did it as an act of charity, and it has brought reward.'

Arif Hikmet champed his heavy blond moustache, and frowned perplexedly till Ferid Bey returned. Then he exclaimed, 'A messenger! Where can I find a messenger who is not likely to arouse suspicion? By this unlucky accident to Basri they now know all our usual methods of communication. I need a trusty man to go to Resna—a fedaï. I, personally, am beset with spies. Five times have I had to change my lodging in a month. Every creature who approaches me is under surveillance. Were I to send a soldier he would be examined in the train, for Allah knows all soldiers are suspected. Basri Bey assassinated! Our despatches seized!'

'You forget that I am not of the initiated,' chuckled Ferid Bey.

'This is no time for joking,' answered Arif Hikmet crossly. 'You are my friend, and I am asking your advice, in earnest, on a matter of extreme importance.'

'What think you of my simple Camruddin?' asked Ferid Bey.

'That man? … An honest fellow, good enough. He is the man, it seems, who sought me at the barracks. My orderly considered that he was perhaps a spy and so, to tell the truth, I hid from him.'

'As little of a spy as I am. They were after him. They dogged him from the barracks, where he went to ask for you, up to the house of my respected uncle, Sâdik Pasha, who is his patron, having known him in the Yemen wars. You and my uncle were the only people in the city whom he wished to see. A curious conjuncture, is it not? … When an attempt was made on Sâdik Pasha's life, this person, going to his house next morning to inquire, was seized by these same spying gentry and arrested. The case looked black against him—and against you, too, my soul, for the spies were able to show plain connection between him and you —when I saw him waiting under escort in the hall of the Serai and, hearing him protest his innocence and say that he was well known to my uncle, I brought my uncle down to look at him. Sâdik Pasha has a real affection for the man. He made the tale-bearers look foolish, and at once released him. His position now is good, for he is known to be in favour with the Commandant; and, in fact, to-night he will be married to a damsel of my uncle's house …

'Praise be to Allah!' said the bimbashi distractedly. 'But where on earth am I to get a messenger?'

'Have I not told you?' answered Deyli Ferid, with a grin.

Chapter X

WHEN CAMRUDDIN came out from Sâdik Pasha's kiosk after the ceremony of the marriage contract, it was late at night; but Ferid Bey informed him there was something further to be done before they both went home to seek repose. The carriage took them down into the city, of which the main streets were still fairly crowded. It stopped before a café full of noisy music, which they entered. The bey exchanged salutes with persons sitting at the tables, but did not stop to speak to any one. He traversed the large room and went out at a farther door which one, who seemed to be upon the watch, held open for him. Then by a corridor he came into another street—a narrow alley, dark and empty, featureless except for the long strip of starry sky above, like a rich awning stretched above a rubbish-pit. A few steps and he turned into a narrow doorway, where he was challenged by some unseen person and replied in whispers; and Camruddin kept ever at his heels.

They stumbled up a flight of stairs in semi-darkness; then came a landing faintly lighted, then a second flight, and then a second landing upon which a lamp set down upon the ground was burning dimly. A lady, veiled, stood guard before a door. She greeted Ferid Bey as an acquaintance, which shocked Camruddin, who thought it shameful that a Muslimah should be abroad so late at night, quite unattended. He began to fear lest Deyli Ferid had beguiled him to some place of sin.

The lady, after speaking with the bey in whispers, knocked three times upon the door. Camruddin caught a glimpse of a revolver in her small white hand, which somehow reassured him on the score of virtue. But to see a lady thus employed as doorkeeper distressed his soul. He thought what would have been his feelings if she were his bride. When the door opened he followed Ferid with reluctance, fearing some indecent sight, but found himself in the presence of a grave assembly.

The room was furnished only with a divan round the walls, on which at intervals five men were seated, four officers and one civilian. The last was a broad-faced man with square, clean-shaven chin which he kept stroking as if in conjuration of a beard—a man of singularly level gaze and rather scornful look, who wore his fez pressed forward on his brow. Of his companions, Camruddin took note of Arif Hikmet Bey and one of quiet mien whose cloak concealed his rank, which Camruddin judged from the precaution to be elevated.

'This is the man,' said Arif Hikmet Bey, when greetings had been finished, indicating Camruddin, who then became the object of all eyes—to his embarrassment, for he was unaware of any reason for such preference.

'But will he go?' asked the civilian sceptically.

'I answer for him,' replied Ferid Bey. 'It is a simple errand. Camruddin Agha,' he cried, 'I need a messenger to go to Resna. I pay expenses and give ten pounds Turk on your return.'

'To hear is to obey,' said Camruddin, in Arabic.

'A man of education!' some one murmured, in accents of surprise.

'Nay, by your leave, efendim,' put in the civilian earnestly. 'The errand cannot be so simple, since the messenger must carry documents. He must know something of the business which we have in hand—enough at least to realise its great importance.'

'I beg to disagree with you, my soul,' said Ferid. 'I can imagine the effect which realisation of the great importance of an errand would have upon a simple creature like myself. It would inflate or else unman me. In either case my manner would invite inquiry. And Camruddin Agha and I are much alike in character.'

'Allah forbid!' said Arif Hikmet, with a grin.

The civilian then raised an objection to Ferid's further presence in the room. 'The rest of us are bound together by an oath which he has never taken. He makes a jest of all our doings. I have heard him. If our meeting is of great importance, as I judge from the personalities assembled, he has no business here.'

'He furnishes the messenger,' said Arif Hikmet Bey. And there ensued a long discussion, which at one moment threatened to grow angry; but in the end it was agreed that Ferid Bey could stay.

The officer whose rank was hidden by his cloak then spoke for the first time. He took no notice of his colleagues, but addressed the messenger,—

'Camruddin Agha, you are a Muslim, you have been a soldier, and you would take up arms again, at any time, if enemies attacked our country. You are not of those who shrink from danger, preferring their own comfort to the public good. Say, is that true?'

'It is quite true, efendim.'

'You know what Power is our relentless enemy, what Power has always been the enemy of progress.'

'Russia, efendim.'

'What Power of Europe was our friend till lately, what Power has always been the friend of progress, what Power is still the most beloved among us?'

'England, efendim.'

'Well, England, seeing our corruption, has despaired of us. The King of England meets the Russian Czar up there in the north. They both agree upon a plan for our complete destruction, regarding us as quite unworthy to exist. How can we escape complete destruction when former friends and foes unite against us? Only by some immediate action which shall make it known that the Turkish nation is alive and bent on progress, that we abhor the Government's corruption, and have not sunk to the condition of unthinking slaves. When that is known, then England will draw back from Russia and befriend us. Do you understand?'

'Eyvet, efendim.'

'The time has come to act. We want a messenger, and you have been commended to our notice as a worthy man. But we will not let you go in ignorance of the tremendous import of your errand, nor of the danger you will run by undertaking it. You will carry papers which every servant of the Government would give his eyeballs to possess. If your purpose is discovered they will drag you to the nearest karakol, and there use every means to make you tell the story of the whole conspiracy. You say you do not know it: they will not believe you. You will be tortured, and then shot or hanged. You see that clearly?'

'Eyvet, efendim,' answered Camruddin, continuing his steadfast gaze into the speaker's eyes, which gave him confidence and peace of mind, together with a growing exaltation, as if the fire of faith which glowed in them had power to kindle like a burning-glass.

'And still you go upon the errand?'

'By Allah Most High!'

'Thou art my brother! Come, let me embrace thee!'

The officer arose and put his arms round Camruddin. As he did so the cloak slipped partly off his shoulder and revealed his rank as that of a field-marshal. He replaced it quickly.

'Well, then,' said Arif Hikmet Bey, 'that much is settled. He will go to Resna. From thence the orders will be passed through all Albania. The messenger will start to-morrow by the train which leaves at the third hour— But no, he cannot; he must have a tezkereh!'

A tezkereh, or passport, was required under the despotism before a man could go from town to town in Turkey. Thus the authorities could keep control of every movement.

'I always make a point, myself,' said Ferid Bey, 'of travelling without a tezkereh. I am by nature fond of talking with all sorts of people, and I find the lack of one a never-ending source of conversation with policemen, soldiers, secret agents, and their sort—persons who would not otherwise address a word to me. I pay a fee into their private pockets, with the result that they approve my surreptitious mode of travelling. Camruddin Agha, let me tell you, is no common messenger, being, in fact, a favourite of the Commandant.'

'The Commandant no longer, more's the pity!' murmured the cloaked officer. 'He is a good man, Allah knows, they may replace him by a miscreant.'

Camruddin was startled by this interjection, of which he would have liked to ask the meaning. But as no further reference was made to Sâdik Pasha, he speedily forgot his curiosity, in thought of matters which concerned him much more nearly.

'I can procure a tezkereh, but not in time for him to start to-morrow morning,' the civilian said.

'The day after to-morrow will be soon enough,' said Arif Hikmet. 'But he must go then, tezkereh or no tezkereh. If we postpone his going further it will be too late.' He whispered then to Ferid Bey, who rose and left the room.

'Well, then, there is nothing more to say,' said the cloaked officer. 'He will receive the written message that he has to carry at the railway station, after he has passed the barrier … Be ready, brother, to receive a paper from an unknown hand. If anybody asks your business say you are going to buy goats at Resna, and name Mehmedoghlou Abbâs, a farmer.'

'Avoid his house, however, for he is a time-server,' put in an officer, who had not spoken until then. A murmur of approval hailed the warning.

'Go to the barracks in the manner of a lounger; enter into conversation with the soldiers. Shall I tell him the words now?'

'Yes,' murmured the civilian, and the others nodded. All were now standing ready to depart. 'Learn well the words that I am going to teach you, and swear by your own life and Allah's mercy not to reveal their hidden sense to any one, for they are words of power. The man among the soldiers there at Resna, who answers you correctly, is a brother. You can trust him with the knowledge of your errand. But confide in no man till you have received the proper answer. The man who gives it will conduct you to an officer, to whom alone you will deliver the despatches. Give not the word alone, which might arouse suspicion, but use it in a sentence as it were by accident. The counterword will be given in like manner. Now tell me what you have to do!'

Camruddin repeated his instructions accurately.

'Excellent!' said his tutor. 'Now, I give the words. Pay close attention. The word which you must say is "Union," and the answer "Progress."'

Chapter XI

CAMRUDDIN HAD looked forward to his interview with the bimbashi, Arif Hikmet, as the termination of the errand with which Basri Bey had charged him; after which he would be free to give the whole of his attention to the business dearest to his heart, the work of preparation to receive his bride. Instead, within a few hours of that interview, he found himself entangled in a vast conspiracy, and bent upon an errand still more dangerous than that from which he had so ardently desired relief. And yet his mood was jubilant. His soul exulted in the very danger. He remembered his sensations at first setting out upon this journey, how, when he turned for a last look at the house beside the flowering orchard, he had experienced a thrill of awe as if the hand of fate was on him. From that time forward, as it seemed, he had been under guidance, strongly impelled towards some purpose quite unknown to him. And now the nature of that purpose was revealed. He was to help, however humbly, to restore the glory of Islâm. Alive or dead, a happy future was in store for him.

Such pleasure, in the prospect of so perilous an undertaking, must seem absurd to those who do not know how great a volume of enthusiasm, thirst for education, and desire for progress, how great a longing for the friendship of the West, was kept imprisoned by the Turkish despotism. A race as disciplined as it was vigorous did not complain. The Christians of the country, who had special privileges which saved them from the worst part of the tyranny, complained; the Muslims never. The latter fought the battles of the Padishah as in old days; but without rapture, as men entrapped fight on despairingly. Now hope had come again. A sense of health renewed was in the people. There were reviving voices in the air: the sky was full of reassuring portents. The pent-up energies of thousands were set free, and with but one direction. The glory of Islâm was not a mere remembrance. The triumph of Islâm was yet to come.

Camruddin had caught a spark of this enthusiasm from the lips and eyes of one whom it possessed so utterly, that many people looked upon him as inspired. And it had lighted up the world for him. That lady, standing guard before the entrance of the council-chamber, the sight of whom had shocked him at the time, now thrilled his memory. At the great moments of Islâmic history, women came out and fought beside the men. The slim, veiled figure, grasping the revolver, stood for the true Jehâd to which all ties were sacrificed, commanding him to put away his heart's desire.

In this exalted mood, on the day following his acceptance by the secret council, he was sitting in the garden, surrounded by the children of the bey efendi, who kept asking for more stories of the Yemen War, when some ladies of the household came in sight at modest distance. They called the children to them and rebuked them, telling them not to persecute good Camruddin Agha when he had business. Camruddin was going to protest that he was far from busy, when he saw a black-veiled phantom beckoning to him from the shrubbery. The ladies of the house were clad in white. He recognised the same old woman who had led him to the bride's inspection, and his heart beat fast and loud as he obeyed her signal. The ladies of the house had gone away again. The old woman waited till he came in earshot of a whisper,—

'The Long Meadow, one hour before sunset!' then fled ungainly as a frightened hen.

Camruddin looked about for some one to resolve the questions which her message left unanswered in his mind. He spied the hunchback dwarf reposing in the shade of the selamlik wall.

'In kindness, tell me. The Long Meadow! Where is that? By what road does one go to it?' he asked politely.

The other yawned and stretched himself. He said:

'You know the karakol? Proceed in that direction, but at the corner by the oak-tree, take the other road. It is a place of concourse in the evening. Any one will show you.'

Camruddin thanked him for the information and set out at once. As there was still some time to spare before the hour appointed, he went first to the tavern bowered in wistaria, remembering that he had not yet told its friendly owner of the favourable turn in his affairs. But the day was Sunday, and the bower was the resort of Christians who sat there drinking arak with their women—a disgusting sight; beholding which he stayed no longer than was necessary to apprise his friend of his good fortune and remonstrate with him for dispensing alcohol. The taverner replied,—

'It is not my affair. The Ghiaours come hither on their feast-days for the view they never look at; and a Christian pays me so much weekly for the right to sell to them abominations. His traffic is quite separate from mine. His stock-in-trade is in the other corner.'

Camruddin was not contented with this explanation, but as it was the tavern-keeper's business he made no reply, but asked his way to the Long Meadow.

It was a run of grass much trodden, and worn bare in places, bordered by old trees, its slopes commanding a fine view of Mount Olympus and the sea. At the moment when he first beheld it, it was brilliant as a flower-garden, being covered with a crowd in many-coloured clothing. Women completely veiled in white or black or mauve sat in still groups or walked about sedately. Men moved in separate troops. Children ran in and out among them, flying coloured kites which hovered overhead like monstrous butterflies; and on the edges of the pretty concourse there were booths devoted to the sale of toys and light refreshments. The voice of singing and the thrum of lutes, the rub-dub-dub of children's little drums, was in the air. The evening sunlight held the picture like a gem.

Camruddin walked about the meadow, then sat down apart. He thought: 'I have been sent here for no purpose. My lady is a tease. It is her pleasure to befool me. She gave the hag the message to torment me for her own amusement, to see how much I would endure from her, just as she tried my patience by making me perform fool's antics when I came beneath her lattice. She may be present in this crowd, observing me; I cannot tell. If I behave as one in search of somebody, she and her companions will be pleased and so prolong my ordeal. But if I seem indifferent, she will reveal herself. Oh, when shall I obtain her for my own, to punish her deliciously for all her games at my expense?'

Lighting a cigarette, he smoked serenely. Some children, playing near, had trouble with a kite. He had set it flying gaily for them and was watching it, when a small group of veiled ones passed quite close to him. One of them said: 'His love is in the sky. He has no eyes for daughters of this earth,' and there was silvery laughter.

The lover was at once alert from head to heels. His eyes pursued those women, looking for a sign, but none was given. He could not tell from which of the four gliding forms the voice had come. He was perhaps deceived in thinking that he knew the voice. How should he recognise a voice which he had heard but once?

Once more he walked about the meadow, waiting for a sign. The time appointed was long past. The light grew rosy, and the shadows deeply blue. It might well be that she had brought him there only to prove her power. Or it might be that she wished to show him to her friends. In any case he had stayed long enough; he would depart. As he came on to the road above the meadow, some veiled ladies were getting into two closed carriages, disputing gaily as to who should go in which. One of them, stepping back, came close to Camruddin, so close that he inhaled her perfume. The movement seemed quite accidental, and so he thought it till she spoke.

'The rose is sweet at sunrise where she blooms beneath the cypress, like true love which smiles at death.'

The words were uttered just as if she were reciting poetry. But, as she spoke, she turned in his direction, and he could feel her eyes intent upon him through the gauze.

He had sufficient wit to feign unconsciousness, but his heart beat so as to confuse his brain and dim his sight. When he again beheld the landscape clearly, the girl was gone; the carriage which, no doubt, contained her was fast disappearing in a cloud of dust.

He had walked a good part of his way before the

meaning of her words grew plain to him.

Where do roses bloom beneath the cypress-tree except in cemeteries? There was a cemetery near the house of Sâdik Pasha, and somewhere in it, doubtless, was a place where roses bloomed. There he must be at sunrise on the morrow.

Without a conscious purpose his feet changed direction, leading him towards the dwelling of his bride. Passing the entrance, he was hailed by the Albanian janitor, who told him news which took his breath away. The Pasha had been ordered to Stamboul by telegraph. He would depart by the first steamboat on the morrow. The ladies and the household were to follow as soon as all the necessary arrangements could be made. In consternation at these tidings, Camruddin went in and craved immediate audience of His Excellency. After a time of waiting he was shown into the upper chamber, with window looking on to cypress trees, which had been the scene of all his interviews with Sâdik Pasha. He found the General seated at a table strewn with papers, in company with Hamdi Bey, his aide-de-camp.

'Your visit gives me pleasure,' cried the Pasha heartily. 'Had you not come I should assuredly have sent for you to say farewell. I am recalled; I see you know the news already. The terms of the command are highly flattering. Our august master learns with deep concern of the attempt to kill me, and would remove a trusted servant from such dangers. But I suspect intrigue. The order comes so timely to prevent my doing something which I meant to do, and which other people, who dislike me, knew I meant to do. I seem to hear those others whisper to our sovereign lord: "That Sâdik Pasha is too easy-going, too indulgent. He grows old. See, he remains inactive while the province which he is supposed to govern has become a hornet's nest." And all the while they know that I have grasped the trouble as no other Commandant could grasp it without months of work. It is evident that there are persons of high influence who do not like my efforts to stamp out conspiracy.'

The General seemed to have grown ten years older in the hours since Camruddin had last set eyes on him. He added: 'I am disappointed, I confess it—ay, and angry, though, Allah knows, my anger is mere folly. I go to safety, it is true. I may be honoured with some safer post. But think, my soul, how you, a soldier, would feel, supposing, in the middle of a fight in which you had the hope to beat your adversary, anybody—even angels— were to pounce on you and bear you off to safety and preferment! Would you not come near to burst with indignation?'

Camruddin smiled at the comparison, as did the aide-de-camp. But Sâdik Pasha, with his hands spread out in demonstration, looked from the one to the other seriously and said: 'That is how I feel.'

Camruddin shed tears at parting from his benefactor, whose hand he kissed repeatedly with deep respect.

Chapter XII

THE TREES, the silver-gray kiosks with dark red roofs, the garden walls, and here and there a dome as white as ivory with tapering minaret beside it, dreamed of night, and wore a sleepy look, although the sky was coloured, when Camruddin walked down the hill by Sâdik Pasha's mansion towards the wood of cypress trees which was the cemetery. At the moment when he stepped into the sacred grove a sudden deepening of the shadows told him that the sun had risen. Under the ancient trees, tall, narrow headstones, higher than a man, inclined this way and that with the disorder of a natural under-growth; and at wide intervals some little cubic build-ing with a dome stood forth among them, marking the burial-place of a reputed saint. Here and there a group of loose-robed figures flitted silently, for it was the hour when men and women love to commune with the dead and meditate upon the mystery of life renewed. The glance of sunlight on some stone or tree-trunk shone like a gem amid the gloom; and at the end of every vista winked the sapphire sea with coloured craft afloat upon it, in full sunshine, the emblem of a full, exultant life.

The vastness of the shady cemetery daunted Cam-ruddin, who knew not which direction he should take. On every side he caught a glimpse of women gliding phan-tom-like or standing still among the gravestones. But nowhere were there any roses that he could descry. Perhaps the rose his love had mentioned had been metaphorical. Perhaps the speech he had heard possessed no meaning. Perhaps the speaker had not been his love at all.

In doubt of everything he sauntered on thinking at any rate to pass the time until the hour drew near when he must start for Resna. At last, in a small open glade, touched by the sunlight, he caught the scent of roses, and beheld a little thicket of them surrounding a small mausoleum the dome of which was finely ornamented with mosaics. Two white-veiled women sat upon the threshold of the tomb. Even as his glance fell on them they both rose. One of them beckoned to him and then moved away, pointing to the other as the proper object for attentions. He stood confronting a white statue of which the drooping head betokened shyness, and the shrinking pose a half desire to run away. The silence growing irksome, he said softly: 'Efendim, here I am at your command!'

'How sweet the perfume of these roses!' was the trembling answer.

Camruddin assumed a boldness he was far from feeling to reply: 'Gul-raaneh is far sweeter to my thinking.'

The word Gul-raaneh means a kind of yellow rose.

'Gul-raaneh grows in royal gardens, not in cemeteries. You do not know me. You know no more than that a girl spoke in your hearing yesterday of roses and the cypress-tree, of love and death—a shameless creature thus to speak before a stranger and use such talk to cloak immodesty.'

'I know much more than that,' said Camruddin.

'Impossible!' she laughed. 'For whom then do you take me?'

'You are my bride, Gul-raaneh.'

'Your bride! Ma sha'llah! Then you do not know your bride! You make that claim to every veiled one who will heed you. You are nicely trapped this time, for you are wasting all your honeyed wiles on an old woman.'

'Your age is twenty years, no more.'

'A lot you know! And if I were your bride, what do you think would be my feelings now I know that you will follow any light-of-love who speaks of roses?'

'I would not follow any woman who did not belong to me,' said Camruddin. Her fencing had, however, raised a doubt in him. 'You are Gul-raaneh Hânum, well I know it,' he replied, but with so much less conviction that she laughed outright at him. 'If you are not,' he added vehemently, 'depart at once. I am no libertine, and only one is mistress of my thoughts at present. Vouchsafe your name.'

'For you I am the rose beneath the cypress,' she replied maliciously. 'You insist that I must call myself Gul-raaneh; so be it! But is it true that you would never follow any other woman, even if she were as nice as I am, and invited you?'

'It is quite true, efendim.'

'O paragon of virtue!' sighed the lady.

'If you are not my bride, as I imagined, I ask leave to quit you,' added Camruddin, offended by her mocking voice.

'You think I brought you hither for a naughty purpose. Suppose that I am in distress and need a champion.'

'No lady in this guarded country needs a stranger for her champion, unless perchance she be imprisoned wrongfully. She has her rights secure before the law. The Câdi of the city is her champion. She has but to make known her wrongs to him … Hânum Efendim, I am but a simple man, a Muslim; I deal not usually in poetic speech, nor have I any taste for love's intrigues. I deemed you one who now by law is joined to me, and so I kept the tryst … But I am not a fool. I perceive clearly that you do but play with me for your amusement. Therefore with your permission I will take my leave.'

'Nay, go not yet, and not in anger, my two eyes. There are still so many questions I desire to ask you. What if this bride of yours—whom you have never seen—should prove upon acquaintance to be very ugly. Would you still regard her as the only woman in the world?'

'Assuredly, if I did not divorce her!'

'Ah, ah! You would divorce her for her looks, poor creature!'

'No, that I should not,' answered Camruddin—'provided that they were not frightful. Let her but be good-natured and soft-spoken—I ask no more, being a simple man. I do not claim the moon nor yet a star.'

'Good,' said the lady, 'and this bride whom you have never seen; why then do you not claim her and behold her? Is she still a child that you refrain from taking her?'

'She is of age, efendim, but she has been used to luxury, being a member of a noble household. I must provide a dwelling suitable for her. She is refined, coming of such a house. I must improve myself before I claim her, lest she scorn my manners.'

'Tell me your name,' the lady exclaimed suddenly.

'My name is Camruddin, the son of Mehemed.'

'And mine is Gul-raaneh of the house of Arab Sâdik Pasha. I find thy manners not too rustic, soul of mine. Rather, thou hast a cunning and a courtly tongue.'

'Praise be to Allah!'

'Thou givest praise to Allah for a thing which may be ugly and ill-natured?'

'No, but because a lady who has charmed my soul by voice and speech and perfume is now lawful to me.'

'But I am loud-voiced and ill-natured, and as ugly as a little toad.'

'I listen and I learn that ugly words are fair that fall from thee.'

'All my companions say that I am ugly as a rainy day. Am I so ugly? I cannot judge myself.'

She raised her face-veil for a moment, and half turned away, then, as she let it fall again, she sighed,—

'I must be going. My companion beckons.'

There was silence between them for a while, and then she whispered shyly,—

'Have no fear, my soul. Thy bride is not the hard, disdainful creature of thy thoughts. Here, take this rose.' She tore a rosebud from the thicket. 'Thou layest it to lips and heart, a common rose, no different from all the others. Why? Because my hand bestowed it. So will it be with all that comes from thee to me.'

So saying, she moved off to join the other woman, who called out to Camruddin,—

'Your eyes have brightened, bey efendim! They light up the grove.'

Camruddin lingered in the cemetery long after the two white-veiled forms had disappeared. He sauntered to and fro among the tombs in dreamy ecstacy until he suddenly remembered that the time wore on, and he was pledged to start that morning on an expedition of some danger; when he retraced his steps to Deyli Ferid's house.

Chapter XIII

BEFORE THE wicket in the booking-office of the railway station, Camruddin found a noisy, surging crowd of people struggling to buy tickets, already maddened by the fear of being late, although it wanted fifty minutes of the time of starting. Each, fighting with his neighbours in the hope to get a ticket, helped the congestion which seemed likely to be permanent. Camruddin, at the sight of such a tumult, gave up hope. But at a word from Ferid Bey, the hunchback, who had come down in the carriage with them, flung himself into the crowd and, by dint of shouting out his wish and pressing forward, obtained a ticket in a little while.

At the door which led on to the platform stood a gendarme in a white, black-braided tunic, light blue trousers, and tall scarlet fez, demanding tezkerehs. At sight of Deyli Ferid Bey, the face of this official, which had been severe, relaxed its gravity. He sprang to the salute, and then, when Ferid Bey held out a tezkereh for his inspection, indignantly repelled it, waving the whole party onwards in the manner of a host with honoured guests.

Out on the platform Camruddin implored the bey to give himself no further trouble upon his account. But Deyli Ferid took no notice of the request. He made the hunchback summon an official of the railway, who bowed before the bey, and said, 'Efendim?'

'Is your high personality the protector of the train?'

'Eyvet, efendim.'

'Then do a kindness which will earn my heartfelt thanks. Take care of this good man, who is not used to travel on the iron road. At his destination kindly see him past the barrier, explaining to the sentry that he is an honest man well known to you, belonging to the house of Arab Sâdik Pasha.'

With that he made a present to the guard, who answered,—

'It is a command, efendim.'

Nor did Ferid's kindness end with that injunction. He made the hunchback buy a bagful of pistachio nuts and a supply of bread and hard-boiled eggs for Camruddin, and stood beside the door of the second-class compartment despite the agonising protests of the latter, to which his only answer was,—

'It is my duty.'

'How can your Honour have a duty towards me? All that you do is condescension, and it is too much.'

'In saying that it is a duty, I but state a truth, and now I see the person destined to relieve me,' said the bey at last. 'I have been waiting here to give you your credentials, without which you would miss the object of your journey.'

A soldier, pushing through the crowd of relatives and friends of travellers which filled the platform, handed to the bey a letter, which he passed to Camruddin just as the engine whistled and the train began to move. Camruddin, in his excitement and importance had been prepared to start without his message. He had quite forgotten it. A blush of shame for his forgetfulness discoloured his last glimpse of Deyli Ferid and the hunchback and all the crowd of people on the platform, waving hands. This small humiliation at the outset was, however, of good omen, the mood which courts disaster being self-conceit.

He placed the letter safely in his bosom and then took notice of his fellow-travellers, who were all companionable. One, an Albanian, had a splendid voice, and charmed the way with songs of his own mountains to the accompaniment of a one-stringed lute, played by his brother, a young lad who hung upon his every word. Two modest merchants travelling to Monastir, a khôja, and a Christian from the Serbian marshes, who told stories of the villainy of priests and monks and all such 'cattle'—his own word—the prices which they charged for absolution, the way they palmed off donkey's bones as holy relics, and many other tricks which edified his Muslim hearers. These were the other occupants of the compartment. There was talk and laughter to beguile the journey. The guard was as good as his word. At every station, he came to the door of the compartment to see how Camruddin was getting on, giving the latter consequence in the eyes of his neighbours. At every station there were persons selling mulberries and nice sour plums provocative of strange grimaces, and water slung in earthen pitchers to the back and poured over the shoulder of the vendor with a sidelong bow. 'Sweet water,' or 'Pine mountain water,' or 'Water from the glen of roses,' was their cry; for in a land of water-drinkers the water of some districts is renowned as wine is in a land of wine-bibbers. These water-sellers did a roaring trade, for almost every one upon the train drank deep at every station. The day was blazing hot, and dust mixed with the grit of engine smoke induces thirst.

Camruddin, in the intervals of conversation, looked out at the ever-changing landscape as the train meandered up into the hills, with here dark-green of forest, here the blue of some deep lake under a cloudless sky. It was not the first time that he had travelled by the iron road, but it was the first time he had been sufficiently at ease in travelling to look around him with such keen enjoyment. This compartment, where he lounged, was vastly different from the trucks into which they packed poor soldier-men. And this was but ikinji (second class). There was birinji (first class) also on the train-compartments like a casket made for holding jewels. And some compartments, closely curtained, were reserved for women, the shrill voices of their inmates being heard at every halt. Everything had been arranged with nice convenience and propriety; the train possessed a cheery whistling voice; the guard watched over all like a proud father. The spice of danger in the expedition was a source of energy to Camruddin, making his mind alert to notice trifles, and filling him with a sense of joyous life. He felt quite sorry when the train stopped at the station short of Monastir, at which he had been ordered to alight. The guard spoke for him to a soldier who was on the platform, with the result that he passed out without the slightest difficulty.

Going to the adjacent village, he there spent two hours in bargaining for the hire of a mule on which to ride to Resna. It was late in the afternoon when he set out upon the mountain-road attended by a ragged lad, who acted as his guide, but whose chief business was to keep the mule in sight and bring it back again.

After an hour or so they reached a village, where the lad proposed that they should sleep, because, if they pursued their way, the night might overtake them in wild places where the road was hard to trace. There was an inn at which, after a frugal meal of bread and olives, they lay down on the ground with other way-farers, the guardian of the mule taking the precaution to tie the spare end of its head-rope round his wrist.

Camruddin arose before the dawn. He wakened his companion, and they both set out again. About the fourth hour of the day they came in sight of Resna, in its smiling vale beside the stream which flows into the lake of Prespa, which was flashing like a mirror in the sun.

Descending to the plain they came at length to a made road beneath an avenue of poplar trees beside a singing stream, along whose banks sat white-veiled women, washing clothes. There Camruddin dismounted and discharged his guide, who, at the sight of unexpected bakhshîsh, called down blessings on his head. The boy went on into the town to bait the mule and rest it before returning to his village. Camruddin sat down beside the water for a moment to collect his thoughts, taking the papers from his bosom to make sure he had them. Then he arose and walked into the town.

Out of the open country he passed suddenly into a labyrinth of narrow markets with scraps of awning hanging bat-like overhead, crowded with all sorts of people— men in turbans, high-crowned fezes, kalpaks, multifarious raiment, and women in striped veils of divers hues. Arriving at a mosque he had a mind to enter and make up his arrears of prayer before proceeding farther; but as he was on the point of doing so he saw a face well known to him within the gateway, and quickly turned away.

It was the spy Khalîl, last seen at Saloniki, the man who had so nearly brought him to destruction on a lying charge. What was he doing in this country town, far from the seat of Government, the source of pay for such as he? Praying that the rogue might not have seen him, Camruddin hastened to the barracks. The sight of his old enemy had made him anxious to bear the letter to its destination instantly.

Chapter XIV

AS CAMRUDDIN was squatting by the barracks-gate beside an ombashi with whom he had just made acquaintance, the town and valley became filled with joyous trumpeting. The garrison was marching back from exercise. Tears of emotion sprang into his eyes as the exciting strains grew louder and the head of the column came in sight, the troops advancing with a gallant swing. The trumpets shrilled out a triumphant air. The drum beat time beneath their exultation, like a solemn thought.

'Observe the officer who walks in front upon the right,' murmured the ombashi. 'He is the man to whom I shall conduct you presently.'

The speaker sprang to attention and Camruddin, from force of habit, did the same, as the dust-stained troops swung by into the yard. When Camruddin had come up to the gate ten minutes earlier, and in his salutation had inserted an unusual word, this ombashi had given the concerted countersign, and after that said nothing till the troops returned, smoking a cigarette and blinking at the sunlight dreamily. After the troops had been dismissed, he whispered 'Wait!' and went inside.

Camruddin waited philosophically, squatting by the wall, a little troubled by the thought of that accursed spy. After perhaps an hour the ombashi returned, paused in the gateway to bestow a careful glance to right and left, and then said: 'Come, my soul!'

He led the way across the dusty square, in through a doorway, down a whitewashed passage, where soldiers jostled one another round the place of washing; then up a staircase, also thronged with soldiers, to the upper story, and along a corridor which had a row of windows upon one side and a row of doors along the other. Some of the men they met put questions to the ombashi, who answered with a name which was beloved of these in-quisitives, to judge from their contented smiles at hearing it. Camruddin, accustomed to the ways of soldiers, gath-ered that he was on his way to see a general favourite—an impression which he found it hard to reconcile with the appearance of a tall, bewhiskered major, sitting writing at a table in a room severely neat, who struck him as the very model of a martinet. This personage looked up a moment from his writing when Camruddin was brought in by the ombashi, and nodded to the latter, who at once withdrew, shutting the door behind him. Camruddin was thus left alone in presence of the officer, who, after bid-ding him sit down, continued writing.

Laying down his pen at length, the major fixed his eyes upon his visitor and said: 'You have a message for me, is it not so?'

Camruddin delivered up the packet which had been entrusted to him.

The officer undid it, and began to read.

For quite ten minutes there was perfect silence in the room, excepting for the rustle of the papers as he turned them over. Then he sat back and fixed his eyes once more on Camruddin who, under that inspection, dropped his gaze respectfully.

'You do not know the contents of these papers?'

'I do not know a word of it, efendim.'

'Yet you knew that they were dangerous to carry.'

'So I was told, efendim.'

'Allah reward you, brother. You are a brave man.'

'I do not think I ran much risk, efendim.'

'You are a friend, I am informed, of Ferid Bey, the son of Zia Pasha. Is he well?'

'Praise be to Allah!' answered Camruddin.

The officer then shouted for the ombashi, who must have waited at the door, for he appeared immediately, and told him: 'Take care of this man, who will remain with us a day or two.'

And that was all the interview. Yet Camruddin, as he went out, felt that a signal honour had been done to him; and the ombashi appeared to think so, too, for he made much of him, calling him dearest brother and walking with him hand in hand across the square.

The ombashi took leave of absence for the day, upon the strength of the command laid on him to take care of Camruddin. They sauntered in the town and the surrounding country, remarking upon all they saw, with that fresh gaiety which marks the birth of friendship between men still young, as if they saw things newly through each other's eyes.

The discovery that both were hajjis, pilgrims of Mecca, made a bond between them. The ombashi's name was Hasan, he came from Trebizond, he was thirty years old. When he heard that Camruddin had been a chaûsh in the army, he seemed to think it quite miraculous until informed that he could read and write, which quite explained the matter to his thinking. 'I, too, begin to read and write a little,' he informed his new-found friend. 'Niazi Bey—that officer with whom you spoke—

gives lessons to all those who wish to learn. He is a pious man—Allah reward him! There is none like him in the world for discipline; and yet he is not churlish like so many who are strict. He speaks little and he seldom speaks a word of blame, a look suffices; but praises freely when a man deserves it. And praise from such a man is worth the having. He is the terror of the Christian bands throughout this province, having crushed them quite. Yet even they bear no ill-will to him, but if they have a just complaint refer it to him. Few of the rich and great are servants of Allah as he is. Most of them become enclosed in pride like silkworms.'

'You say truly,' answered Camruddin.

Late in the afternoon they went into a cook shop, and Camruddin paid for a pilaf of pigeon-meat, which they discussed together. They were about finishing the savoury dish when Camruddin gave a start and muttered: 'I seek refuge in Allah!'

Hasan inquired: 'What ails you, brother?'

'I saw an enemy pass by—a spy. I think he saw me.'

'A spy! What kind of spy? Say quickly, brother!' Camruddin told the story of his past acquaintance with the man in question, which Hasan interrupted, saying,—

'This is serious. A headquarters spy in Resna at this juncture! There must be leakage of instructions somewhere. Our business is to stalk that man and capture him. If it is you he seeks, do you engage him in any kind of talk and lead him towards the barracks. I will meet you. My present business is to warn Niazi Bey. Now watch the street and tell me if you see that spy again.'

Camruddin answered: 'There he is. The man in the white dust-cloak talking to the sweetmeat-seller.'

'I will not hide from you that we may have to kill him. But first we have to ascertain that he has no confederates.'

'Well, shall I call him to us?'

'Nay, I know not. Wait a minute. Let me think! I must not go too far in this without authority. Ay, call him hither. You and I are chance acquaintances. You are a spy as he is. I am an informer. While you are talking with him I will leave you. But do you keep him here till I return; or if he will not tarry in this place lead him towards the barracks.'

'Good,' said Camruddin. He stepped to the front of the eating-house and, smiling at the man in the white dust-cloak, cried: 'May your evening be prosperous, efendim!'

The spy seemed startled, but he crossed the way and came to Camruddin, saluting almost humbly.

'May your honoured evening be prosperous,' he cried. 'Wallahi, I could not be sure that it was you until you gave the sign, or, if it was indeed yourself, that you would deign to recognise me. Allah knows how I have longed for an occasion to ask your pardon for that most unfortunate mistake.'

Up to this point the man's demeanour was disarming. He went on to ask: 'What business brings you here?' and with the question a slyness crept into his smile. 'Again it seems you have an errand to the garrison?'

'By no means,' answered Camruddin. 'I came here seeking a relation whom I have not seen for years. I happened on this ombashi, a former comrade, with whom I have been chatting for an hour.'

The spy then shrugged as if he thought the matter not worth arguing. He changed the subject, asking: 'When did you arrive?'

'To-day, efendim.'

'And when will you depart?'

'To-morrow, in sha'llah

The ombashi here asked permission to depart, taking affectionate farewell of Camruddin.

The moment he was gone, the spy unmasked. He drew a stool up close to Camruddin and whispered 'You are here on behalf of Sâdik Pasha, is it not so? Why hide your business from me when we come from the same camp, although there may be some small matter of ill-feeling since your patron has been ousted from the post of Commandant? I can sympathise with his displeasure at some people's conduct. By Allah, in his place I should have washed my hands of the whole business; I might even have gone over to the other side, for vengeance. It surprises me to find that he still takes an interest … But why withhold things from me? I know everything.'

'I do not think that likely,' murmured Camruddin.

'Well, now, listen! The King of England meets the Czar at Reval. They make a project detrimental to this realm, some people say. Those people wish to overthrow the Padishah, and set up a republic, as if their overthrowing monarchy would please the King of England or the Czar! It is certain that some order of extreme importance went forth yesterday—or, Allah knows, it may have been the day before—what say you?' The spy kept eager watch upon his hearer's face.

'I say all that is nonsense. I know nothing.'

'You will not tell me anything, as once before. Beware, I say. Remember what befell you!'

'Do you remember! Another such mistake might cost you dear!'

'I have no wish to quarrel with you, but you are annoying. Why keep me in the cold? I could assist you. Be not of such a selfish nature! Be a comrade! This place is not convenient for a quiet talk. Come, let us walk together and survey the town.'

'In which direction go you?'

'Faith! I care not for an hour.'

'Then let us go in this direction.' And they walked together slowly towards the barracks till they met the ombashi returning.

'A safe man,' said Camruddin.

The spy's face brightened. He looked really grateful for the confidence. Camruddin added: 'I have found out something, and I seek for proof. Say, have you any helpers in the town? We need a score of hands.'

'Alas, I am alone, efendim.'

This last was spoken in the hearing of the ombashi, who said as one in full possession of the matter:

'Then we must wait till night. I have got leave of absence.'

The three turned back again into the town. The spy, in friendly company, became so amiable that Hasan whispered that it was a pity he had got to die.

When it was dark they took their captive to a lonely place and there informed him that his hour had come, but gave him leave to pray two rekaas, to make all things comfortable. It then appeared that he was not a Muslim, for he feared death, becoming frantic at the prospect, whining shamefully. It made the necessary execution horrible. Hasan despatched him, and they hid the body in a dust-heap.

Chapter XV

CAMRUDDIN SPENT that night beneath the shelter of a public fountain on the outskirts of the town; and the ombashi, to his surprise, stayed with him. When he asked the reason, Hasan answered simply: 'I have orders.'

They rose at dawn and went together to the mosque. Camruddin's devotions were of the accustomed length, but Hasan's were unusually prolonged. When Camruddin inquired the reason for such supererogation he was told: 'To-day is Friday. I must miss the noonday prayer. Moreover, there is work before us which may keep me in the field for many days.'

'Tell me one thing truly, O my soul! Am I, in any sense, a prisoner?'

'A prisoner? My soul, that is absurd!' said Hasan, with a touch of indignation. 'A friend detained for safety in a friendly way is not in any sense a prisoner.'

'Until when am I detained?'

'You will be free to leave us ere the sun shall set again, though Allah knows my hope is you will choose to stay with us.'

Camruddin felt relieved. His errand being now accomplished, his wish was to return to her he loved, on whom his thoughts had run through all the night, preventing sleep.

His worship ended, Hasan sent a servant of the mosque to fetch some food, on which they breakfasted together with the messenger, beneath the cloister. While they were thus employed a sound of military music filled the air, announcing that the garrison was marching out. Camruddin glanced inquiringly at Hasan, who smiled and said: 'It is not our affair. We have our orders.'

A little later, when they were alone together, he explained,—

'They go against a foe who has no real existence. It is a ruse of Niazi's, to employ them in the wrong direction.'

Camruddin was not inquisitive, feeling content to loiter in the shade beside his friend, telling his beads and lazily observing the play of pigeons on the sunlit pavement round the fountain of ablution. This idleness continued till the call for noonday prayer trilled forth from the adjacent minaret. Then Hasan scrambled to his feet and whispered: 'Come!'

'But it is sin to turn our backs upon the call,' protested Camruddin.

'The call to prayer is the appointed signal. Come with me.'

The barracks-yard was quite deserted when they reached it, but just outside its precincts near a hundred men, most of them in civilian dress, stood waiting, and others from the town arrived continually. An officer, passing between the waiting groups, unnoticed, as it seemed, entered the square. It was Niazi. There must have been some signal, although Camruddin did not perceive it; for suddenly the idlers moved of one accord. They also passed into the square and formed in ranks. 'Keep beside me!' said Hasan, in the ear of Camruddin. 'You are to come with us an hour or two upon the road:

that is the order. And after that you will be free to go your way if you desire to leave us, which God forbid, for this is true Jihad.'

The armoury was broken open by command of Niazi Bey, and rifles were distributed, two to every man excepting Camruddin and a young Christian priest whom Camruddin first noticed in this distribution. Hasan explained: 'He is a hostage, but no harm will come to him. The sister of a great Bulgarian bandit, whom Niazi punished, came to Niazi yesterday for justice. A band of Serbs have carried off her child. Niazi promised, with the help of Allah, to restore him to her. Therefore he takes this Serbian priest along with us. Henceforth the nations must give up their wickedness. They will soon learn, in sha'llah!'

There was some delay, the cause of which was not discernible, but Hasan said that their commander was engaged in writing a receipt for the munitions taken; and then the men fell in as if by instinct, formed fours, turned left, and marched out in good order from the town of Resna while most of the inhabitants were still at prayer. Camruddin kept close beside his friend, the ombashi.

Soon they were climbing up the western hill, following in single file a winding path which traversed a dense undergrowth of scented shrubs with here and there a group of forest trees.

'There are some here who do not belong to us,' Hasan told his friend. 'They fell in because we did, knowing nothing of the business, just like sheep. Niazi must have noticed. He sees everything.'

The burdened men kept halting on the uphill road to wipe their foreheads. Niazi cheered them on with pleasant words, though he was carrying no less a weight than they were. He clapped the Serbian priest upon the back approvingly for shouldering a pair of rifles like the rest.

On a green summit which commanded a majestic view of lakes and mountains, forests, fields, and villages, and three fair towns, another band of forty men awaited them—volunteers from Persepe, as Hasan whispered. Here a halt was called. The men piled arms, loosed belts, and flung themselves upon the ground, plucking the grass and looking out over the sunny land. Some lighted cigarettes. Their chief, after some conversation with the officer from Persepe, came and lay down among them. Having given time for their repose, he said: 'My children, listen! Most of you know the reason of our coming forth, but some are here in ignorance; so I will state it, to the end that no unwilling man may share our danger. We have sworn by the Unity of Allah to give our lives for the salvation of our fatherland. The nation expects you to set a bright example of Osmanli chivalry, worthy of imitation through the ages. Are you prepared never to see your homes again until the safety of your country is secured; are you ready to die gladly for your country?'

There were murmurs of assent.

'We are all Muslims—servants of Allah, with plain commands. Look at our Muslim land to-day. See what has been made of it by faithless servants. Despotism is forbidden by the Sacred Law, so is oppression, so is selfish gain, so is the sale of justice, so is usury. It is no use saying: "We are not the rulers." It is the duty of all Muslims to preserve the Muslim body from corruption. That body is, or ought to be, a living witness to the truth of the august Coran, which shows the only way of progress for the world at large. The judgement of Allah is one for all mankind, even as Allah is One for all mankind. We have more perfect guidance than the others, therefore our sin is greater if we go astray. What if the Muslim empire under the Khalîfa is not more godly than the other kingdoms of the earth? All of you can answer: it deserves destruction. It is in danger of destruction at this moment. Seeing its present state in which freedom of speech and thought, learning, education —the rights conferred on every Muslim, every Muslimah —are suppressed; in which corruption has become the way of government; seeing the condition of the Christian nationalities, the Powers of Europe think it time to make an end of us. England and France, who were our friends, now side with Russia, our most deadly enemy. For thirty years the Muslim people of this realm have seemed to acquiesce in this iniquity: that is the reason why they deem us past all hope. But there is hope. If we can vindicate Islam by re-establishing the Constitution of the blessed martyr Midhat Pasha, the Constitution sanctioned by the Ulema, of which we have been robbed for thirty years, then England will draw back from Russia and support us. Of old the Muslim empire was the only country in the world in which religious tolerance was law. Now other countries are ahead of us in that respect. The bitterness of never-ending war has made us scornful towards our Christian brothers, has caused us to forget that conduct, not belief, is the one field of rivalry for servants of Allah, the way of human brotherhood prescribed for Muslims.'

'The Constitution gives equality to all Osmanlis, irrespective of creed or race. We, as the heralds of the Constitution must remember that. We are fedaïs, who have said farewell to life. Our enemies are many and will surely slander us. Take care that no one shall have reason to speak ill of us. I charge you, while you wander through this country, to respect the honour of the people as your own. Be guilty of no act of oppression. Steal nothing, though the pangs of hunger urge you. Respect all women of the country. Practise chastity. If one of you transgresses even in the least degree, his punishment is death, and I will see it executed. There can be no other penalty for men engaged in such a work as ours, so high, so sacred. The safety of our fatherland demands severity. I give each man three pounds for the support of his family, and two medjidiehs for tobacco. I undertake to keep you all in food and clothing. These are the terms of service. Say, do you accept of them?'

'By Allah! In Allah!' came as a triumphant shout.

'Let those who feel a weakness or reluctance turn back now. They sacrifice their lives who come with me.'

There was a moment of dead silence, then from every throat rose an impassioned sigh: 'Allahu Akbar!'

Only four stood up and asked permission to return, in accents of profound apology. They had joined the band in error, they explained, supposing they were to be led against the Bulgars. They had come without religious preparation, in no fit state to enter upon true Jihâd. Niazi Bey commanded that their rifles and their ammunition should be confiscated; then, taking out his notebook, wrote a line or two which they could show as proof that force had been employed against them, giving the page to one of them.

The four departed down the mountain path, turning to look back enviously at the gay fedaïs, who kept waving hands to them and shouting: 'Pray for our success!'

The call to arms was given and the men arose. The leader's eye then fell on Camruddin.

'My friend,' he said, 'your work has been well done. Allah reward you for it. You are now at liberty. Go back along with those four men. You are not one of us, although a helper.'

Camruddin strove for words. At last he blurted out,—

'Efendim, when I am not one of you, then know me dead!'

Niazi Bey looked hard at him, then turned away, commanding,

'Give him a rifle and two hundred rounds.' Camruddin leapt for joy. He trod on air. His bride, his mother and his other relatives, the hopes and plans which he had cherished that same morning, appeared like lovely objects in the plains below. He stood upon the heights.

Chapter XVI

LATE IN the afternoon the band arrived at Labcha, a mountain village into which they marched with cries of 'Allahu Akbar!' 'La ilaha illa 'llah!' The people, summoned from their work in the fields, applauded them and offered prayers for their success. Niazi Bey addressed the multitude, explaining the committee's plan of action and the part which they and all the Muslim peasantry could take in it if they would lay aside old jealousies and false distinctions and once more practise true Islâmic brotherhood.

One of the Labcha elders, a vigorous, white-bearded man but bowed with age, who said that he had been a sergeant in the army, asked leave to join the band and share its dangers. 'Refuse me not this blessing,' he implored, 'for even if we fail, true martyrdom can be obtained in this endeavour.'

But Niazi answered: 'No. My heart would have you with me, but this village needs you; for I mean to make of it our base and place of refuge, and your experience is wanted here.'

The chief men of the village were initiated and instructed in the proper method of self-government; and Camruddin, with half a dozen more of the fedaïs who, like him, were new recruits, received instruction with them, and were sworn in as adherents of the Committee of Union and Progress. Then, after they had eaten and refreshed themselves, the band set out again, amid a storm of blessing from the villagers, to march all night among the hills under the friendly stars.

At evening of the next day, being near to Ochrida, they halted in a cherry orchard and there bivouacked while Niazi, under cover of the night, went on into the town.

'He is too venturesome,' said Hasan to his friend. 'This town is strongly garrisoned and full of spies. Pray Allah that no harm befall him, for he is our life.'

The ombashi said that as they lay down to sleep, while still pale ghosts of daylight peered beneath the fringes of the orchard; and when they woke soon after sunrise, Niazi Bey had not returned. Then there was real anxiety on his account. Scouts were thrown out in the direction of the town, and Osman Efendi, as the second in command, summoned a council to decide what should be done in case of some untoward accident. But, about the third hour of the day, reports came in that he was safe and on his way to join them; and half an hour later Niazi himself appeared, accompanied by certain of his friends from Ochrida. He had spent the night in writing and despatching letters to the great Albanian chiefs, and the Bulgarian brigands.

Later, some men arrived with a supply of leather water-bottles, such as soldiers carry on the march, and other things which the fedaïs needed—a gift which gave much satisfaction to the mind of Hasan, who was a stickler for correct equipment.

They lay up in the cherry orchard all that day, inhaling with delight the perfume of its shade; until the sunset prayer was said, and then the order came to march again. 'Praise be to Allah!' exclaimed Hasan. 'In sha'llah, we shall soon be able to breathe freely. This place is much too near the lion's den to be agreeable. To run the risk of being killed or captured at the outset, before we have done any of the work appointed, and just when I have found a friend more to my liking than any I have ever had before in all my life, annoys me. I pray to fight beside thee once or twice before the lead comes crash into my heart or brain. Allahu Akbar!'

It was rumoured in the ranks at starting that their destination was the town of Dibra, on the Kara Drin. It meant a respite, because all that district was wild country in which the Government had little real authority.

When dawn came, it revealed a mountain landscape— a deep, meandering gorge with wooded cliffs so steep that it was a marvel how trees rooted there, and, high above, a range of peaks which caught the light like a great wave about to break on all the country. The notes of newly-wakened birds resounded solemnly. Then, as they turned a promontory of the mountainside, they saw a village amid fields and orchards on the farther slope, and halted for a while to rest before approaching it.

And then began the most wonderful three weeks in all the life of Camruddin—a space of time filled with events so strange, so rapid in their sequence, that they seem even now miraculous to all who had the privilege to bear a part in them. The blessing of Allah was visible on every effort of that little company. They sped from place to place among the mountain, bringing hope; and soon their march was a triumphal progress. None knew fatigue, none hankered for the life which he had left behind. If it was prayer-time when they came into a village, they all went to the mosque, where Niazi climbed the pulpit and addressed the folk. At other hours they held their meeting in the open air beneath some tree. In almost all the Muslim communes their success was instantaneous. Only two refused a hearing to their message, threatening armed resistance, and were left in peace, Niazi's orders being strict against attacking any one except the actual agents of the despotism; and from one of those two villages they afterwards received a deputation of the elders asking pardon. The council had been misinformed of their character and intention; it had deemed them a rebellious, plundering band, like those which for so long had terrorised the country. But now, perceiving that they came as peacemakers, the village offered gifts of food and full adherence.

As peacemakers, the band appeared to all the mountain people. By preaching holy war upon a state of things which was the enemy of all alike, by giving to the warring clans a common purpose and a common hope, they caused blood feuds to be at once abandoned and confidence to take the place of jealousy. The sight of persons who, the day before, could not have met together without bloodshed, standing side by side, both listening with the same emotion to Niazi's eloquence, impressed the common people as a sign from God. Another sign from Allah was the gentle conduct of the band. Even in the Muslim villages this caused astonishment, for roughness was expected from armed men. But when they came to visit Christian villages, where any Muslim force was looked on as in nature hostile, the surprise at their polite behaviour was intense.

It was not till tidings of his band's good conduct had had time to penetrate the country, and his letters to the Christian leaders time to take effect, that Niazi led his men to a Bulgarian village. Cries of alarm were raised at their approach, and when they came into the streets they found them empty. The shops were shuttered and the houses barred. To knock at any door would have produced a volley. So Niazi halted in the square before the headman's house, and there announced his peaceable intentions loudly, calling on the elective council of the village to tell the people that he came in all goodwill. The headman soon appeared and greeted him respectfully, exclaiming: 'We have heard your good report, efendim, and if we had been sure that it was you and your fedaïs, be sure that we should not have fled into the houses, but gone forth with songs to meet you on the way.'

The people soon assembled, and Niazi thus addressed them,—

'Brethren, children of the same fatherland, I know that you have suffered from this cruel despotism, of which the pleasure is to set us by the ears, and that your sufferings have driven you to seek the help of foreigners. You know that, as a soldier, I have been your enemy; but even when obliged to put down insurrection, I perceived that you yourselves were not to blame for the disorders, and I, and others with me, sought a remedy for your distress. The remedy is found. We Muslims, who, as you well know, have suffered more than you have from the despotism, have determined to enforce the Constitution by which equal rights have been secured to all Osmanlis. With sincerity of heart we offer you the rights of brothers, and what is more, the love of comrades who defend their common home against a common enemy. You have said: "We are not Turks, but Bulgars. Our fatherland is Bulgaristan." That is not true, for Macedonia is your fatherland; and in Macedonia four-fifths of the population is composed of Muslims, Greeks, and Serbs. You are one fifth. The Serbs say just as you do: "We fight for Serbia."

The Greeks: "We fight for Greece." Where will this end, except in grave injustice, shocking cruelty. For suppose Bulgaristan should conquer Macedonia, four-fifths of the inhabitants would be oppressed. The same would be the case if Greece were the invader' —An angry murmur went up from the crowd.- 'Only under the Khalîfa's government, even at its worst, have conquered people any rights at all. Under the Constitution they have equal rights, and Muslim, Christian, Turk, and Greek and Bulgar are not distinguished by the law. All are Osmanlis. Is it not better for all of us, children of Macedonia, to be members of the free Osmanli Commonwealth than to struggle to impose upon our country some foreign rule obnoxious to the great majority?'

Here there were shouts of 'True!' The rest of Niazi's speech, an eloquent appeal for brotherhood, was interrupted by applause. When he had finished speaking, the headman of the place stood forth and said:. 'This much we know, efendim: No man, of all the races in this country except a Turk, would have the generosity and scope of mind to speak as you have spoken to men who have stood up against you as your enemies. Allah knows that, at the worst, we Bulgars never felt against the Turks the hatred we have felt against the Greeks and Serbians. The Turks are brave and upright, they have manners, they have honour. If the despotism goes, they are in truth our brothers.'

The Christian crowd then pounced on the fedaïs, leading them away to take refreshment in the houses. There were shouts on one side of 'Long live Islâm! Success to the brave Turks who fight for justice and equality,' and on the other of 'Long live Osmanlilik! The brave and honest Bulgars are our brothers!'

But one man held aloof from the rejoicings. It was the village priest, who moved amid the crowd in the distracted manner of a hen whose chickens have become unmanageable. He drew near to a Christian, who had seized the arm of Camruddin, and whispered something in his ear. The man retorted angrily, and when the priest had gone, laughed out and said,—

'To day is gall to him. He is a Russian!'

From the balconies the Christian women rained down flowers on the fedaïs as they marched away.

In Muslim villages, after the first few days, women and marriageable maidens were permitted to converse with Niazi's men; and it was strange to Camruddin that he felt no temptation from their charms, but only exaltation in this freedom from imposed restraint. When he remarked on this to an old man who was his host one night, he got for answer: 'You are true Mujahidlar; your conduct proves it. If all men were like you, there would be no more need for women to go veiled. The example of your good behaviour, seen of all, has made more converts than the preaching of Niazi; for no men who were not sincere could thus restrain themselves, nor would they do so for a cause which was not holy. We, who have seen the passage of so many bands, all fighting for some cause which they themselves thought excellent, notice the difference. Not one rude word, not one ill act, has been observed from you.'

The fedaïs were in truth in such a state of inward fervour that outward things were merely objects offered to their sight or hearing, which succeeded one another as such objects do in dreams. And all, with the exception of a few like Hasan, were men possessing education and the power of thought.

They had been nine days in the mountains when they first had news of what was passing in the outer world. A messenger, from the Committee, came to Niazi Bey one night in the village which he used as his headquarters, and in the morning all the tidings he had brought were topics of discussion on the march.

Shemsi Pasha, the Commander-in-Chief at Monastir, had been assassinated just as he was leaving the Telegraph Office, in his carriage, to join the force which he was going to lead against Niazi's band. He was shot dead by an officer in uniform. Fifteen hundred people were around his carriage at the time, yet the executioner was able to stroll quietly away. Nevertheless the troops had started in pursuit of the fedaïs and must be now close on them, for the news was four days old; and Government agents were at work among the villagers.

The bimbashi, Enver Bey, had also taken to the mountains with a company, and was at work some five days journey towards the east; and other officers had done the same at other places.

The representatives of the Committee now sat openly at Ochrida, a town of which the garrison had declared for liberty.

The news, though hopeful on the whole, commended caution, for at any moment they might meet the troops sent out to finish them. It became mere prudence to remove their quarters to a distant village. They were on their way there when a man came riding at full gallop to tell them that two regular battalions with machine-guns were behind them. Again the plan was changed, the village first selected being in the danger zone. And then, for the first time since they began their wandering life, the cold wind of misfortune blew on them.

Being pursued, they had to prepare for a long march; it was necessary to lay in a fresh supply of bread and cheese, their usual diet. But approaching a large village with intent to purchase these necessities, they were opposed by the inhabitants, who came out armed against them, incited by a person of superior rank, no doubt an agent of the Government. Their chief protested that his wish was only to buy food. They would not listen, but threatened an attack if he did not at once withdraw. He gave the order to retire accordingly. It was not the strength of those deluded villagers which overawed him, but the reflection that the two battalions in pursuit were gaining ground through this delay. He gave up thought of purchasing provisions, and left the lower slopes where there were villages, for the high mountains where pursuit was quite impossible. In a thicket, among rocks beside a mountain tarn, the little army of the Constitution spent that night, sending down scouts in three directions to look out for news. In the gray dawn one of these scouts returned, bringing a messenger whom he had intercepted on a bridle-path which led to Dibra. A little later came another with a good supply of bread and cheese, which had been given to him by some friendly villagers. Soon after sunrise, when the men had bathed and were refreshed, Niazi Bey announced that he had orders to bring his men to Ochrida without delay.

Chapter XVII

AT OCHRIDA, they spent a night among the gardens, while Niazi and his staff went on into the town itself. Early next morning the command was given to pack up at once and march towards Istarova. It was pleasant going in the early morning along the sandy fringes of the lake, where the Bulgarian fisher-people of the villages along the shore gave them a hearty welcome. But when the sun attained full strength the men grew silent, too much oppressed to smile in answer to the welcome, which was even more enthusiastic when they came to Muslim communes. The news which Niazi had received from the Committee leaked out upon the march, and was discussed at evening, when the growing coolness eased the men and made them once more talkative. The revolutionary movement was extending rapidly. Many spies and agents of the Government had been destroyed. The whole Bulgarian community declared itself in favour of the new ideas, though still unwilling to give armed assistance. The darkest spot on the horizon now was Monastir, where Marshal Osman Pasha had been sent to take the place of Shemsi Pasha, who had been assassinated.

'Hast ever served with Osman Pasha or with men who knew him?' Hasan inquired of Camruddin, who showed surprise at the profound impression which the news of this appointment made on everybody. Camruddin shook his head. 'Then thou canst never guess the sort of man he is. A man of iron, and of such renown in war that every soldier is constrained to take a pride in him. A man whom no one ever disobeyed. You know that I am heart and soul for the Committee, as are all men here. Well, if Osman Pasha were to come before us now alone on horseback and cry "Follow me!" I do not feel quite sure at heart that I should not obey him. If that is the case with one of us fedaïs, imagine what must be his influence on men still doubtful. The task of hunting us has been entrusted to him. That is bad news.'

'He must be such another as my patron, Sâdik Pasha,' chuckled Camruddin.

'Just such another, I have heard!, assented Hasan dryly. 'All the troops would be heartbroken if we chanced to kill him.'

Niazi had been praised at Ochrida for the behaviour of his band, and sent to a safe region for repose, with the express warning that he and his men would shortly be required for serious work. The district they now traversed was already won for liberty, and there was little danger of pursuit. At Istarova they were welcomed by excited crowds; the people offered food and drink; the council of the village begged to be informed what they could do to show the strength of their enthusiasm for the cause of Right. The region was well governed. The Caïmmacâm, the only person who refused to meet Niazi or take any part in the rejoicings, was said by all to be a good and upright man. The peasants were not overtaxed. The land was on the whole well cultivated. The communes in this district did not need reorganising from the very ground-work, as had been the case with those round Ochrida and Dibra. What could the people do to show their will for progress? Niazi told them: 'In all your county, prosperous as it appears to be, I have not come across a single school; and everywhere I find the mosques dilapidated. Without a cultivated understanding there can be no progress; without the bond of public worship no true Union and Fraternity. Build schools, instruct your people, and repair your mosques.'

He was standing in the lofty pulpit of the mosque of Istarova when he spoke the words, looking down upon a boundless throng of eager faces, which stretched far beyond the shade of the old walls into the outer sunlight. The words were hailed with cries of 'True, by Allah!' There and then a fund was started for the holy purpose, everybody giving what he could afford. After the sunset prayer a feast was spread for the fedaïs in the open air; and all night long there was a sound of music in their honour, and occasionally sounds of firing also, as fresh adherents from the country came into the village, each party firing in salute and to announce its coming. Before noon of the following day more than four thousand men had come to Istarova to swear allegiance to the new régime. In sight of that armed crowd, the hopes of the fedaïs rose.

'Allah! Allah!' murmured Camruddin impatiently. 'Why do we wait? We have but to enrol the people to obtain an army which no common army could resist. It is time that we came forth into the open. Our secret work of preparation is accomplished; we have roused the world.'

'Gently, my soul,' said Hasan, his habitual confidant. 'It is true that all these people are now one with us. But suppose that Osman Pasha with but one battalion were to come among us at this moment. I think that most of them by instinct and the force of habit would submit to him. So long as Osman Pasha holds command at Monastir our hope of victory is far from sure. You and I—even Niazi—are but the hand in all this business. The Committee is the head, possessing eyes and ears. They watch the country. When the time is ripe they will inform us.'

From Istarova, where Niazi held his court two days, the band was suddenly recalled to Ochrida. It stayed there but the time required for taking orders and then, with reinforcements, marched to Resna.

'Wallahi, now I think thy wish will be fulfilled,' said Hasan to his chosen comrade. 'We are going out into the open, Allah help us!'

Near Resna further reinforcements joined them, and they took the mountain road towards Monastir.

'What did I tell thee?' Hasan said to Camruddin. 'We go to beard the lion in his den.'

Nothing had as yet been said as to their destination, but all men judged from the direction of their march and from their numbers that nothing less than an attack on Monastir was in the wind.

At night, when they were traversing a deep ravine intensely dark, although the moon was shining on the heights above, a sound of firing close at hand surprised them. A halt was called. They waited in dead silence, listening to the clamour of a battle near at hand; until a scout came in to say that all was well. Two companies upon their way to join Niazi had come together in the moonlight on the hill above and, being ancient enemies accustomed to salute each other with a hail of bullets, had fired their rifles in the air with all the movements of a

mimic battle, to celebrate their new alliance in the cause
of Progress. Half an hour later, when the column issued
from the gloom of the ravine on to a moonlit down, it
was received with joyous shouts by some five hundred
men, who there awaited it. There was a halt while Niazi
Bey inspected these recruits and put some questions to
their leaders.

'It is an army, well appointed and well led, and what is
more, inspired with holy zeal. In sha'llah, we shall have
success,' said Camruddin.

'In sha'llah,' answered Hasan, 'yet I do assure you that,
if Osman Pasha's voice should chance to reach this army,
it would melt away.'

'Allah forbid!'

'I do believe it,' answered Hasan. 'If only he were with
us, not against us, I should feel more comfortable.'

The column rested later at a village where many other
volunteers awaited it. The streets were crowded in the
hours before the dawn with people come from far to give
their blessing and small gifts of food to the fedaïs. The
sun was up before the army marched away.

About the fifth hour of the day a halt was called
among the rugged heights of Mount Pelista, underneath
a scorching sun.

The men were formed in twenty companies; the roll
was called; then Niazi Bey explained the purpose of the
expedition to the men of Resna, while Eyub Efendi did
the same for those of Ochrida.

'Comrades,' he cried, 'we have forsaken comfort and
our wives and families to work for the salvation of our
country. We have made our lives a sacrifice for this most
sacred cause. You all, my brothers, have suffered many
hardships uncomplainingly. Fatigues which men in ordi-

nary times and for a lesser cause would think intolerable, you have cheerfully endured. Endure a few hours longer and our troubles will be past, for, if God wills it, we shall have attained our object and rescued our beloved country from affliction. Relying on the help of Allah and the inspiration of His Prophet (may Allah bless and keep him) we are on our way to the headquarters of the vilayet of Monastir, in obedience to an order which we have received from the Committee. Our business is to kidnap the Field-Marshal Osman Pasha, to capture him and carry him away out of the very midst of his force without injuring a hair of his respected head; simply to prevent his putting into execution the project he has formed to injure the Committee and the Fatherland. Therefore, every one of you, my comrades, must obey religiously the orders that you will receive. The strictest discipline must be maintained. May Allah grant complete success to this, our effort in the way of duty.'

There were shouts of joy, and when the word to march was given, the men, forgetting their fatigue, set forward at the double on the mountain road. At a turn they suddenly encountered half a dozen bashibazouks who were on their way to meet them, bringing a young roebuck they had found astray among the hills and coaxed to follow them with food and petting.

'We bring you luck!' exclaimed their leader, pointing to the pretty beast, while all the soldiers who beheld it offered praise to Allah for its beauty, and for the gracious trustfulness which it displayed towards sinful men. Thenceforth it trotted on before the column, stopping often to look back and give them time to follow, and always. in the right direction, towards Monastir. The men beheld the creature as a Heaven-sent guide, its movements as of happy omen for their expedition. Its presence kept them in good spirits, gave them energy so that they performed an almost superhuman effort without knowing it, and reached a village close to Monastir before the sun set. Here there was a halt for food and rest, while Niazi Bey conferred with persons from the town who had come out to meet him.

Camruddin spent a good part of his leisure in writing letters for some comrades, among whom was Hasan, whose veneration for his friend's attainments in the way of learning demanded frequent exhibitions of the same.

'To-morrow we shall be victorious, with Allah's help; either on earth or else in Paradise. Now is the time for every man to send a word of farewell and instruction to those near to him, and I know one who can compose a letter worthy to be compared with any work of scribe or khôja. It is Camruddin Agha, the chaûsh, now our lieutenant,' he went round saying to the men who had no scholarship; and several of them took advantage of his invitation, a person of the village giving pen and ink and paper, while every one sat round and watched the writer with blessings on the skill which moved his hand. One letter was unfinished at the call to arms. Its owner would not let it go among the others to be sent off as occasion offered by the friendly villagers. He thrust it in his bosom jealously, remarking that, please God, the time would come when Camruddin would condescend to finish it.

Niazi Bey once more addressed the men when they were in their ranks, bidding them be steady, silent, and obedient. When the order to advance was given, the fedaïs doubled; their feet, in sandals, making little noise upon the dusty road. In a short while they reached the outskirts of the town. It was then near midnight. Once again a halt was called, while members of the Monastir Committee arranged the plan with Niazi and Eyûb. Eight hundred men, divided into several companies, advanced by different roads into the town in perfect silence, while the main force remained among the suburbs. Camruddin and Hasan went with others of the band straight to the residence of Osman Pasha. Their guide, a member of the Monastir Committee, imparted scraps of information in a whisper as they went along. The telegraph wires had all been cut, so that the General in command could not communicate with his own staff, much less with Yildiz or Stamboul. And all his possible coadjutors would soon be guarded.

'It is the lion himself whom we are going to assail, is that not so?' said Hasan to his friend in awe-struck tones. 'I ask to be defended from the voice of him. The sight alone would not perhaps confound me utterly. But if he shouted: "About turn! Quick march!" I fear I should obey the order, may the Lord forgive me!'

Chapter XVIII

NO light was visible in all the town except the lantern carried by their guide. The buildings rose in silhouette against a sky alive with stars as they went forward silently. The air was cool and sweet, except where heaps of rubbish exhaled fetid odours. The dogs, prowling about their business, took no notice of the stealthy march of men, reserving all their noise for their own quarrels, which were the cause of furious barkings now and then. The officers sent back a warning which was passed by touch from man to man. They were approaching a large building. A momentary halt, and then they rushed to the attack. Camruddin, who, acting as an officer, was in the front, pounced on a sentry who stood in his way. The man submitted. Out of six men thus taken by surprise one only offered serious resistance, and he was overpowered before he could let off his rifle. Most of the band remained in the courtyard. But twenty men went on into the house, the guide preceding them. Along a passage and upstairs they went, until they reached a door which proved, on trial, to be locked. A charge of three strong men removed that obstacle. They found themselves in Osman Pasha's bedroom. The officers advanced to the bedside, while Hasan, who had matches, lighted all the candles, of which there were a number in the room—'for honour,' as he told his comrade afterwards.

The old Field-Marshal, wakened out of sleep, first stared at the intruders in bewilderment and ordered them, at once, to leave the room. The officer in chief command assured him that his honoured life was in no danger, but that they, who thus had ventured to invade his privacy, had orders to convey him, with all reverence, at once to Resna; to confirm which statement he presented a letter from the Committee with every symptom of profound respect.

The Pasha sat up, looking straight before him. His face was flushed; the veins stood out upon his forehead; his mouth was working underneath the gray moustache. He seemed about to speak his mind, but managed to control himself and merely ordered,—

'Bring a light here, one of you.'

Hasan sprang forward with a lighted candle in a candlestick, and held it so as to throw light upon the bed.

Osman Pasha tore the envelope, perused the letter to the end, and then said calmly,—

'I am your prisoner, efendilarim. I ask your leave to go into another room to dress.'

With that he rose up, took the candlestick from Hasan's hand and walked sedately through the midst of his opponents, who would have let him dress alone had it not been for Hasan, who caught hold of Camruddin and whispered in his car: 'He means to kill himself; I saw his eyes. The yuzbashi must go with him, and you go, too!'

The yuzbashi was grateful for the hint. He and another officer attended on the Pasha while he dressed; but Camruddin preferred to go with Hasan and the soldiers, who now rejoined their comrades in the courtyard.

Presently Osman Pasha came, attended by the two

young officers, who might have been his children, so insignificant and meek did they appear beside him. A horse was ready for His Excellency. Hasan held the stirrup for him as he mounted.

Respectfully escorted by his captors, he was taken to the spot where Niazi, with the strength of his battalion, waited on the outskirts of the town. And then the army of the Constitution quitted Monastir. A cool breeze, heralding the dawn, was rustling in the poplars. The murmur of the running waters was exceeding loud, seeming to fill the whole vast hollow between earth and sky. Before the sun rose they were far upon their way.

The day was very hot, the road was mountainous, and only short rests were allowed, for fear of a pursuit. It was during one of those brief halts upon the summit of a ridge that a noise like thunder, in the distance, reached the ears of the fedaïs. It was not very loud, and yet it shook the ground. Some birds among the brushwood on the slopes below them were disturbed. 'Cannon,' the whisper ran, and men sat up to listen. There was silence for a minute, then the same dull sound, seeming to cause a tremor in the very sunlight.

'The guns of Monastir!' cried a young man, in gay apparel, who happened to be lying near to Camruddin. 'The city is perhaps besieged, or torn internally.'

An interval, and then again the noise was heard.

'That is no cannonade, but a salute of honour,' said an old man, who had once been in the Sultan's bodyguard.

Then some one near Niazi raised the cry: 'Long live the Constitution!' which was repeated by the men in a tremendous shout. And everybody knew that distant booming meant that Monastir was won.

Chapter XIX

THE NEXT day was a day of wild rejoicing. From early morning until late at night the streets of Resna were alive with a dense throng of people—a medley of good Muslims, Bulgars, Greeks, Serbs, Valachs, Jews, embracing one another, laughing, dancing in a veritable frenzy of enthusiasm. The Constitution was proclaimed in Macedonia and Albania. Banners with the inscription: 'Liberty, Equality, Fraternity, Justice,' fluttered in the breeze, and sounds of festive music came from every side. Niazi sat in council with the leaders of the Christian bands, who had come in to take the oath of loyalty to the Committee. His men, the object of their federation being now achieved, had twenty-four hours' leave in which to seek the consolation of their wives and families; and those who came from Resna and the country round—the great majority—availed themselves of the permission and were no more seen. Hasan, the ombashi, being of the lucky ones, Camruddin was all alone on that great day. He tired of strolling aimless in the noisy crowd. The fatigue of the past weeks, unnoticed at the time amid excitement, now oppressed him. He felt as one who wanders in a dream, with full perception of its unreality. He thought of his own native village, of his mother and his sister Melek, and wondered if his brothers had had tidings of the great event. He thought of cypress-groves and roses and his bride, Gul-raaneh. His soul was far from Resna, with its noisy crowds and decorated streets.

As the day grew hot he wandered out into the fields, lay down in the deep shade of trees, beside a stream, and slept. He dreamed. He saw Gul-raaneh in the sunlit space within the cypress-grove, but he was prisoned in the shadow and a long way off. She stretched her arms to him but he could not approach her, the shadow being hard around him like a wall. Then suddenly a voice beside him muttered: 'Kerata!' The landscape changed and he was in a carriage facing Deyli Ferid Bey, beside whom sat the old Field-Marshal, Osman Pasha. They were on the tops of mountains, and the wheels rolled smoothly though there was no road. Then they were standing with Niazi in a crowd which shouted for the Constitution, and Camruddin beheld his mother and his sister Melek in the distance beckoning. He was going towards them when Niazi called out: 'Stay! Your vow is still upon you. The work we swore to Allah to perform is not accomplished, nor will be till all evil has been banished utterly.'

And then the world was darkened, there were flashes, thunder-claps, and men were groaning round him in the gloom. It was the final war. The men beside him were laid low, and he himself was sorely wounded, yet fought on with faith, remembering his vow. Among the faces of the dead, he recognised the chief supporters of the despotism, and was surprised to know that they were not the enemy. What was the enemy? He meant to learn before he died. He heard a cry and saw Gul-raaneh, together with his mother and Melek, in extreme distress. They had been captured, and men of bestial appearance were assaulting them. He ran to their assistance, but before he reached them he fell into a gulf and so awoke.

The evening sun was shining on the country; the shadows of the poplars lay in long blue stripes across the fields. The mountain-ranges had assumed rich purple hues. From the town still came the shouts of joy, the sounds of music. Flags waved upon its roofs, and from the minarets. After gazing for a while upon the scene in a bewildered way, still under the impression of his evil dream, he rose and sauntered back into the town. He went into the mosque to pray. A tall, white-turbaned, black-robed khôja was discoursing eloquently, and Camruddin, when he had done his duty, sat and listened. He noticed many Christians in the congregation, a thing unknown, until that day, in all the land.

The Khôja said that now at last Islâm would be complete, since Jews and Christians joined with Muslims in the fight for righteousness, as Muhammad (Allah bless and keep him) had invited them to do by God's command. He quoted:-

'Say: "O people of the Scriptures, come to an equitable proposition between us and you: that we shall not serve any but Allah, and we shall not associate anything with Him, and that none of us shall take any others for lords besides Allah." But if they turn away, then : "Testify that we are His submissive servants."'

'You believe in one God, all of you,' the khôja cried: 'then come into the one Theocracy! Give up your fighting over details of belief. The test in Allah's kingdom is not creed, but conduct. The true jihâd is not of those who say "We are Muslims" against those who say "We are Christians." The true jihâd is of good against evil, beginning with the conquest of a man's own lusts and ending in the battle which we are now waging for righteous conduct in the government of man. That is the teaching of Islâm. From the refusal of the Jews and Christians, in the old days, to hear the message, from their attacks upon the Holy Prophet and his followers, has risen all the trouble in the world since then.

'But now the People of the Scripture have grown more enlightened, praise to Allah. The highly-educated Christian nations of the West no longer hate and persecute the Muslims for their faith; they have long ceased to torture and to kill each other on account of little differences of belief; the test to-day in all their courts is conduct, in accordance with the sacred law of Islâm. Please God, to-day the message will be heard and all men, irrespective of their creed and form of worship, will now acknowledge Allah as their Lord and King.'

It was the truth! Camruddin sat spellbound, listening to the good words which exorcised the gloom remaining from his evil dream. In view of that great truth, what matter though misfortunes came upon him and those dear to him; how long the struggle lasted, so long as he remained the faithful servant of the Lord of Heaven and earth. The end was written, and it was success, though that success might be deferred a thousand years.

When the khôja had finished speaking Camruddin rose and went out quietly. He was slipping on his shoes upon the threshold, when some one touched him on the shoulder, saying: 'Peace be on you. What is your opinion of that khôja's sermon?' He turned and, to his great surprise, found Ferid Bey beside him. 'Allah reward him good for it!' said Camruddin, with deep emotion. He wished to kiss the hand of Ferid, but the latter stopped him, crying: 'I ask forgiveness of Allah! You, a fedaï! I, a rotten idler! No, it shall not be!' Taking his friend's hand, he walked beside him, adding: 'That was the best religious speech I ever heard. The Christians present were impressed by it. They are, all of them, our loving brothers for the moment—until their priests get hold of them again! The priesthood organises evil, as I know, by Allah, having studied in a college which was ruled by priests. May they go blind! But most of them are blind already, by their doctrines, to such a light as this which shines to-day.'

It was evident to Camruddin that Ferid Bey, despite his cynical address, was deeply moved.

'Where are you going?' Ferid asked.

'Efendim, to the barracks. We parade at nightfall.'

'So I have heard. You march again to Monastir. Have you any particular desire to go there, may I ask?'

"Efendim, no; but I am a fedaï.'

'Your vow is expiated. Whither would you choose to go, supposing you were free and had the means to make a journey?'

'Either to Stamboul or to my native village.'

'Which, for choice?'

'Stamboul, efendim, for my bride is there.'

'As it happens, I am going thither. I will see Niazi.'

With the abruptness usual to him, which had much to do with his eccentric reputation, Ferid Bey then let go of Camruddin and walked away.

Some two hours later, when the fedaïs were assembling in the barracks-yard, a yuzbashi came up to Camruddin and said: 'You are required for special duty, efendim. Go in through that gateway and knock at the third door in the passage on the right.'

Camruddin obeyed.

He found Niazi Bey in conference with some civilians.

The leader said: 'Give up your rifle and equipment, for we are sending you upon an errand to Stamboul. Here are some letters which you must deliver personally. Let no one see even the cover of them. Go to the konak and join Ferid Bey who there awaits you. His wealth will make your journey quick and easy, in sha'llah!'

So Camruddin forsook the band of heroes and set out from Resna. His grief was that he had not said farewell to Hasan, and that he might never see that perfect comrade in the world again.

Chapter XX

'AN ICY winter wind has this advantage, that it blows away all kinds of stinging pests which thrive in summer. The despotism banished men like that!' said Deyli Ferid, as he sat by Camruddin upon the steamer's deck. The man referred to had that minute left them—a Turk from Paris and an advocate of all things French. He was, like Ferid Bey, a first-class passenger, but, unlike Ferid Bey, he had his meals in the saloon, and spent the daylight hours in talking to the Frankish travellers of the great changes he was going to make in Turkey. And he wore a hat. Ferid Bey, who understood French perfectly, had overheard remarks of his which much amused him, and so had entered into talk with the Parisian. In the end, he had beguiled him to that portion of the deck allotted to the second-class, in order to make sport for Camruddin, with whom he (Ferid) spent a great part of his time. To lead the boaster on, he had assumed the character of an extremely simple-minded Turkish notable, to whose intelligence all that the other had to tell of Europe caused intense surprise. Camruddin's surprise was quite unfeigned and mixed with horror. With two such listeners the apostle of French culture had aired his views complacently, untroubled by the slightest doubt of their inferiority.

The Revolution, it appeared, was all his work. It was he, at any rate, who had first thought of it. He had prepared the way for it in Paris, where he had been a member of

the Committee of Union and Progress which had exist-
ed there long before this other, purely local, Committee
was formed in the Ottoman Empire. Overjoyed at the
success of his idea, he was now upon his way to take
control and give direction. He told them of the various
reforms he would at once inaugurate, foremost among
them being a decree that every Turk should throw away
his fez and buy a hat.

'Then Europe will be sure that we are civilised,' he
told his listeners.

'And if the people, as a whole, object?' asked Deyli
Ferid, in an awestruck tone.

'Then the reform must be enforced, since it is necessary.'

With that the maniac left them, having promised certain of his Frankish friends to play a game of cards, as he
explained. As soon as he was out of earshot, Ferid Bey
made his remark about the icy wind and stinging pests.

It was already night, and they were past Gallipoli. The
island of Marmora appeared before them, a dark mass
of mountain rising from the tranquil sea. The stars were
large and bright, though far astern a gleam of sunset still
threw up the outlines of the land.

'They call me mad,' said Deyli Ferid chuckling. 'My
wisdom is despised because, through modesty, I cloak it
generally in facetious terms. Yet every one will listen to
a man like that.'

'No one would listen to him patiently except your
Honour!'

'What do you know of people! His proposals will
not be approved—at least, I hope not—but they will
be discussed quite seriously. Whereas, if I proposed
that we should all resume the splendid dress of the old

Turks—a really picturesque reform which would appeal
to Europe—I should be derided.'

Ferid Bey was silent for a while. When he resumed,
it was in quite another tone, a tone of sadness. He observed: 'They call me mad. The fashion of the day seems
mad to me. I had a Frenchman for my tutor—he was mad.
They sent me to a college kept by Frankish priests—all
mad. And since I am grown up I meet with traces of that
madness everywhere; and all against our country, so I
do not love it. I keep apart, and every one rebukes me. I
have rendered considerable services to the Committee;
there are men belonging to it for whom I have the highest admiration, though all are tinged with the insanity of
which I speak. They look askance at me because I laugh
at some of their ideas. You are quite sane, my soul, that is
the reason why I take such pleasure in your company. And
you are a fedaï! Allah, Allah, I would give my wealth to
have the soul of a fedaï—the commonest of Allah's gifts
among Osmanlis. I had it at my birth, but foreign education killed it. I saw the falsehood of the Franks, which
saved me from the madness of that fool who spoke to us
just now; yet their ideas impressed my mind sufficiently
to prevent me from becoming a whole-hearted Muslim.
I was latterly against the despotism, though it never hurt
me personally, who have been regarded by all parties as
a harmless joker; but since we heard, at Saloniki, that the
Padishah had granted our demands I have been almost
sorry, doubting what may come of it. And now that fool
to-night has made it all seem madness. I thought that I
could share in the enthusiasm; but now I see that I must
still look on and jest.'

'Efendim, may I offer a suggestion?' put in Camruddin.
'It is that you should not expect completeness in a thing

until it is complete by Allah's mercy. Only by Allah's mercy can the end be gained. Our part is the intention and the effort. Your Honour's judgement would be far more useful to the cause than that of the misguided person who just now addressed us. But his judgement will be heard, and yours unheard simply because you will not state it seriously.'

'There are hundreds more like him in Paris. They will all be flocking to Stamboul like birds of prey. There are good men in exile, but not more than five or six. The fools, alas! are numbered by the hundred. What chance have I of being heard amid that jabbering crowd—I, Deyli Ferid, whom men call a trifler.'

'If your Honour would but condescend to humour their insanity and use the kind of speech acceptable to their intelligence, and if you would but deign to take a part in government!'

'No, that I will not,' answered Ferid Bey decidedly.

Camruddin said no more. He feared that he had already said enough to give offence to one whom he perceived by intuition to be highly sensitive. It was that faculty of being hurt by incidents which men of coarser fibre hardly noticed, that made his patron shun the thought of public life. Ferid Bey said good-night to him, and sauntered off in the direction of his cabin. Camruddin rolled his cloak into a pillow and lay down upon the deck. He remained awake a long while, thinking of the man from Paris and the strange effect he had produced on Ferid Bey. It made him anxious and unhappy till the thought of Allah, the protecting friend of men of honest purpose, returned to fill his heart with hope and confidence, and then he fell asleep, his last thought being,—

'England will befriend us now.'

In the morning when he rose he saw the glory of Stamboul uprising from the sea, its ridge of noble mosques in one line with the coast of Asia, its minarets like spears caught in the sunrise. It was an hour before he could make out the entrance to the Bosphorus, and then, next minute, they were in the strait. Ferid Bey was at his side among a crowd of passengers, all gazing with emotion at the panorama of the city as it opened out. The lighthouse and the mosque of Sultan Ahmed, Aya Sophia, the old palace glided by. There was the Golden Horn with all its shipping and, throned upon the hill above it, the Cathedral Mosques.

Far up the winding Bosphorus, as blue as borage-flower, the mosque of Ortakeuy rested on the water like a swan. The pretty villages among the trees, the solemn cypress-groves, made Camruddin cry 'Praise to Allah!' constantly. And then the steamer drew up to the quay of Ghalatah, and was at once invaded by a crowd of touts and porters who cried: 'Long live the Constitution!' 'Long live Freedom!' 'Long live England!' as they ran on board. A group of several fezzed, frock-coated individuals of some importance, each carrying a silver-headed cane, approached the gentleman from Paris, who for the ceremony of landing had put on a fez.

'He will make them throw away those scarlet caps and put on hats directly,' said Ferid Bey. A minute later, having watched their meeting and called attention to the air of triumph of the man from Paris, he suddenly laid hold of Camruddin and said: 'Come on!' He led him close to the frock-coated group and then cried out for all the ship to hear: 'Long live the Constitution! Here is a fedaï straight from Resna. One of the men who captured Osman Pasha!'

At once the man from Paris was deserted. His very friends forgot him in their eagerness to clasp the hero. It was half an hour ere Camruddin could get ashore, and long before he did so the man from Paris had completely disappeared.

'I meant to put that braggart in his place,' said Ferid Bey.

Chapter XXI

ALONG THE quay a crowd of his admirers followed Camruddin, calling to passers-by that here was a fedaï of Niazi's band, with the result that he was stopped perpetually by men of all conditions who insisted on embracing him. Ferid Bey was entertained by his embarrassment in this position, till an excited Christian pedlar mistook him (Ferid) for the hero of the hour, and flung his arms about him, provoking hearty laughter from the multitude; on which he very quickly hailed a carriage.

The driver had some difficulty in starting, owing to the throng, but by dint of shouting: 'Long live the Constitution!' he managed, by degrees, to reach the entrance of the Bridge where toll is paid, and after that whipped up his horses, leaving the crowd behind. No end of painted kaïks with people in them were moving to and fro upon the dark-blue water. The shipping in the open strait was gay with bunting, which fluttered also from the buildings of Stamboul and Ghalatah, and up the reaches of the Golden Horn. Across the Bosphorus, which was a dazzle in the sunlight, Scutari, too, was all beflagged beneath the hills of Asia.

The crowd upon the footwalks of the bridge was not an ordinary crowd, for everybody greeted everybody; and when a Muslim met a Christian of his class the pair embraced.

At the Bridge-end the carriage stopped; the driver turned round with a shrug to face his passengers, at the same time pointing onward with his whip. The open space before the Sultan Valideh mosque was covered with a throng of people, many of them sitting on the ground with goods for sale spread out on mats before them. There was no clear roadway.

'Liberty,' explained the driver in indulgent tones. 'Every one sits where he likes. And if one shouts, they do not deign to move until the horses are upon them. They seem to think that everything to-day is harmless. It seems a pity to disturb them, Bey Efendim.'

'Kerata!' said Ferid Bey resignedly. 'I am at liberty, it seems, to walk, for all my money. But being of a lazy nature, I shall not do that. I meant to take my friend here to the War Office. He is a fedaï of Niazi's band, and has an errand thither. But since the journey must be done on foot, I leave him here. Proceed, my soul, in Allah's keeping. I look to see you in the evening at Eren-keuy. Arabaji, turn back! The landing-stage!'

So Camruddin went on alone up crowded streets, bewildered by strange sights at every turn, until he came to the great square before the Ministry of War. Here at last was quiet and some show of discipline. He made inquiry of some lounging soldiers, showing his credentials. They bade him wait and presently brought out a sergeant who, learning that he was Niazi's man, embraced him fondly and then led him into the great building, along sounding corridors.

'Everything is out of gear,' his guide informed him. 'There is no proper Government. The orders come from private persons whom we do not know. All the officials here are idle, and in great anxiety. The man to whom your letter is addressed is not here, and I know not where he is. But I am taking you to one who can no doubt inform you.'

Camruddin was brought into the presence of a white-clad officer, who seemed extremely weary, for he yawned continually. On being told that Camruddin was a fedaï, he murmured 'Bravo!' but without enthusiasm. Then, having heard the nature of his business, he took a pen, dipped it in ink and wrote out an address upon a sheet of note-paper. This he handed to the sergeant, saying simply: 'Indicate!'

The sergeant studied the handwriting all along the corridors, and when they came again into the blazing sunlight of the square, he said,—

'I am not sure. Wait here a moment. I will question some one.'

Camruddin waited there an hour, and had just arrived at the conclusion that he had been cheated, when the chaûsh returned, bringing another man, a private, with him. He pointed to that man, exclaiming,—

'Go with him. He knows the place.'

The place, in fact, was close at hand—a large house in a modern street, one half of which was occupied by business premises. His guide led him upstairs into a room where several men were sitting round a table, while others sprawled at ease upon a couch against the wall. They took no notice of the new arrivals till, the guide approaching one of them with a request in which he chanced to mention that he brought a member of Niazi's band, they all applauded frantically, and Camruddin became the butt of eager questions.

'Give me the packet, for it is, I hear, addressed to me,' said one, who seemed to have authority above the rest. As he received it, he stared hard at Camruddin and then said: 'We are old acquaintances, are we not, efendim? And so that errand, upon which we sent you, led to glory!'

It was the civilian of the Saloniki secret conclave, the same who had betrayed dislike of Ferid Bey.

'Praise be to Allah,' answered Camruddin.

'How did you come?'

'I came with Ferid Bey.'

'With Deyli Ferid! How is he, as mad as ever?'

'I do not think him mad, efendim.'

'The madness is, you think, assumed, like that of foxes?'

'I think he is the best of men, efendim.'

The other laughed and said: 'He is not bad, perhaps; only too cautious, and too sceptical to be of use.'

He then became absorbed in the perusal of a letter, while the others questioned Camruddin about Niazi's doings in the mountains, and the raid on Monastir.

At length the great man folded up the letter, saying,—

'This was written before the Padishah had granted our demand. Events have answered it. But, in a postscript, we are asked to give promotion to the bearer, who is said to be a trusty man of good intelligence. I say not no. But things will not be as they were. No man henceforward will be thrust into a post because he is the friend or relative of So-and-so. As soon as the administration is remodelled, and we know what vacancies are to be filled, I recommend you for employment; I can do no more. But you will have to show your fitness in examination,'

'Good, efendim.'

'Leave some address where we can always find you.'

A secretary beckoned Camruddin, who went to him

and, being given pen and ink and paper, wrote his name and the address of Ferid Bey's kiosk. He then departed, with due thanks and reverence, feeling a good deal daunted by the promised favour, for he was far from sure of his ability to meet the views of men who were not soldiers. The soldier who had brought him from the Ministry of War said: 'That is where the orders come from now. Those men, whom you have just seen idling, arrange what needs arranging. It is liberty!'

There was a touch of sarcasm in this statement, which made Camruddin suspect that the speaker was a secret lover of the despotism. Before they parted he asked if he knew where Sâdik Pasha lived.

'Which Sâdik Pasha?'

'Arab Sâdik Pasha.'

'Allah knows! I think I heard them say he was arrested.'

'Arrested! For what crime?'

'Who knows. They pounce on anybody.'

The sunlight became livid in the sight of Camruddin; the sounds of popular rejoicing seemed a cruel farce. 'Can you not tell me where his house is situated?'

'No, that I cannot. But some other can, no doubt. Brother, where does Arab Sâdik Pasha live?' the soldier called out to a tall Cavass who happened to be passing.

'He lives at Kasim Pasha, brother, in a great kiosk,'

'Go to the waterside above the bridge and take a boat. That is the nearest way,' the soldier counselled.

Camruddin thanked him, and set out in great anxiety, with only one idea: to get to Kasim Pasha quickly; but in spite of himself the unaccustomed sights, the changing pageant of the streets, beguiled him into loitering upon the way.

Chapter XXII

FROM ALL sides came the sound of music and the happy shouts of 'Liberty!' 'Long live the Constitution!' 'Long live our Padishah!' 'Long live England!' 'Long live Progress and Fraternity!' Before a lovely tomb in a side street he saw a crowd assembled and, drawing near, found a white-bearded khôja preaching in the open air.

'The Christians and the Muslimans are brothers once again. Praise be to Allah!' he was saying. 'Before the days of Abdul Hamid, the Muslim and the Christian women used to nurse each other's children.'

A little farther on he found a priest of the Armenian race preaching in like manner, using almost the same words. Before the days of Abdul Hamid's arbitrary rule the Christians and the Turks had been good neighbours, and now, please God, they would be so again. England, the friend of liberty, would now befriend them, and help them to defeat the evil aims of Russian tyranny.

He met a long procession, led by many khôjas, advancing to the sound of loud Takbîrs, and asked its object of a bystander.

'They go to the Armenian cemetery to pray for those who suffered innocently years ago,' was the reply.

'Allahu Akbar!' exclaimed Camruddin devoutly.

But the strangest outburst of enthusiasm he beheld was by the fountain in the square, before the mosque of

Sultan Bayazid. A street hawker, selling buttons from a basket, was shouting: 'Made in England! English work!' and everyone who heard him rushed to buy, vociferating 'Long live England and the Constitution!' 'Down with Germany and Despotism!'

Camruddin himself was caught in the excitement and went up to purchase with the rest, but by the time he reached the object of his struggle the last button had been sold. The hawker turned his basket upside down and sat on it, shaking his head at all the would-be customers, and striking his hands together, cymbal-fashion, to express finality. He was a wily Greek of dissolute appearance. Camruddin remarked that he had driven a brisk trade. The rascal winked as he replied: 'I owe a trifle to St George who taught me to transform those things, which once were German, into English goods … Long live England! Down with Germany!' he shouted, as he put the empty basket on his head and walked away.

The muezzin's chant was over all the city like a song of birds. Camruddin turned into the mosque of Bayazid. After the prayer he lingered in the shady cloister, watching the evolutions of a crowd of pigeons, and drinking most delicious water, icy cold. He entered into conversation with a man who sat there, in appearance a small Government official. From him he learnt that Sâdik Pasha was at liberty, though, like all the chief supporters of the despotism, he was under surveillance.

Camruddin set out again with mind relieved. He sauntered in the shade of roofed bazaars, where the rich goods displayed on either hand delighted him as decoration, down to a landing-stage upon the Golden Horn, where he engaged a boatman. The water sparkled in the sun. Before him rose the hill of Kasim Pasha with silver-gray kiosks and red-tiled roofs among the trees; behind it the high ridge of Pera with its crown of Frankish buildings, and ancient cypress-groves upon the slope beneath. Behind him was the vision of Stamboul, mosque after mosque, with stately domes and soaring minarets, ennobling the dense throng of wooden houses. The kaïkji, seeing that he was a stranger, pointed up the water to a spot beyond the city where domes and minarets peeped out from a dense grove of trees beside the shore. He said: 'Sultan Eyûb.'

That that was the point to look at was implied in his address, a mild rebuke of Camruddin's preoccupation with Stamboul itself. There, on the shore of Europe, lay a little earth which once had been the Standard-bearer of the Holy Prophet.

Camruddin vowed to go there ere the week was out.

The boatman, who was well acquainted with the house of Sâdik Pasha, provided him with full directions how to reach it. The ladies of the household sometimes honoured his poor boat, he said. They were lively, amiable ladies, and their talk was pleasant to him as the voice of nightingales.

'My bride is of the damsels of that house,' said Camruddin. 'Perhaps you know her?'

'I could not tell the mistress from the slave. They are all sisters,' was the answer. 'And now they are all equal, so they say. Slavery is abolished! Why should they abolish slavery, efendim? An empty edict which will alter nothing, for not a slave would quit his service willingly.'

'It is to please the English, who are now our helpers. They hold slavery in horror, because when they kept slaves they treated them with frightful cruelty,' said Camruddin, repeating words which he had heard from the fedaïs.

'Ma sha'llah!' said the boatman. 'Well, we live and learn. These are strange times, efendim. A plain man like me requires instruction not to lose his way in them as in a maze. In sha'llah, you will hire my boat again and teach me further. May Allah give to you. With safety, go.'

Thanks to the instructions given to him by the kaïkji, Camruddin found his patron's kiosk without delay. After some conversation with the servants in the vestibule, he was shown into the Pasha's presence in the garden. Two other visitors were with His Excellency, both of them men of rank, to judge from their appearance.

Camruddin met, at first, a cold reception; for Sâdik Pasha asked why he had disappeared from Saloniki without a word of warning or of explanation. They had thought him dead. His bride had been in terrible anxiety.

Although His Excellency spoke in quiet tones, the visitor was made to feel his stern displeasure; and Camruddin had ground for thinking that the explanation of his conduct, when he heard it, would displease him yet the more. He told his story therefore in a shamefaced way and was amazed when Sâdik Pasha cried: 'The praise to Allah!' his anger turned miraculously into joy. 'And you have come to claim your bride?' he said. 'Then we will have a splendid wedding now, directly. A daughter of my house weds a fedaï with my full consent; the matter was arranged before the Revolution. How will that look, efendilarim, think you?'

One of his friends said dryly: 'You are fortunate. Invite us to the wedding at the least, efendim, that we may show our love of the fedaï in the sight of all.'

The Pasha waved his hand towards Camruddin, who murmured in confusion: 'Highly honoured.'

'I had no wish to end my days in Tripoli, much less the

Yemen, where I have already wasted five years of my life,' said Sâdik Pasha. 'And Camruddin Agha saves me from that fate, in sha'llah!'

'It will not last, this great enthusiasm,' said the other. 'They call out "Long live England!" We shall see!'

'I do not see why England should not help them, since the Revolution has been bloodless and complete, two things I never thought it could be,' said the General. 'I say "Long live the Constitution!" if they let me be. It is a blessing to be free to think and speak and read without the fear of spies.'

The other two kept silence with a guarded look. Their host then craved permission to withdraw a moment. Signing to Camruddin to follow him, he led the way into another portion of the formal garden divided by a high, thick hedge from that in which they had been sitting.

'And now, my soul, since all are free and like the English, I suppose that you may meet your bride, if she desires it. I should not say so, I will tell you frankly (being an old-fashioned person), if she had not suffered much in health from the uncertainty about you which depressed us all. Leylah Hânum has been worried upon her account, and through anxiety, and not the Revolution, she allows to-day what otherwise she would esteem an impropriety. Wait here, I have informed the ladies of your presence, and if your bride desires to see you she can do so. I rejoin my friends.'

He walked away and left the favoured lover in a state of nervousness approaching panic. His heart beat so that he could neither see nor hear distinctly. The perfumes of the garden took his breath away. He spied an arbour tunnelled in the solid hedge, in which there was a seat, and there took refuge.

Chapter XXIII

THE arbour was so placed as to command a curious view—a picture, all in length of sky and water, and a section of Stamboul between them. Across the lowest portion of the picture glided kaïks, and now and then a sailing boat. The whole was held as in a frame between a wall of the kiosk and the clipped end of a tall hedge of evergreens. From time to time some steamer, out of sight upon the Bosphorus, released its siren, and an awful din reverberated in the seven hills. The ordinary noise was that of children playing, and the pulse of industry.

As Camruddin beheld and listened, he recovered confidence. The Constitution was restored, and he was a fedaï of Niazi's band. The girl was keeping him a long while waiting. If she could show displeasure, he could tease her.

But suddenly he saw her coming, attended at a distance by an older woman, and his courage dwindled. He was reclining on the bench for comfort, and it pleased him to remain so and pretend to be asleep. He closed his eyes and waited, breathing deeply. After a while some missile hit his face a little harder than he thought quite necessary. He yawned and stretched himself and rubbed his eyes, then started up as if in great amazement, crying,—

'I ask a thousand pardons, honoured lady! My fatigue was great.'

Gul-raaneh was attired in white with a white head-veil. She made no answer but stood there confronting him with long, disdainful eyes and pouting lips. Suddenly she darted past him and sat down upon the bench from which he had that minute risen. Perceiving her design to place him at a disadvantage, for he could hardly sit beside her in the sight of the duenna, he sat down on the ground and waited till she chose to speak. When she did speak, at length, her voice choked with rage.

'Well, what have you to say to me, efendim?'

'Efendim, I must say that I am much ill-used!'

'Ill-used! I trust my soul to you, I show you favour, and then at once you disappear—no one knows where —doubtless to more congenial company … I said I was prepared to come to you, however poor, which meant that you could claim me instantly; instead of which you ran away from me … Have I not cause to be offended? Say!'

'Efendim, hear my story and then judge. That very morning I set out for Resna on an errand, thinking to return after a day or two. My errand brought me into contact with the hero of this age; I heard him speak, and from his words my soul caught fire. He preached the true Jihâd for the salvation of the world. I laid aside all human ties and took the vows of a fedaï. I went into the mountains with Niazi Bey. We started not two hundred men; but soon we were an army, by the help of Allah. In three weeks less a day, with Osman Pasha as our prisoner, we heard, from far off in the hills, the guns of Monastir salute the Constitution. Praise to Allah! Then we returned to Resna where they feasted us. I had no joy in the festivities, but wandered out into the fields. At evening, in the mosque, I met his Honour, Ferid Bey, who asked me to what place on earth I would be going if I had my choice. I answered: "To Stamboul, because my bride is there!" He answered: "I am going to Stamboul, and thou shalt bear me company." His grace obtained permission for me from the leaders. This morning we set foot together on the quay of Ghalatah, having performed the journey without one delay. That is my story, judge me now, efendim!'

Gul-raaneh's pretty face expressed a childish misery. She moaned: 'Alas for us and our ill-fortune! Our hope is dead, and you have helped to kill it.'

'I do not understand ...'

She plucked a bunch of Banksia roses which had strayed into the arbour, and began to tear the petals from them as she told him miserably,—

'We shall all be exiled. Some have gone already. The people tore the hated Fehim Pasha limb from limb at Brûsa. We hear terrific stories of the cruelty of those whom you have helped to bring to power.'

'All lies,' said Camruddin.

'I tell you they tore Fehim Pasha literally limb from limb.'

'Not they, my gilly-flower! The people he had injured and oppressed dispatched him.'

'What do you know about it? ... Anyhow, it is quite certain—everybody says so—that the strong supporters of the despotism will be banished. Sâdik Pasha was the strongest. And Leylah Hânum is resolved to go with him, even though it be to far Arabia. So you and I will soon be parted, so it seems to me.'

It was evident that she knew nothing of the Pasha's plan to have the wedding in a week with unexampled splendour. And Camruddin, desiring to explore her mind, did not enlighten her.

Feigning amazement, he exclaimed: 'But you are free, efendim! Do you not know that slavery has been abolished?'

'I was emancipated on the evening of the marriage contract, so their law does not apply to me. But when my people are in trouble, I belong to them. Do you think I would forsake them in this great calamity, when Leylah Hânum and my more than sisters have such need of me? The hired servants will forsake them, the slave never; and least of all the slave whom they have freed so generously. I do not think in all Stamboul there is a girl in my position who, hearing of this foolish law, will leave her people. If there is, I scorn her.'

'Alas, my grief! What then am I to do? My life is now made desolate!' moaned Camruddin.

'Unless you will come with us to our place of exile and there make a home for me so near that I can wait upon my ladies daily, you may as well annul our marriage from this minute,' she replied, with spirit, 'for Allah knows if we shall ever meet again. You spoke of true Jihâd and how your soul caught fire, how you laid aside all thought of our relation when you went into the mountains with a gang of rebels. Well, this is true Jihâd , and it has fired my soul to share the exile of my kind protectors. Come with us!'

'No, that I cannot,' answered Camruddin forlornly, knowing full well that her forebodings were all moonshine. 'I am still a fedaï of the Revolution.' That was true. 'And I am now a person of some small importance. I have been offered a position in the Government, and I was thankful for it, for your sake, efendim. But if you will forsake me— well, it is my portion and I must make the best I can of it. My duty is to save the country. I have made a vow.'

'And I have made a vow—to help my people.'

'Good. But I perhaps could help them more efficiently. I might obtain for them a choice of places and some reduction of the term of banishment.'

Gul-raaneh stared at him in blank amazement, which quickly turned to scorn. She cried: '*You* help them! *You* help to save His Excellency Sâdik Pasha and his noble family! Truly the world is upside down, as Leylah Hânum says. If you have influence you must exert it to the utmost upon our behalf, that is your duty; for Sâdik Pasha is your patron just as much as mine. Unless your influence is great enough to stop our exile or, on the other hand, you will consent to share it with us, I must now say farewell to you, efendim.'

She rose as she said this, and, drawing her white robe around her, made as if to go.

Camruddin murmured: 'Then you do not love me as I love you, efendim.'

'You are a fedaï. You have told me: I am naught to you.'

'I said not that!'

'Not in those words, perhaps, but you implied it. Do not misjudge my feelings, my two eyes. I know that you are pious, brave, and honourable; and I can understand your fervour for the Revolution, although I cannot share it since it is against my people. I would accept you as my husband gladly, if things were as they were when last we met. The world has changed since then. You have assumed new duties, so have I; and those new duties lead us far apart.'

'It is evident,' said Camruddin more frankly, 'that I

must claim my bride at once, to stop your exile.'

'How could that stop the exile of the Pasha Efendi, which involves my lady?—You have annoyed me all this afternoon by foolish talk.'

'You do not know the worth of a fedaï of Niazi's band! When it is known that Sâdik Pasha has bestowed a daughter of his house on one of them, it will be the same as if he swore allegiance to the Constitution. He will not be exiled. His Excellency himself said so, in my presence, half an hour ago … Allah is my witness, I came hither as a humble suppliant, expecting him to frown on me; and so he did at first, though not so terribly as you have done. But when he heard I was a member of Niazi's band, he was transported and vowed we should be married in a week with splendid ceremony.'

'You knew this all the while you were tormenting me?' exclaimed Gul-raaneh, tears springing in her eyes for the first time. 'You knew you had me in your hand, and yet you let me chatter! That is atrocious. I will never speak to you again.' She dealt him a last glance which he found quite inscrutable, than went to her duenna and returned into the house.

Camruddin went back to the selamlik to take leave of Sâdik Pasha, who told him to consult with Ferid Bey about arrangements for the wedding; and then he strolled down to the waterside and took a kaïk for the Bridge.

The boatman had two other passengers who occupied the stern—strange-looking persons, prematurely old, who wore the dress of men of education, though the dress was shabby. Their cheeks were very lean and their eyes haggard; they looked about them with bewilderment and, as it seemed, with caution too, as if they feared too wide a vision of the actual scene. One of the two, especially, who seemed the elder, was so manifestly nervous that he shrank as in alarm and trembled when he met the gaze of Camruddin. A minute later he was weeping silently. The other took his hand and, with a movement of the lips which, but for its exceeding sadness, would have been a smile, explained,—

'The world is strange to us, efendim, and its beauty daunts us. We tremble every minute lest it vanish and the walls close in once more. My comrade here has been in prison fifteen years, I eight. We were released at noon to-day.'

'What was the cause of your imprisonment?' asked Camruddin.

'I was a clerk in the Ministry of the Interior. My age was twenty-one. I happened on a day of rain to say : "I wish I could escape out of this rotten country." A colleague brought it to the knowledge of the Palace. I was put away.'

'And your friend, efendim?'

'He does not know the reason why he was imprisoned. Nobody told him, and he had no crime upon his conscience … Pardon our tears, my soul; it is so long since we beheld the sunset on this glorious scene.'

The boatman cried: 'Long live the Constitution! Down with despotism!' and the cry was taken up in other boats and by the concourse on the Bridge. 'Long live the Constitution. Long live England, friend of liberty and justice! Freedom!' Amid a volley of such shouts they reached the landing-stage. The sun had just that minute set. The waters of the strait were cold and gray, although a glow still lingered on the town of Scutari and on the hills beyond it on the farther shore. The men released that day from prison heaved a sigh of vast relief. The sun had grown so unfamiliar to them as to seem an enemy.

Chapter XXIV

CAMRUDDIN SAT under a Paulownia tree in Ferid Bey's enormous garden, and meditated on the chances of this mortal life. Occasionally the accents of his host, who was inspecting the work of the gardeners, came to him, occasionally he could hear a dog bark in the distance, or the hooting of some steamer's horn upon the Bosphorus. Otherwise he was alone amid a hum of insects which conduced to reverie. Warm, heady perfumes floated in the shade. Before him was a great tank overgrown with water-lilies, pink and white, above which dragon-flies kept darting with the flash of gems. Beyond that was a zone of heavy shadow cast by a little chestnut-grove, between whose stems was seen a space of vineyards and of cornfields newly reaped, in blazing sunlight, extending to the boundary wall of Ferid Bey's domain—a wall which had collapsed in many places. Beyond that again were trees and fanciful kiosks, backed by a cooling vision of blue sea with sunny islands resting on its surface.

He thought: 'It is two months since last I sat in happy idleness. Then, suddenly, the sound of firing came to break the stillness. I wonder will some such disturbance come to-day; for Allah knows that my contentment is too great to last. It is like Paradise. Or is such happiness to be henceforth the lot of every Muslim? The power of

England will now stand between us and our enemies. It may be Allah's will that we shall live in peace henceforward. But I must keep the heart of a fedaï, or I slay my soul.'

He recalled the hardships of his time of military service, the hardships of his pilgrimage to Mecca, and could distinguish plainly those which were the consequence of men's ill-doing from those which were imposed by God's decree. The former hurt, the latter fortified the soul. If all the accidents men had to fear were those which come upon them from the hand of God, the world would be a happy place to live in.

He thought: 'If I had remained with my mother and my sister and my brothers two months ago, instead of setting out, I should not, certainly, have known the rapture of sublime endeavour, nor yet the peace of mind which goes with it. For all those years my life was like a river pursuing its appointed course, but underground. But now it is released by Allah's mercy; it reflects the sunlight; it is bountiful; it has a portion in the life of all things—praise to Allah!—and so may it continue to the end. For the word of Allah says that "Verily with effort goeth ease." I must not set my heart on earthly blessings which make men unsociable. In Allah only is true brotherhood.'

A bee came humming close around him. He raised his hand to fend it off. A minute later came a flutter, followed by a dreamy cooing. Two doves had settled in the branches overhead. Their music brought to him voluptuous thoughts. His bride was sweet, and in three days she would be his.

The wedding festival was all arranged. Ferid bestowed upon the pair a charming house, which stood within his grounds but had a separate entrance on a quiet road, close to the ornate mosque which Zia Pasha, Ferid's father, had built in memory of a beloved wife, Ulviyeh Hânum.

I wish to keep you near me,' he remarked, when Cam-ruddin protested that he was too kind. 'It may be partly for a selfish purpose, for all this land and wealth of mine was gathered by my father in the service of the Government, and a fedaï on the premises may save inquiry. But it is true that I take pleasure in your conversation more than in that of men who think themselves the patterns of the age for fashion, learning, and diplomacy. It is because you are yourself, and unashamed to be so. Talking with you, I feel I talk with an Osmanli, whereas the others make me feel at times as lonely as if I were the sole survivor of that race.'

'Efendim, look around you; there are thousands. Here on your domain your servants all are true Osmanlis.'

'I know,' was the reply, 'but if I spoke to them as I now speak to you, they would be stupefied, and when my back was turned would shrug their shoulders, smiling at my madness. You are the man whom I have all my life been seeking, sincere and unaffected, yet of good intelligence.'

'Istaghfaru'llah,' murmured Camruddin, with an incredulous smile. 'The truth is, I suppose, that I am something new.'

'And something old, that is the charm of you.'

As he remembered all the goodness of the rich young bey whom people blamed for levity, his heart was full of an affection which was not less strong for having in it a perennial source of laughter. He had arrived at this point in his recollections, when he heard the sound of footsteps, and saw a black-robed and white-turbaned figure drawing near under the trees. It was the khôja who instructed the three children of the bey—a worthy man, and staunch supporter of the Constitution. His face as he approached betokened news. He said: 'My soul, I bring a message from the bey efendi. He begs that you will go at once to the selamlik. There is a visitor who much desires to meet you.'

'What kind of visitor?' asked Camruddin, as they returned together.

'A young man of fair complexion with blue eyes, dressed as a military officer. My lord embraced him with an outcry when he first appeared. It seems that all his friends had thought him dead. No sooner were the greetings over than he asked for you.'

Camruddin could think of no one who would answer this description, and saying: 'Ma sha'llah!' resigned himself to wait for the solution of the problem till he saw the personage. Very great was his surprise when, in the cool reception-room of the selamlik, he saw Basri Bey, the officer whom he had found, two months before, lifeless beside the mule-track leading to his native village; the man at whose request he had set out upon the journey which had had such wonderful results. Camruddin was inquiring of his health respectfully, but the young man sprang upon him and embraced him, crying,—

'Welcome, efendim. I am now your brother.'

'As the explanation bids fair to be lengthy, I will now leave you,' chuckled Ferid Bey. 'When it is finished, come to luncheon, both of you.'

Basri Bey made Camruddin sit down beside him on the divan and, keeping firm hold of his hand, poured out his story.

After Camruddin's departure from the little house beside the orchard, Basri Bey had lain in bed nearly three weeks. More than once in the bad time, when his mind wandered, he had fancied that he saw an angel bending over him; and, as his sight grew clearer, he beheld a maiden of the name of Melek (angel), a sight much more agreeable to him since it spoke of life. While they supposed him on the point of death, her mother and her brothers had let Melek help in nursing him; but when they saw him on the mend, they veiled her from his sight. And he was desolate. By dint of longing for her presence he fell deep in love; and, when he was once more upon his feet, he asked her brothers for her hand in marriage. 'They would have granted my request at once, for we were friends,' he said, 'had it not been for the behaviour of your Christian neighbour, Lefteri. That queer old fellow has the nature of a spy and, having come to know of my existence in the house, I have no doubt but that he told the village mukhtâr, who passed on the communication to the Caïmmacâm. Lefteri kept on letting fall dark hints that I should soon be shot or hanged, and bring misfortune upon them all, which gave your brothers much alarm on my account. They told me that it was no time to talk of marriage. My horse, from idleness, had grown too strong for me to ride, so they procured a pack-horse upon which they set me one fine night, your brother, Mehmed, riding my own horse beside me. The Revolution had begun, and there were rumours that an army of fedaïs was at no great distance. Mehmed Agha brought me to them on the following day, and, having seen me safe, returned to his own place. On the very night of my departure, I heard afterwards, the mukhtâr and an agent of the Government, assisted by a lot of cringing Greeks, ransacked your homestead with intent to kill me. Yet a week later, when our band came to the village, the mukhtâr and the elders swore fidelity to the Committee, and Lefteri wept tears of joy at sight of me!

'Again I made my suit of Melek Hânum; your mother and your brothers were agreeable; and on the day on which our Padishah restored the Constitution we were married amid general rejoicings. Your mother feared the bride would be too homely for my people. But that is not the case, I can assure you. My mother and my sisters praise her modesty, and my father—the old Pasha—calls her a true Turkish maiden, and says young men are fools who marry foreigners. Directly after luncheon you must come with me.'

Accordingly, that afternoon, they drove to Eski-dar and thence took boat to Beycos on the Bosphorus, where Ahmed Pasha, Basri's father, had a yâli (seaside house). Camruddin would not have recognised his sister in the stately, white-robed lady who advanced to greet him in a room entirely white-white walls, white hangings, and a thick white carpet on the floor—if she had not come towards him with a cry of joy. Basri Bey then left them to converse awhile, returning after half an hour with all his family, who gave the kindest welcome to the visitor. The ladies of the house had heard of his approaching marriage; the younger ladies were acquainted with the bride, who was to visit them upon the morrow.

'There is only one thing I complain of in your sister's conduct,' said the lady of the house to Camruddin. 'It is that she will never tell us what she likes. She falls in with our ways too perfectly. It makes me fear that she is still in awe of us, although our one wish is to make her happy.'

It was evening when he took his leave, and Basri Bey led him down into the cellars of the house, where he was surprised to find a vault whose floor was of deep water. A boat manned by four servants of the house was there in waiting. They both got into it, and at a word from Basri darted out into the strait, aglow with sunset light. As the boat sped along the foot of cliffs and terrace walls and palaces, with Stamboul looming up against the setting sun, Basri observed: 'There is one favour I would ask. It is that I may join your escort on your wedding night. You have not asked me yet.'

'I feared to do so, because the rest of my attendants are not men of rank, but upper servants of the house of Ferid Bey.'

'What does that matter? I have known them from my childhood—the tall Albanian with his pan-pipes, and the little hunchback with his lute! But do not think that you will be without more pompous followers. I hear that half the tyrants of the old régime are going to send their sons to bear you company in the name of Liberty, Equality, Fraternity, and Justice.'

And so, indeed, it proved. Because the bridegroom was a stalwart of the New Turk party, the wedding was attended largely by supporters of the old régime. The ceremony was both lengthy and elaborate, nicely designed to tantalise an eager lover. It began in Sâdik Pasha's kiosk upon the Golden Horn, and ended at Eren-keuy on the Sea of Marmora, when Camruddin was led, in slow procession, with lights and music to his own house where the bride was waiting.

The stars winked down at the procession through the trees in Deyli Ferid's garden. Every now and then it halted while the hunchback, to his lute, sang an epithalamium, the crowd repeating the last words of every strophe in impressive chorus. The little hunchback had a powerful and lovely voice. When they had brought the bridegroom to his gate, and taken leave of him, he sang a song which ended in a wail of anguish. To that strange music, Camruddin went in, keenly aware of every perfume in the garden.

Chapter XXV

WITHIN A fortnight of his marriage Camruddin received a small appointment at the Ministry of War. At first he thought that this was due to the Committee's influence, but later learnt that Sâdik Pasha had procured it. The men who made the Revolution did not touch such matters. Intending shortly to reform the whole administration, they let it run meanwhile, and watched its working carefully. Camruddin's post was not a lofty one. He was a sort of overseer of the various ushers and attendants—most of them non-commissioned officers—who loitered in the corridors from morn till night. If one of them was at a loss he came to Camruddin, who sat behind a little table in the hall beside the entrance to the Minister's apartments.

He rose before the sun and said his prayers in the adjacent mosque, then broke his fast, and paced the garden with Gul-raaneh, or walked with her by the sea-shore until the sun was high, when he set out along a shady avenue which led him shortly to a railway station bowered in foliage. The train then carried him to Haïdar Pasha, whence a steamer bore him over laughing waters to the bridge of Ghalatah, which spans the entrance to the Golden Horn. There was always the same crowd of men upon the train and steamboat, who came to know each other and converse as friends. Each person carried in his hand his chosen newspaper, which he perused in intervals of conversation, of which the subject was invariably politics. Camruddin did not say much upon his own account, but won approval as a deferential listener. Arriving at the Bridge, his first concern, as that of everybody, was to have his boots cleaned of the dust of the suburban roads. That done, he crossed the bridge amid the crowd, and, choosing shady pavements, went up to his Ministry. There he remained until the fifth hour after noon, smoking cigarettes at intervals, and drinking cups of coffee. There was much leisure, which he turned to good account by studying the French and English languages, and mathematics. On three days of the week, after he left the Ministry, he went with an Armenian colleague, Dikran Efendi, to the latter's lodging for an hour's instruction.

At that time everybody was, or feigned to be, a friend to the Committee of Union and Progress. The moderation of the victors, the enthusiasm of the populace, and the approval which the Ulema accorded to the revolutionary programme; above all the presumed support of England; combined to crush all open opposition. Even the most ferocious of the late supporters of the despotism called themselves Unionists, and hastened to enrol themselves as members of the various lodges. The bad elements in the Christian communities, which for years had looked to Europe for their orders, discarded their ambitions not without relief, supposing Europe looked with favour on the new régime. Everything promised well when, one fine morning, a bolt fell from the blue upon the Turkish peoples. Austria had annexed Bosnia and Herzegovina, and Bulgaria had thrown off the Ottoman suzerainty.

Boundless was the indignation among Camruddin's fellow-passengers when they read the tidings in their news-papers upon the way to town. It was a blow aimed at the country at the moment of its greatest weakness, when all its strength was needed for the mighty task of reconstruction, education, and reform. It was a violation of the Berlin treaty, made by England. Surely England would chastise the mean aggressors, making them retract immediately. All creeds and schools of thought were of one mind upon this subject, so long as it was thought that England would defend the Turks.

But when days passed without decided action on the part of England, when it was known that England acquiesced in the injustice, and had advised the Turkish Government to be content with an indemnity, there was a change of sentiment in many quarters. Friends of the old regime could point with shrugs to this, the only tangible result of the new order. Those Christians who had served the aim of foreign Powers to weaken and disintegrate the Empire awoke from their brief trance of illusion, and shrewdly guessed that there was no remission of those aims. They would have preferred the peace and reconciliation which the Constitution had appeared at first to promise; but if the Turkish Power was doomed, no matter what its promise, what earthly profit was there in supporting it? They took their way to their respective embassies, to draw their money and receive instructions as of old. Dikran Efendi, his Armenian colleague, explained to Camruddin the situation while deploring it. He was a red-hot partisan of the Committee.

'We alone are faithful,' he exclaimed, 'for we Armenians have no country we can justly claim, nor have we any friends or patrons but the Turks. I speak of the majority, for well I know that there are miscreants among us who serve foreign Powers for gold. That is another reason for our loyalty, the Turkish power being our sole protection from those malefactors who by torture, rape, and murder extort money from our wretched people and intimidate them. If any foreign Power took Anatolia, those male-factors, as its servants, would become our tyrants. No fate more cruel could await a nation. Allah forbid that it should ever come to pass! Our happiness is bound up with the Turkish Government. It is not so with Greeks and Serbs and Bulgars, who hope to fix their yoke upon their neighbour's shoulders by the power of Greece or Serbia or Bulgaria; though the Ottoman Bulgars would, I fancy, have been loyal to the Constitution if Bulgaria had not denounced the suzerainty; the Greeks were traitors from the first. We had the measure of their friendship in the late elections, when they cheated so outrageously, with help from Greece, that they have made free election quite im-possible, every one demanding Government control.

'If England and France had threatened war against Bulgaria and Austria, they would have saved us and the world from endless misery. But now, Lord help us, I am much afraid.'

The stout and dignified official swelled with ire, invoking every evil on the Powers of Europe. 'I belong to the most wretched of all nations,' he would sigh occasionally. 'In all the world the Turks alone have any love for us; the others hate us, and employ us only for their selfish ends. They would persuade us to betray our only friends in order to destroy us the more easily; and—Allah, pity!—there are found Armenians who will listen to their poisonous suggestions.'

Camruddin retailed the views of his Armenian friend to Basri Bey, who said,—

'Things are not quite so bad as he imagines. England does to some extent support our claims. She insists on the indemnity, and is in favour of our boycotting all Austrian goods till it is paid. But this is true: her attitude is far from that which we expected, remembering the actions of the great Disraeli. It is cautious, critical, repressive; almost as if our liberty embarrassed her.'

Basri was in the circle of the leaders, so was able to impart authentic information.

Those leaders had not seized the highest posts. Personal ambition was forbidden by the oath which they had taken. They had put forward men of good repute among the statesmen of the former Government, and merely kept a watch on their behaviour. They conceived that their chief duty, now that the political revolution had been achieved, was to prepare for the social revolution by founding modern schools throughout the Empire, and enlightening the grown-up people by means of public lectures and debates, for which the numerous local branches of the Committee gave facilities. The local clubs or branches organised festivities and held receptions periodically, at which any one who cared to do so might discourse. They thus were centres of social and intellectual, no less than of political, activity. That was the public organisation of the Committee of Union and Progress. It had also a secret organisation, of which the function was to watch over and guide as well this work of social evolution as affairs of state. But the secret organisation, though it had tremendous power, was anything but irresponsible; the executive being chosen by an elected committee, which was, in turn, elected by a larger body, of which the members were appointed by the district committees representing the initiated of the various branches in each district.

Conscious of inexperience in face of so immense a task, the leaders sought the help and counsel of the British embassy. They were received politely with expressions of goodwill, and given plenty of advice, but all unpalatable, in the nature of repression or discouragement. Among the statesmen of the old regime were men of mind and energy, still in the prime of life, well suited to the post of Grand Vizier. England would hear of none but Kiamil Pasha, a man of eighty-seven, of repute in Europe, but chiefly known in Turkey as a partisan of England. He did not share the vision of the strong reformers, was timidly averse to any change. The old man was a mere encumbrance, yet they bore with him for full six months to please England; and if England showed no particular pleasure while he filled the seat of power, she showed displeasure when he was removed from it. And afterwards, whenever they desired to make some overture to England, there was nothing for it but to put him back in office. It was as if that timid, senile inactivity alone could rouse enthusiasm at the British embassy.

During the four months which elapsed between the granting of the Constitution and the meeting of Parliament, the Committee appointed and deposed ministers and provincial governors and ordered the movement of troops. The British embassy approved this as an interregnum, but held that on the day when Parliament assembled the Committee should have been dissolved. In vain did its apologists point out that the elections had revealed the need for its continuance, and that Parliament itself, composed of inexperienced men, required both guidance and protection. In vain they pleaded that the Revolution was but just beginning. The representatives of England said that Parliament was

Parliament, and Parliamentary government had certain rules. The Committee should become a Parliamentary party, making its voice heard in Parliament and nowhere else, while the executive authority was entrusted the loving care of certain bulwarks of the old régime.

'It is as if,' said Basri Bey, 'they did not care a jot for human progress or reform, but only loved mere names like Parliament and Kiamil Pasha—names, you will observe, associated with the name of England. To do what they demand at present would be to hand the country over to the forces of reaction, which are none the less redoubtable for working underground. Do you remember—No, you were not present; but I remember well the feast to celebrate the circumcision of a hundred boys in honour of the Constitution, which was celebrated by permission in the garden of a Frankish gentleman. The owner of the garden spoke to some of us. He said: "What you have now to do is kill ten thousand men. The Europeans look for bloodshed in a revolution; unless you do it they will think it incomplete. The men are known to you. Do not be squeamish! Your country's sufferings to-day are due to the reluctance of the Turks to killing in cold blood. If your ancestors, the conquerors, had ruthlessly wiped out the conquered, or by force converted them, as any Christian victors would have done at the period, you, their descendants, would have dwelt secure to-day. You do not even get the credit of your clemency, for the Europeans (who are fifty times more ruthless) think you bloodthirsty. To kill ten thousand bad men now will be to save ten million harmless men in time to come."'

'What said his hearers?' questioned Camruddin.

'We laughed at first, supposing that he jested, but when we found he spoke in earnest, became indignant, saying that it was contrary to our religion to do such a deed.'

'What said he then?'

'He said: "The Europeans are without religion. They have that great advantage over you."'

'Allah forbid! The man was, then, an atheist?'

'He spoke in bitterness, as one who hated Europe. He has dwelt here long and feels for us,' said Basri Bey. 'He wished, perhaps, to throw cold water on our too great hopes. It is true that we expected far too much from Europe, and from England in particular. We see that now … One thing is certain: had we killed ten thousand persons, as he told us, the Committee could retire to-day, as England wishes.'

'A very wicked man, indeed,' said Camruddin.

Chapter XXVI

BESIDES HIS lessons with Dikran Efendi, Camruddin attended lectures at the Military School in view of an examination which he was to undergo. In his own home he practised French with Gul-raaneh, who possessed a little knowledge of that tongue, and got much help from Ferid Bey, his neighbour, who was something of a linguist.

The call to the examination came upon him suddenly, while he was still unready in his own opinion. It took place in the Military School near Haïdar Pasha. Except for himself and some alaili officers—men who had won promotion without previous schooling—the subjects of examination were young men of lofty rank. Under the despotism it had been not unusual for a man, by influence, to be a General at the age of twenty-one. A Pasha who had not long passed that age—a handsome, merry-looking youth—came forth with Camruddin at the conclusion of the ordeal.

'What are you now, efendim?' he asked gaily.

'A mulâzim, Pasha efendim, who heretofore was but a chaûsh. The praise to Allah!'

'The praise to Allah! I, too, am a mulâzim. It is the rank to which my age and skill assign me. Call me not Pasha efendi! I shall be bey efendi now for many a day.'

A crowd of the examined then came out, cursing

the Constitution and its works and ways. They came to Camruddin's companion, whose cheerfulness appeared to rouse their curiosity. Camruddin sauntered on. Half down the hill to Haïdar Pasha Station, he was hailed and shortly overtaken by the cheerful one.

'I feel a good deal lighter. I could run and jump with pleasure. Those other fellows take it badly. It is hard on them, for none of them can ever hope to rise above the rank this day assigned to him. But did you notice the dark, silent little man, rather like a Japanese, whom I saluted in the gateway? That is Hasan Riza Pasha, now degraded to the rank of bimbashi. It matters not a jot to him who is our greatest strategist. In a short time he is quite certain to regain his rank.'

'And you, efendim?' questioned Camruddin.

The blue eyes twinkled. 'I shall try, efendim.'

'You do not curse the Constitution like your friends, efendim.'

'I bless it from the bottom of my heart! … Efendim, you are sympathetic; deign to hear my story! I am by nature of an easy-going, happy mind, fond of consorting with all kinds of people, fond of liberty. From the time when I was old enough to wear a sword I have been cramped by ceremony, and encased in etiquette. I was put into the palace, in the bodyguard. I loved with all my heart a girl I used to play with in our garden, a beautiful and artless soul, the daughter of an upper servant. They made me wed the daughter of a high State dignitary, who made my life jehennum to me with her wealth and pride. It was her house, her servants, her dignity, her precious family, every day and all day, till I cursed my destiny. I was nothing but an appanage of her exalted state. And then the Revolution came, praise be to Allah! The fear of her relations was removed; so I divorced my lady straight-way, and married her I love. And now to-day I am released from ceremony—in sha'llah, till old age shall make its stiffness dear to me. Long live the Constitution! I am all in favour of it.'

He asked where Camruddin was living and, hearing it was not far distant from his own abode, expressed the wish to come and see him one fine evening.

He came, in fact, a few days later and spent a long while in agreeable conversation with Camruddin and Ferid Bey, whom he already knew. Two deputies, professed adherents of the Committee, had that day been shot as they went into Parliament.

'There are too many malcontents,' said the ex-Pasha, chuckling, as he did at most things, good or evil. 'And some of them have got together and plot mischief. They tell me nothing; I can see it in their ugly faces. You, too, efendim, must know something of it?'

He turned his boyish face to Ferid Bey, who seemed embarrassed, and replied a little hurriedly,—

'I take no part in politics, efendim.' He added: 'I am mad, you know,' with a light laugh, which none the less contained a note of bitterness.

Was Ferid Bey against the Constitution? Camruddin had asked himself that question more than once of late; for Arif Hikmet Bey, the bimbashi from Saloniki, had been staying with him, and Arif Hikmet, though a maker of the Revolution, seemed now to nourish some tremendous grievance. It was only since his coming that a change had been observable in Ferid Bey, who, though he was as kind as ever, treated Camruddin with an indulgence reminiscent of the manner of avowed reactionaries towards one whom they regarded as beneath hostility.

'There is something in the wind,' said the ex-Pasha, chuckling, when Ferid Bey had taken his departure. 'And you and I may find it well to leave this neighbourhood.'

Camruddin paid little heed to the remark, being immersed in private speculations with regard to Ferid, and when his new friend left him, as he did immediately, he banished such abstruse conjectures from his mind for thoughts of love.

He had forgotten the whole incident when, one dark morning, on his way to town, he was stopped upon the quay at Haïdar Pasha, just as he was going to the steamboat, by some one saying: 'Back! The city is not safe for you. I come from thence. Some of the troops have mutinied, and they are killing all the New Turks they can find. Hark! you can hear the rattle even now.

Camruddin listened, and could hear, across the stormy water, a sound of rifle and machine-gun firing. Then he looked round to see the person who had warned him. It was the hunchback dwarf attached to Ferid Bey.

Chapter XXVII

THE LIGHT was darkened in the sight of Camruddin as he turned back into the railway station with the hunchback, who assured him that to go on to the Ministry would be for him to court destruction on that day; since the city was in the hands of the reactionary party, whose hirelings— spies and bravos of the old regime—were putting down all partisans of the Committee.

When he reached home he told his wife the shocking news, then sat down by the stove to nurse his grief. A bitter wind was tearing at the trees around the house. It seemed to him the darkest day the world had known.

Gul-raaneh tried to coax him with her woman's art, but, finding he did not respond, relinquished the attempt and set herself to guard his solitude, making the old woman who performed the service of the house keep quiet, and confining her own talk to whispers as she came and went. She brought him food, but he would not partake of it. Late in the afternoon he started up distractedly, and went to visit Deyli Ferid Bey in search of news. The servants of the great house wore long faces and when he came into the presence of their lord he found him talking gloomily with Arif Hikmet Bey. Whatever may have been the latter's grievances with the Committee, it was apparent now that he had not desired this thing. It was also plain that Ferid Bey was angry with him.

'This is the end of all your dreams of peace and progress!' muttered the latter in a bitterly sarcastic tone.

'It is the end of all things!' moaned the yuzbashi.

While Camruddin was sitting with them it came on to rain. Through all the many windows of the great reception-room of the selamlik, the trees and bushes of the garden were obscured by falling water. Of what was happening they knew no more than he had heard already.

When he returned to his own house, and was taking off his goloshes in the porch, Gul-raaneh came to warn him that there was a visitor—a gentleman who had arrived just as the rain began. It was Dikran Efendi, who, at sight of Camruddin, dissolved in tears.

As soon as he recovered speech he told his story: how, that morning, going to his work as usual, he had found the building in possession of the enemy; had seen some of his friends and colleagues killed outright and others dragged to prison in a brutal way. He had escaped because of his Armenian nationality; the ruffians having, it appears, strict orders not to interfere with Christians, in order that the Powers of Europe might have no excuse for intervention.

'They have been working secretly for weeks past,' he informed his colleague, 'sending out spies disguised as khôjas, dervishes, and students of theology to every province of the empire. Here in Stamboul they show respect to Christians, but in the provinces they have been calling on the Muslim folk to rise and slay them, as the simplest method of discrediting the New Turk Government in European eyes. Armenians have been slaughtered in the vilayet of Adana; where the preaching of their agents took effect because of the rebellious conduct of Armenian malefactors which enraged the Muslims. Everywhere else the Muslims seized the agents and handed them over to the Government for deportation. Alas, we are the most unfortunate of nations, our most deadly enemies being men of our own race.'

The storm of wind and rain continuing, Dikran agreed to spend the night under Camruddin's roof, when suddenly he recollected that his hospitable entertainer was a well-known partisan of the Committee. Then he cried,—

'I must not stay, it might be dangerous. Suppose that they should search the house and find me here! It might be said that I was in conspiracy against their wickedness. They might be moved to shoot me, even hang me, in a place so far from others of my own community. No, I must go. One thinks of one's own skin.'

He consented, however, to accept the offer of a waterproof and umbrella, which Camruddin was destined never to behold again.

The next few days were horrible to Camruddin. Ferid, whose attitude towards events was resolutely philosophical, assured him he had nothing personally to expect from the usurpers, being so small a man and linked by marriage to the house of Sâdik Pasha. Basri was safe in hiding, Camruddin had only to keep quiet for a while, and he would not be troubled. But it was not for himself that Camruddin was apprehensive; his fear and grief were for the Revolution and its golden hope. The capital was altogether in the hands of the reactionaries, and no news whatsoever reached it from the provinces. This he ascribed at first to Government suppression; but by-and-by, as the days passed, a rumour ran that the capital was isolated by command of the Committee, whose power was still supreme in all the rest of Turkey. The Sultan, Abdul Hamid, famed for his astute perception, evinced no favour for the counter-revolution, although the men who made it were his partisans. The mutineers were quarrelling among themselves already. Trade was paralysed.

Gul-raaneh was her husband's solace in those anxious days. Her talk of politics was an 'Alas! for men's ambitions.' He knew that she was far from sharing his emotions, but she sorrowed for his grief and strove to cheer him, often succeeding in the feat for hours together. He praised their Maker for the gift of such a sweet companion. One evening, as he sat with her before the stove in the reception-room —a large apartment, sparsely furnished, which was cold in winter—there came a tap upon the iron shutters and the voice of someone asking leave to enter.

'Who is it?' asked Gul-raaneh.

'Mustafa, once a Pasha, now a poor lieutenant, by the grace of Allah,' came the answer.

'It is my friend of whom I spoke to you,' said Camruddin. 'Go, tell Ferideh to make coffee and arrange a dish of sweetmeats.'

'I will myself arrange things. She has gone to rest,' Gul-raaneh answered, going to the kitchen as Camruddin unbolted the front door.

The former Pasha was, as usual, in high spirits. Having paid the proper compliments upon arrival, he sat down near the stove and broached his business.

He was weary of inaction, he informed his friend; disgusted with the state of things prevailing in Stamboul … If he sat still much longer waiting for events he would go mad, he felt quite certain; so he had determined to break away and go and join whatever army, anywhere, might still be fighting for the cause of freedom. Would Camruddin go with him?

Would he not? The bold proposal coincided with his heart's desire. But whither should they go? How far afield?

'I think of sailing to Rodosto,' Mustafa informed him. I have gathered from inquiry that we get news from San Stefano, but not beyond; therefore Rodosto should be well outside the baneful zone. Once there, we strike inland to meet the army; for an army must be marching up from Saloniki. The troops there are devoted to the Constitution. It is only here that there are many traitors, and if we stay here they may call on us to help them. It would be worse than death to me if they should win, for then my first wife's people would regain their influence. I swear to you, efendim, that I dread that lovely lady—for she is a beauty, that is undeniable—and her relations, more than their artillery.'

'When do you propose to start?' asked Camruddin, considering.

To-night. To-night. My carriage waits,' was the reply.

Camruddin experienced a deathlike pang at thought of parting with Gul-raaneh so abruptly, but he preserved his countenance.

When she came to the room door with cups of coffee and some home-made cakes upon a tray, he told her simply,—

'I am going with the bey efendi and may not return.' The colour left her cheeks, and the tray shook a little as she gave it to him, but she replied as simply: 'Very good, efendim.'

'We shall take good care of one another,' chuckled

Mustafa, to reassure her. Turning to Camruddin, he added: 'Grant me one more favour. Condescend to let your gentle lady console my life's companion in my absence. I dare to ask that you will let her be the honoured guest of Selimeh Hânum till we both return. She can come with us in the carriage, if you like. The night is dark and we are friends of liberty!'

Gul-raaneh said no word, but her eyes brightened as she looked to Camruddin for his decision. When he answered: 'If she will,' she uttered heartfelt thanks, and hurried off to don her charshaf and collect her things.

Two hours later Camruddin and Mustafa descended steps cut in the cliff, below the latter's garden, down to a ledge of rocks beside the sea, each with a black-veiled figure at his side. The moon was peeping in and out of driving clouds; the sea, a little ruffled, slapped the rocky coast below the hill of summer palaces. It was intensely cold. Reaching the water's edge, the men turned round and each took leave of his beloved with consoling words, then stepped into a boat in waiting, which pushed off at once. The girls stood on the rocks and waved their hands long after their two figures had become invisible to those whose course they sped. Then, hand in hand, they went back up the steps and through the garden to the lonely house.

Chapter XXVIII

A SHORT WAY from the land the mariners ceased rowing and put up a sail, by help of which the boat sped swiftly out to sea, until the lights which mark the entrance to the Bosphorus and those along the coast of Asia had grown small behind them. Then they conferred with Mustafa, whose orders were that they should lie out on the track of shipping, on the watch for some large sailing-boat or coasting-steamer. The dawn was coming up; the land to eastward was taking shape out of the night; a whiteness grew behind it visibly, and in another minute the same pallor was around them like an emanation from the surface of the sea. It was still neither day nor night, when a craft loomed close to them, appearing ghostlike, its great sail like a moth's wing, in the magic air. The rowers gave a hail, and bent to their oars; and in a minute Camruddin was being helped on to the deck of a Greek trader where Mustafa Bey already stood stamping his feet, for it was very cold. They were taken to the galley, where there was a fire, and presently regaled with coffee, bread, and olives. The sun rose, making things seem once more reasonable. The morning lost its chill, the wind was favourable; Mustafa carried with him a little volume of old Turkish poetry from which he read aloud to Camruddin; and in the afternoon they reached Rodosto, where they once more heard the shout of 'Liberty!' The local governor, informed of their arrival, came to them and insisted on their resting at his house until such time as horses could be found for them. He told them all the news so long withheld: how Mahmud Shevket Pasha had collected a great army at Saloniki, and now was marching towards the capital, the country people flocking to his standard as he went along. The counter-revolution had had no effect upon the provinces which, without exception, remained staunch to the Committee, except at Adana, where there had been fighting with Armenians and much bloodshed, the work of emissaries of the party of reaction.

They spent the night in comfort, and set out betimes next day, on horses which left much to be desired for looks, but proved good travellers. Mustafa had purchased them outright after an hour's experience, dismissing their proprietor, who had come out prepared to follow them through all the world, if necessary. Their road lay up and down through settled country. There were some heavy rain showers, causing mud, which made slow going a necessity. It was towards evening of the second day, when, following a shower, the sun shone out, that from a rising ground they caught their first sight of the army—a troop of cavalry, which disappeared and was succeeded by an endless march of infantry, the evening sunshine glinting on their arms. Camruddin, who had experience of warfare, explained the order of the march to the ex-General, and pointed out the proofs it gave of proper discipline.

'You ought to be Mushir, my soul,' said his companion flippantly. 'Praise be to Allah, we at last behold them. Now, we shall see some fighting, in sha'llah. I wish to slaughter the relations of my former wife.'

Soon after sundown they came to a large village beyond which, along a waste where grew some stunted and misshapen trees, the army was preparing to encamp. The little place was all beflagged and overflowing with a rapturous crowd of country people mixed with soldiers and fedaïs.

'The first thing is to sell our horses,' argued Mustafa, 'for we can hardly hope to keep them unassisted in so great a multitude. And they would cramp our freedom with a sense of property.'

At the entrance to the place, where many people were assembled, they dismounted and began to cry: 'Who wants a horse? Here are two steeds of unexampled beauty. Who will buy?'

At once they were surrounded by a joking crowd. The horses were examined by all sorts of men and fun was made of their appearance, which was far from good.

'What men are you, who deal in gipsy bargains?' inquired a person of superior air.

'Two officers escaped out of Stamboul to join in the great work of liberation,' answered Mustafa.

At that there was applause, and men began to look with much more favour on the horses. While the auction was in progress, Camruddin felt a hand laid on his shoulder and, turning round, beheld the grinning face of Hasan, once an ombashi, but now a sergeant in the Resna regiment. After embraces and much praise to Allah, he asked what Camruddin and his companion meant to do. Camruddin passed the question on to Mustafa who, having got his money for the horses, came to join them at that moment.

'We mean to serve as volunteers with any company which will receive us, no matter what the kind of service,' said that cheerful soul. 'By Allah, I would act as mule to drag a gun, just for the hope that it might blow to pieces some relation of my former wife!'

The chaûsh stood stiffly to attention, saying: 'Then, efendim, you cannot do better than return with me to the headquarters of the National Battalion of Resna.'

'Lead on, and Allah bless thee,' answered Mustafa. He led the way beyond the village to a tent in which sat several officers about a table.

There was a moment of dead silence at their entrance, then a chorus of amazement: 'Merciful Allah! It is gyuzel Mustafa Pasha!'

At sight of all those staring faces of dismay, the cause of their amazement burst out laughing.

'No longer Pasha,' he explained; 'a mere lieutenant like my comrade here. We have escaped from the Abode of Happiness which has become Jehennum, and seek to be enrolled as volunteers in your battalion, of which my comrade is a former member.'

'Welcome!' was the cry. 'But what has come to you? You were the Sultan's aide-de-camp, the pampered favourite, the very peacock of the despotism!'

Mustafa told his story briefly, concluding with the wish, enforced with comic oaths, to do some damage to his former wife's relations. He then took the oath, which the officer in charge was going to administer in turn to Camruddin, when another interposed, exclaiming: 'Quite unnecessary. Camruddin Agha is an old fedaï whose name is always on the roll of the battalion. I and Niazi are his sureties. Let him be.'

The speaker was Osman Efendi, who had been second in command of Niazi's band of old. Camruddin had not till then marked his presence in the room. The kind words made this re-enlistment seem like a homecoming, his comfortable sojourn in the capital an aberration; and that impression was not weakened in the days which followed, for old comrades were continually hailing him with words of joy, and Hasan came to talk with him at every halt. Of Mustafa he saw but little, for that cheerful youth was in demand among the chiefs; but the ex-Pasha came to him whenever he could spare the time, and introduced him to the heroes of the hour; for that army, though well disciplined, was a great brotherhood where, when off duty, everybody talked to everybody. The father of them all, and source of all this order, confidence, and kindly feeling, was Mahmud Shevket Pasha, the Commander-in-Chief, whose praises were in every mouth. From Hasan, who was his fanatical admirer, Camruddin heard how at Saloniki, when news of the rebellion came, the army called for Mahmud Shevket Pasha with one voice, and Mahmud Shevket Pasha was away on leave.

'He has the happiest of homes. I know his servant, and he says that Mahmud Shevket's house, wherever placed, is Allah's blessing on the neighbourhood. All are the better and the happier for it. No wonder that he values every moment of his times of leave. Messengers were sent to him, but he did not return. It needed a direct command of the Committee to produce him. And when he did arrive, he said: "Why send for me? I see before me half a dozen men at least as capable as I am of conducting such an enterprise. Why cheat me of a week of my brief holiday?" That might be policy in others, but he means it,' Hasan said. 'He is quite without ambition, though so highly qualified. But, having once accepted the command for duty's sake, he works both day and night; he does not spare himself. That is the kind of man

who should be made the ruler, with liberty and proper
leisure to recruit his strength; for such a man, so modest
and God-fearing, could never be a despot if he tried.'

The army reached San Stefano and camped there,
waiting an attack. But all that came to them were friends
escaping from the hostile area. The city was in chaos, they
were told, all business at a standstill, the Government
resigning every day, the rebel troops, through fear of
punishment, alone preventing unconditional surrender.
The army of Thrace arrived and camped to northward
of the force from Saloniki. Parliament assembled at San
Stefano under the protection of the National Army, and
issued edicts which were printed there and passed into
Stamboul by friendly hands.

At length the order came for the advance. A battle was
expected at the city wall; but there was no resistance,
and at the third hour of the day the vanguard of the army
marched into Stamboul.

Chapter XXIX

IT WAS a day of sun refreshed by a cool breeze. Cam-ruddin beheld, as in a dream, the cheering crowds, the solemn mosques, the soaring minarets, the clouds of startled pigeons wheeling overhead; and here and there, between gray houses, caught a glimpse of dark blue sea with ships afloat upon it, and blue hills beyond. It was a day of joy. The world was once more won for goodness, and in the evening he would see Gul-raaneh. Praise to Allah!

All at once there came the whiz of bullets, the crack of rifles, and a man fell dead before him in the ranks. Another staggered to the wall and leant against it, with hand pressed to his side and coughing desperately. Commands rang out. The soldiers scattered and took cover, and with a din of shouts to clear the ground, first one machine-gun was set up and then another. Soon their crackling fire reduced all other sounds to insignificance. The place they were attacking was a barracks garrisoned by mutineers. Camruddin had fired a hundred rounds into the windows, and had taken part in two attempts to rush the building, before the white flag of surrender was hung out by the besieged. Then, when the place was captured and its occupants disarmed, the troops were ordered to make haste to Pera. They crossed the long bridge at the double, blind to the lovely prospect upon either hand, and deaf to the excited plaudits of the crowd; and so on, panting, up the hill to the Tash-kishleh Barracks, where a battle raged. Upon the open ground before it there were human forms displaying frantic energy, and others lying motionless like bundles. The arrival of so strong a reinforcement was hailed with shouts of joy by the assailants. The machine-guns opened fire, the riflemen spread out and kept on taking rapid aim at puffs of smoke, or faces seen a second at a window. Some were killed and more were wounded, but at last the white flag was displayed, the sign of victory. The tired fedaïs flung themselves upon the ground and lay awhile as quiet as the dead beside them, so that some gentlemen and ladies, who came offering refreshments, made absurd mistakes. Mustafa, begrimed with powder-smoke, lay down by Camruddin and, when he had recovered breath, remarked,—

'Praise be to Allah we are both alive. When you are rested, come with me and ask permission. Now that the game is over, I would fly to her I love.'

Permission was obtained quite easily. Within two hours they were at Mustafa's kiosk upon the Sea of Marmora, the owner seated in a summer-house with his beloved, Camruddin wandering with Gul-raaneh by the shore, the very thought of war and politics completely banished.

The counter-revolution had been crushed effectually. The Sultan, Abdul Hamid, who had been the pretext for reaction, though he took no part in it, was with all due solemnity deposed, and the saintly Muhammad Reshâd was girded with the sword of Osman in his stead. The chief conspirators were tried and hanged, and Mahmud Shevket Pasha was acclaimed the saviour of his country.

At that moment, the whole empire wished him to become dictator; but he, of all men, most possessed the spirit of the Revolution, which kept personal ambition strictly in the servant's place. He was content to do his duty as a general officer towards his men, a man towards his family. He honestly believed that any number of his friends were better qualified than he was for the highest place; and eagerly resisted all their efforts to exalt him, hating the strife attendant upon place and power, desiring, above all things, quiet, as the first condition of creative work. When Minister of War, he led the life of a recluse amid the clap-trap of his office, demanding only money from the Government, with the result that in two years the Turkish army, down to its remotest unit, was clothed and fed and regularly paid—a vast reform. Only by threats to treat him as a traitor did the Committee force this singularly upright man upon the path which led him through a maze of envy to a martyr's death.

But if the victory of Mahmud Shevket Pasha gave pure joy to Camruddin, there were people in Stamboul to whom it seemed a great disaster, and those people were beloved of his bride.

Gul-raaneh, taking steamer to the Bridge one fine spring morning, quite unprepared for any sight of fear, saw human bodies swinging upon gibbets. She had been going to the town to do some shopping, but could not pass along that ghastly avenue. Nauseated, nearly fainting, she made her way home, somehow; and once at home her weakness soon gave way to boundless indignation.

When Camruddin returned she told him her experience, expecting him to share the sentiments which it had roused in her. He said 'You ought not to have started for Stamboul this morning. I should have warned you, but I did not know the rebels had been executed until I saw what you saw, going to my office. It is a horrid sight, but it is necessary in order that all men may know how the Committee deals with malefactors of a certain kind. Allah have mercy on them.'

'Malefactors!' screamed Gul-raaneh. 'Do you not know that Leylah Hânum's brother is among them? Alas, poor lady! Black indeed must be her grief to think her brother has been done to death in such a way, by people of low origin.'

'What talk is this, efendim?' Camruddin exclaimed, in great surprise, for, never having spoken much of politics to his beloved, he was altogether unprepared for this disclosure of hostility. 'Mankind all come from Adam, who was made of earth. All Muslims are the servants of Allah, and if they prove bad servants and betray their trust they merit death, since they corrupt the world. What is this talk of high and low origin? Power, education, wisdom, virtue, rank—all these I know, but not this new distinction. Our leaders are well educated, most of them are virtuous; they use the power which Allah has entrusted to them for a righteous purpose. Whatever be their "origin" they are more noble than persons who for selfish aims conspire to wreck the state.'

'You defend them! Oh, how dare you, bey efendim! They are no better than wild beasts, than savage dogs. Say you do not defend them, I entreat, for both our sakes.'

'I will defend them and their sacred purpose with my life at all times.'

'Mercy!' exclaimed Gul-raaneh, with a look of high disdain. 'Then you, too, are no better than a savage beast, Allah knows I can no longer honourably live with one who triumphs in the murder of my lady's brother. Efendim, you have said enough. I beg you to divorce me straightway without more ado … Oh, never mind the money owing to me; I renounce it. Support me through my time of separation, that is all I ask. In sha'llah, I shall find a more congenial husband.'

'You say this seriously?'

'Have no doubt about it. I will not stay with you another night. I go at once to Leylah Hânum. Deign to send my things to me to-morrow or as soon as is convenient to you, bey efendim.'

A minute later she was in her charshaf hurrying to the railway station, weeping behind her veil, convinced that she had been subjected to unheard-of insult, and was fleeing from a very wicked and malignant man.

Chapter XXX

GUL-RAANEH'S anger, which appeared to Camruddin as sudden madness, had been a natural growth of her surroundings. Because she came from Sâdik Pasha's house, most of her friends were of the class which benefited by the old régime—the daughters and dependants of State dignitaries whom the Revolution had deposed. This class had lost its power but had retained its fortunes, and might have been content with the new order if the freedom and prestige, to which their education, as they thought, entitled them in any State which claimed to be the home of progress, had been accorded to its members. In those great Turkish houses where Oriental rules of decency had been observed with outward strictness, there had for years been foreign tutors, foreign governesses. The women were well read in European, but altogether ignorant of Turkish, literature. They subscribed to European journals, followed European movements, and regarded all things Turkish as old-fashioned and pathetic. Considering themselves as of the European world, they had been secretly impatient of the decencies imposed by Eastern custom and had transgressed those decencies occasionally with a reckless daring which was purely Turkish, the cause of many scandals and some tragedies. These ladies were at first delighted with the Revolution, expecting it to bring the freedom which they long had coveted. Some of them went out boldly and took part in the rejoicings— too boldly, for their misbehaviour caused a scandal. They were mobbed. If the new Government had then supported them, they would have been its staunch adherents. But it punished them, therefore it was a foe to liberty and progress, the very things it claimed to champion: a delusion and a lie. Their grievance was analogous to that which many of the Paris exiles had begun to cherish. They knew the way of progress as old-fashioned Turks could not, yet, far from being treated with due deference on that account, they were thrust in the background—reprimanded, even punished. Where was progress? Where was liberty? They went from house to house abusing the authorities, in terms which no one would have dared to use under the despotism.

There was another matter of complaint, affecting a much larger circle. The men had thrown off Oriental decencies. They claimed the right to go to Frankish houses, to associate, and even dance with Frankish women.

Reshideh Hânum, one of Sâdik Pasha's married daughters, came one day to see Gul-raaneh, in an agony of rage and shame. The Committee was to give a ball to all the European colonies at Fener-Baghcheh, and not a Turkish woman would, of course, be present. She had told her husband, Shukri Bey, that he was not to go. He had replied that, as a steward, he was bound to be there. Angry words had passed between them for the first time since he raised the wedding-veil. What was she to do? She wept in her friend's arms.

Gul-raaneh coaxed her to be reasonable. If Shukri Bey was an official of the ball, of course he must attend it, but he would not dance.

'Dance!' Reshideh exclaimed, her tears dried up by indignation. 'To take half-naked, shameless women in his arms, and clasp them tight and jump about with them—in public, too—is that a pastime for the father of my children? I will mix his drink with flower of laurel. I will poison him.'

'Be sure that he will not so far forget his dignity,' replied Gul-raaneh; and Reshideh Hânum went away much comforted.

But on an evening when Gul-raaneh had retired to rest a little earlier than usual, there came a knocking at the iron shutters of the house. Camruddin asked: 'Who's there?' 'I seek an audience of Gul-raaneh Hânum,' came the answer in a woman s voice. He opened the door and in slipped a girlish figure veiled in black, coquettishly, and wearing long white gloves. It offered thanks to him, in passing, and fled into Gul-raaneh's room. His wife came presently to say that it was Reshideh Hânum, who was in great distress, and wanted shelter for the night. He bade her welcome, secured the door, and went to bed. The world of women was a mystery to him.

Gul-raaneh got no sleep at all that night. Reshideh Hânum would not stay indoors but insisted upon sitting out on the veranda, wrapped in shawls. It was moonlight, and the frogs were noisy in the garden tanks. Reshideh was in tragic mood, no longer tearful; and as she stood and told her story, with pale face uplifted to the moon, she looked so lovely that Gul-raaneh thrilled with sympathy for her, and anger at the clumsy power of men to hurt such loveliness. Reshideh had tried to make her husband promise that he would not dance at Fener-Baghcheh; and when he refused, she had forbidden him to go at all. But he had only laughed, and recommended her to keep her orders for her underlings. He had set out in uniform, at last, without farewell, for she had hidden from him at the moment of departure. After he had gone, she bade the eunuch call a carriage and, putting on her charshaf drove to Fener-Baghcheh in company of her old nurse, 'to hear the music.' At Fener-Baghcheh she had got out of the carriage, telling Lulu she would not be gone a minute, and had walked about the wooden building whence came sounds of gaiety, until she saw a waiter going in. Him she entreated to tell Shukri Bey that some one from his home with serious news was waiting. After a minute Shukri Bey came hurrying out; when, drawing out a whip which she had concealed beneath her charshaf, she had beaten him with all her might. He had not touched her; he had stood up straight under the blows until a crowd collected, when he had divorced her publicly.

'So now I am no longer anything,' she said, 'for Shukri Bey was all the world to me. I went back to the carriage. No one followed. Then I came to you, dismissing Lulu. To-morrow I shall go home to my parents, and send for my two children. He cannot withhold them; they are still too young … what is that you say? Oh, no, beloved, he will not forgive me; do not think it for a moment. He is much too proud. And I shall never love another man. The beauty of this night is torture! Why did Allah make such beauty to become the scene of cruel deeds?'

In the last hours of darkness, when a light sea-breeze began to stir the foliage of the garden, she was seized with a desire to walk abroad. Gul-raaneh could refuse her nothing, so they stole out through the garden and along the lane. Reshideh led the way to a small village cemetery where, amid the gloom of cypress trees, slim headstones congregated like a crowd of ghosts. She flung herself upon a certain grave, and lay there sobbing a long while.

'Now I feel better,' she declared, when she at last arose. 'I feel as if I had been buried with her and come forth anew. It is the grave of Alia Hânum, my maternal aunt, who died quite young in happier days than these. How simple and how beautiful were Turkish women's lives, before the world went mad with Frankish customs!'

They got back to the house just before sunrise, and then lay down to rest till the old servant came with cups of coffee and two clusters of ripe grapes, on which they broke their fast. Then Reshideh Hânum asked to have a carriage called to take her to the railway station. Her wish being conveyed to Camruddin, he went to satisfy it.

'Last night I was a lioness, but to-day I feel more like a little mouse,' were her parting words to Gul-raaneh; who cried out against such self-depreciation on the part of one whom she regarded as a heroine of high romance. Bred up in close attendance upon Reshideh and her sister Safet, sharing their lessons and their pastimes and adoring them, she could not have imagined either of them in the wrong. This incident, which was the cause of so much misery—for it was months before the quarrel was arranged—rendered Gul-raaneh very hostile to the new ideas. And it was not the only one within her circle of acquaintance. A girl, whom she knew well, committed suicide because her husband was seen driving through the streets of Pera with a bare-faced foreign woman of disgusting character. Another—it was quite an open secret—killed her husband by mixing poison in his coffee, for a similar reason. Wherever she went, in the great Hamidian houses, she heard the leaders of the Revolution mentioned as the worst of men. They knew not how to govern; they were ruining the country; they were needlessly offending all the foreign embassies of which the ladies had the latest gossip from their menfolk, ex-officials and diplomatists, who went there to denounce the failings of the new régime. They were men of no breeding, *canaille,* mere adventurers. Among the Turks this class-distinction was a novelty, the very latest thing in European manners. The Hamidian clique of Arabs, Kurds, Circassians, picked up from any quarter at the tyrant's will, now loudly claimed to be the Turkish aristocracy, losing thereby the tone of perfect breeding which marks the Muslim nation as a whole from labourer to Grand Vizier. But even in this eagerly adopted snobbishness there was a Turkish frankness, for it was reserved for enemies. The people whom these ladies liked were never 'low' no matter what their station in the world. They sneered at Enver Bey and his relations, while showing sisterly affection to the washerwoman and the baker's wife.

The truth was, party feeling ran extremely high. Men perfectly acquainted with the diplomatic game felt outraged by the first mistakes of men quite new to it. Everything was being ruined by those honest blunderers, who had no business in the seat of power. The feeling of the men found vent in private lamentations to the foreign diplomats, and still more private conversations with their wives and intimates. They all deferred to the Committee outwardly. Among the women of a certain circle discontent was open, and prayers were heard for the Committee's downfall. Gul-raaneh never guessed the source of all that bitterness, implicitly believing the remarks of women whom she loved and reverenced. She thought the New Turks really wicked men. Her husband had expected great things from the Revolution, like everybody else; but as he never condescended to discuss such matters with her, she supposed that he, like everybody else, was disillusioned.

The counter-revolution, and the butchery of New Turks in the capital, alarmed her greatly for the sake of Camruddin; and the ladies of her circle also were alarmed, denouncing it as premature and much too violent. So she was not surprised that Camruddin should go to join the revolutionary army; and she, with everybody else, felt much relieved when Mahmud Shevket Pasha marched into the capital, restoring order and security of life and business. But then the Sultan Abdul Hamid— the idol of her ladies—was deposed! But then a number of important persons were arrested, summarily tried and hanged; among them being Leylah Hânum's brother and Aïn-ul-Hayat Hânum's husband! It was horrible.

Chapter XXXI

GUL-RAANEH wept behind her veil in the woman's compartment of the train, and in the saloon reserved for women in the steamer, hearing the chatter going on around her as a tiresome noise a long way off. Arrived at Ghalatah, she went to the other side of the Bridge and took a kaïk. Afloat upon the Golden Horn amid the sounds of evening, her mind grew calmer; but the sight of Sâdik Pasha's house, her childhood's home, revived her grief. It was so short a time since she had left its walls, so full of hope!

The eunuch at the door of the haramlik recognised her voice and wished to gossip. She could not answer his polite inquiries, but let him see her face, beholding which he shrugged his shoulders and led on. In the large ante-chamber sat the maids of honour, as the slaves of such a house might well be called, at needlework. They also wished to talk, assailing her with eager questions, but she could do no more than greet them tremulously.

A minute later she was in the presence of the Lady Leylah and her youngest daughter Sâmieh Hânum, not yet ten years old. The child was ordered to embrace Gul-raaneh and then run away.

Alone with her now sobbing visitor, the wife of Sâdik Pasha took Gul-raaneh's hands and forced her to sit down upon the couch beside her, pouring out words of welcome all the while to give her time to conquer her emotion. When that object had been gained to some extent, she asked,—

'Well, rosebud mine, what is the trouble?'

Gul-raaneh was inclined to cry again, but she controlled the inclination by an effort. Fixing her gray eyes upon the kind face of her more than mother, she replied with horror,—

'My husband is become a miscreant.'

'Merciful Allah!' cried the elder lady, much concerned. 'In what way, now? It seems incredible, for Sâdik Pasha was his surety, and gave an excellent account of him! Has he ill-used you? Does he slight you in the house? Has he imposed upon you some indignity? Or have you heard that he frequents bad women? Tell me the facts, my lamb, at once, that I may judge his conduct coolly and, perhaps, advise you.'

Gul-raaneh shook her head at each new question, and at length confessed that she had always counted him the best of men until this very day.

'And then, what happened?' urged the lady. 'Did he divorce you in a sudden rage?'

Gul-raaneh shook her head decidedly. 'I spoke with horror of a sight I saw this morning as I was going to Stamboul. It made me ill. I had to turn and go back home again, and all day long I mourned for your most noble brother, dearest lady, and cursed the malefactors who had dared to hang him like a gipsy. And-and-I told Camruddin Bey what I thought about them, and he dared to defend them—to my face!' She sobbed anew.

'Ah, now I understand what it was all about,' said Leylah Hânum. 'But what is that between you and your husband?'

197

'Efendim, see! He is the partisan of wicked men. He said that he would do their bidding to the death. He would himself have hanged your honoured brother, if he could!'

'My honoured brother is, it seems to me, already hanged —Allah have mercy on him!—and between ourselves, my fawn, he had well earned his fate. He was no hot-head, but a selfish and ambitious man, who found his profit in the despotism. He plotted to restore the state of things by which he profited, well knowing the result of failure; and he failed. My blossom, there is nothing tragic in all that. I wept a little for him yesterday, but more in shame than anger. I recalled him as a boy, but since he grew up he has never pleased me, and of late years I have seen but little of him, because Sâdik Pasha never could abide his sight.'

'But hanging—for a man so noble, of so high a family!'

'Beloved, how your words remind me of a story! It was of a flea, I think, if I remember rightly, who dwelt amid the fur of a small mouse's back, and called the mouse a noble beast in consequence. I do not wish to wound your soul by that comparison; I only wish to bring you to your senses. Sâdik Pasha has held high positions. We have lived in luxury. But who was Sâdik Pasha's father? Tell me that! A simple khôja from Angora, who obtained a good position under the Sheykh-ul-Islâm. And as for me, my father was the Admiral Pasha, but of his father I can tell no more than that he was a Muslim of Bulgaristan. We were exalted by the will of Allah, and by His will we may at any moment be abased. You have conceived too lofty an idea of us, and in so doing, as I fear, have put on airs of grandeur, as one of us, towards your husband,

who, as Sâdik Pasha says, is really one of us, being a good
Osmanli. My two wild daughters have great love for
you, they call you sister; I fear the licence of their talk
at times is bad for you. It may have made you proud and
boastful, in imagination, and full of condescension for
your husband. I wish that either of them had as good a
man.'

'But everybody says the Unionists are miscreants!'

'And if they were, what matters it, beloved, provided
that your husband fulfils all his duties and is sweet to
you? Factions and government, my dear one, are not our
concern. I take my husband's word, when he vouchsafes
one, on such subjects, and pay no notice to the words of
other women, who usually are repeating only what their
husbands tell them. Men understand their own affairs,
we must suppose, and what they do outside the home
with other men does not affect us. You do not know,
perhaps —how should you?—that Sâdik Pasha is in
favour of the Unionists. He calls them honest, zealous,
and sincere. Their only fault, he says, is inexperience;
and that will mend with time. Most of his friends are
of the other faction. He hears from men the talk which
you have heard from women; but he disregards it. With
Mahmud Shevket Pasha he has old acquaintance. He
has been offered a command and will accept it. So your
trouble, in so far as it arose from a desire to champion
the opinions of this house, was groundless. Stay with us
a day or two, and then return to Camruddin Bey as if no
angry words had passed between you. That is my advice,
my little dove from Allah.'

Gul-raaneh was in tears again, no longer angry. She
now wept despairingly.

'He said no angry words to me,' she moaned. I—I

insulted him. I swore that I would not return. I urged him to divorce me. I cannot go back, for shame. It is impossible; I, myself, in madness, made it so. O Allah! O my grief! What have I done? ... Let me remain here till my mind can frame some project. I have nowhere else to go.'

'Stay with us and welcome, little honey-flower, and we will do our best to make you smile again,' said Leylah Hânum, patting her upon the cheek. 'You shall go now to the Hammam with Suz-i-dil, who afterwards will rub your skin with rose-leaves to refresh you. By then it will be time to sup and go to bed. To-morrow, in sha'llah, we will go shopping to Bey Oghlou in the carriage. My pet, the sun will shine again to-morrow.'

The lady clapped her hands. A pretty girl appeared with reverence, who, at an order, put her arm around Gul-raaneh, leading her away. Left alone, Leylah Hânum looked out of the window at the gathering night. Then, with a smile, she murmured: 'Little fool!' and quietly resumed the work of checking household linen, with which she had been occupied before the interruption.

Chapter XXXII

ON the morning after his domestic cataclysm, Cam-ruddin repaired as usual to his Ministry and performed his wonted duties, at first in a bemused condition. But after sipping two small cups of coffee and smoking half a dozen cigarettes his mind grew clear again, and he thought simply: 'It was written that this trial was to come upon my head.'

After that he ceased to brood on the calamity, facing the new conditions of his life with courage.

Three days later when, returning from the city, he reached his country house, he found his sister Melek and her husband waiting in the garden. It being a fine evening, one of the servants of the great kiosk had brought out coffee to them in the arbour.

'What has happened?' they inquired, with real anxiety. 'We came two hours ago to find the house locked up. A gardener of Ferid Bey informed us that it had been so for days … Where is Gul-raaneh Hânum?'

'Allah knows! She said she would return to Sâdik Pasha's house.'

'Where is the old woman?'

'She decamped through modesty.'

'Where is that lame man whom you had about the place?'

'I put a present in his hand and said farewell.'

'But how then do you live?'

'Praise be to Allah! My food and rest are in the house of Ferid Bey. His Honour is away. The servants love me, and the khôja who instructs the children is my friend.'

'Ma sha'llah!' exclaimed Basri Bey. 'But what has chanced between you and your lady?'

'She chose to go, being possessed with sudden horror at the sight of me. She is a servant of Allah as I am, in account with Him.'

Camruddin took his key and let the visitors into the house, which Melek set to work at once to tidy.

'But tell us the whole story,' pleaded Basri Bey.

Camruddin told the story of the quarrel briefly, and answered briefly the astonished questions of his hearers. Melek said,—

'So that is all? And she has gone to Sâdik Pasha's house? Be sure, my soul, that she has been well scolded for her foolishness. The house of Sâdik Pasha is respectable.'

Camruddin answered: 'She does not return.'

'No doubt she is ashamed to do so, being proud and modest. You ought to have recourse to Sâdik Pasha as an intermediary. Write her a letter saying that she is forgiven.'

'If you had heard her when she last spoke in this room you would not talk about forgiveness as from me to her, my sister; nor do I truly think the word is mentionable. She has her own opinions: I have mine. They clash. It seems to me a simple matter. She, not I, objected to her staying here. It is for her to state her pleasure to return or not return. I ask you to remember she is not my slave.' Something of iron in the tone of the deserted husband warned his companions that no useful purpose would be served by further agitation of the subject. They were silent for a space, and then began to speak of other matters.

But Melek Hânum called next day at Sâdik Pasha's house, and, after talking for a long while with the Vâlideh Hânum, saw Gul-raaneh. Two days later she saw Camruddin again, and in the course of conversation mentioned that, according to the talk of women, there was reason why his wife should not desire him to divorce her.

'What?' he inquired.

'She is with child by you.'

Camruddin flushed with pleasure at the tidings, his eyes grew bright, but he constrained himself to answer calmly: 'She is blest, the praise to Allah!'

'It must be sad for her apart from you.'

'The house is here and so am I,' he answered.

'You will never make him beg her to return,' said Basri to his wife. 'They will simply go on nursing grievance one against the other, making you their confidante.'

'She makes me her confidante; he does not. Yet she is more implacable than he is. She expects him to entreat her to return. I see no hope at present.'

That was her opinion from her observations; but it happened otherwise. Pushed on by Leylah Hânum and her married daughters, enticed by Melek, teased by her companions, Gul-raaneh did go back to Camruddin, but in a state of mind which left it doubtful whether her intention was to stay with him, or merely to confirm their quarrel and depart immediately.

By great good fortune he was in the house when she arrived, though generally, by that hour of the evening, he had gone to Ferid Bey's kiosk. Had she found the house locked up the disappointment to emotions strung for an encounter would have been disastrous. As it was she coolly walked into the house, traversed the room in which her husband sat without appearing conscious of his presence, and went to her own place.

A visit from Mustafa Bey, the ex-Pasha, had detained Camruddin beyond his usual moment of departure. His friend had come to tell him they had both been named by the Committee among the officers to be employed to put down brigandage. It had been a custom of the despotism for Ministers of State and Court officials—indeed, for all rich men—to keep hired bravoes, whose business was to silence protests and enforce respect. After the Revolution, all those ruffians, thrown out of their employment and de-prived of patronage—exposed, moreover, to the anger of the populace—either vanished into private life or took to brigandage, the latter course appealing to the greater number. Most of them were Albanians, men by nature proud and lawless and averse to compromise. They now distressed whole districts by their raids and robberies; and the Committee had resolved to hunt them down. It was an adventurous service, which appealed to Camruddin; and after Mustafa had gone he sat and contemplated its attractions, chief among which was the idea that in a life of movement he would more easily forget the loss of a be-loved wife. And while he sat thus musing, the door opened and a veiled figure glided through the room.

'Praise be to Allah!' he exclaimed within himself and sat awaiting further manifestations. She reappeared without her veil. He bade her welcome. She answered in the terms of strict politeness as she crossed the room and passed into the kitchen. He waited till she came again and then inquired,—

'What is your will, efendim?'

'To go again into the road since my appearance gives no joy, efendim.'

'Your presence always gives me joy,' said Camruddin. 'You have the strangest manner of expressing rapture! Give up these sorry efforts at politeness which cannot deceive me. Your love for me is dead, that is quite evident. You never came to seek me, never wooed me to return. A lover would at least have shown some interest.'

'Efendim, I considered that you knew your mind. You said you hated me; you asked me to divorce you. Who am I that I should seek to force your inclination?'

'A lover would have tried to alter it, efendim.'

'A lover who was not a husband, yes! But marriage is, it seems to me, a contract of which the first condition must be mutual inclination. Where either of the twain detests the other, it had best be terminated.'

'The Franks have other notions,' said Gul-raaneh dryly.

'Well, I am not a Frank, though I have heard how they pretend to honour women but in fact degrade them. They worship the relation of the sexes, esteeming it the goal of life.'

'What is the goal of life, in your opinion?' asked Gul-raaneh scornfully; but she sat down before him.

'It is surely not communion with a fellow-creature. That search must end in disappointment always. The soul of every living man and woman is solitary from the cradle to the grave unless it finds, by service, that communion with Allah for which, in truth, it was created. When that is found it is at one with all the other servants of Allah, but not before.'

'So you are a Sufi, are you?' said Gul-raaneh, interested.

'I am a Muslim, and not learned,' he replied. 'But this is clear: I have my personality and you have yours, both given to us by Allah; I cannot make you me, nor my thoughts yours; nor have I any right to seek to do so. Your mind and soul, and mine, are independent of each other. But we are travelling the same road, we are servants of the same Lord. In Allah and our life's conditions is our bond of union, and that of all men, if they only knew. I love you, and I praise the Lord of Heaven and earth for giving me the comfort of such sweet companionship upon a portion of the road. But if you love me not, then go your way; for you are a free servant of Allah and it were sin for me to keep you here against your will …' He stopped because a sob came from Gul-raaneh. She pressed her face upon the floor and clasped his feet. In compassion he leant down to hear what she was moaning, and he heard,—

'My dear, you should have beaten me and locked me up!'

Chapter XXXIII

THREE DAYS later Camruddin was sent to Brûsa, where he was given a command of twenty men, with orders to proceed into a certain valley on the eastern slopes of Mt Olympus. After a month's campaign the outlaws who oppressed that valley were surrounded and compelled to fight. Their leaders being killed, the rest surrendered. And Camruddin was ordered to another neighbourhood. Such was his occupation for a year, during the whole of which he never saw Gul-raaneh, though they wrote to one another constantly. It was at Eski-shehir he received the news that she had been delivered of a boy, and gave the largest sum he could afford in alms therefor.

The sense of doing righteous work sustained him; and he could not but exult as he observed the changes which were taking place even among the peasants in far mountain villages. Of old, the people being full of grievances, had nearly always sided with the outlaws secretly; but now they sided with the Sultan's troops, which made their work much easier. On every hand he heard the cry for education, sanitation, and improvements of all kinds. In many places schools were being built, the gift of rich men who approved the new ideas; and, meanwhile, lessons of the modern sort were given by old-fashioned khôjas in the mosques, who studied hard and anxiously, learning themselves the subjects which they taught their pupils. It was no uncommon thing to hear of men of means devoting sums of money to the education of a number of poor children from the mekteb to the University. There was a demand for better roads and railways, a demand for hospitals and better regulations for the public health. Above all, there was a demand for knowledge upon every subject—the knowledge which enables men to help themselves. The printing-presses of Stamboul and Brûsa, Smyrna, and Saloniki were at work on Turkish literature, turning out cheap editions of the classics, old and new, as well as modern text-books and translations from the European languages; and Camruddin, who now read every book that he could lay his hand on, received new publications regularly through Gul-raaneh, who got them from her friend Reshideh Hânum. Even in the mountains he was asked to lend them, by persons who were proud of their new power to read. In many of the villages informal courts were held to settle small disputes concerning land and neighbours' quarrels inexpensively, a practice the Committee had encouraged by an edict. The spies were gone. The bravoes, too, were gone. The brigands were upon the way to be exterminated. Free movement, free expression of opinion, was now the right of every Turkish subject. Old-fashioned persons who disliked the new ideas aired their objections freely in the village café or the marketplace. The very air seemed sweeter and more wholesome than of yore.

After a hot encounter with a robber-force upon a mountain-top, Camruddin joined bands with a lieutenant who had brought his men up to the battle from another valley. Approaching that lieutenant as a stranger, he was overjoyed to recognise the former Pasha. The friends embraced and then sat down upon the ground and gossiped, comfortably, while their troops were resting. They were together after that for many days, bound by the common duty to convey their captured brigands down to the coast for deportation to Albania.

In a well-watered, richly-wooded valley, full of the song of birds and creaking of huge wooden water-wheels, they came towards evening to a great kiosk. The house had been a fine one, but was now dilapidated. The garden had become a perfect wilderness; its weeds encroaching on the terrace and its climbing plants engarlanding a large part of the house itself. A path led from a gate—which had long since fallen off its hinges, and now lay buried in a growth of tall blue nettles—on to the aforesaid terrace where, in solitary state, upon a chair, sat a correct efendi, surrounded by a group of peasants, sitting cross-legged on the ground. The person thus exalted, seeing soldiers passing, bade them enter. The voice appeared to Camruddin familiar, and when, obedient to the invitation, he with Mustafa arrived upon the terrace, he saw its owner was no other than the yuzbashi of Saloniki, Arif Hikmet Bey. He recognised them both and made them welcome. Chairs were brought. The soldiers, having piled their arms and loosened their equipment, presently joined the group of peasants on the terrace floor, partaking of the conversation of the chaired ones. The prisoners, also, were allowed to join the circle.

'What does your Honour in so rustic and remote a place?' asked Camruddin, when greetings were exhausted. 'Doubtless it is but to repose a little after your unheard-of labours in behalf of liberty.'

It was enough. From then until they went to rest, the moody Arif ceased not to expound his grievance. 'I am not wanted. I am too sincere, and know too much about the conduct of affairs to be accepted in an age when ignorant rascals are preferred to sage and upright men,' he answered; and he went on to explain how the Committee of Union and Progress had gone all astray, the Revolution had been made a failure, and the state of the whole country had grown worse than ever; simply, it seemed, because the leaders had not sense enough to perceive that Arif Hikmet was the soul of progress. He talked so much, so vehemently, and withal so vaguely, that it was impossible for his hearers to discover the real reason of his bitterness; which, none the less, had been sufficient, after vain remonstrance with the men in power, to drive him to self-exile on this wild estate of his; where every day it added to his grievance that no deputation came to beg him to return. The Committee could not function properly without his help. It was a manifest disgrace as well as loss to Turkey that such a man, at such a time, should rust in exile.

Mustafa Bey and Camruddin emitted sympathetic murmurs. The soldiers shrugged their shoulders as they listened to his fierce complaints. His place of exile seemed like paradise to weary men. A fertile valley between wooded hills, concluding in a glimpse of purple sea, the peaceful scene embellished by the evening light, seemed very good to them. They looked with envy on the peasants, dwellers in that happy glen, who also shrugged in disapproval of the great man's talk.

The troops marched early on the following morning, sped with goodwill by Arif Hikmet Bey. As the two lieutenants rode together down by leafy lanes towards the sea, Mustafa observed,—

'He is an ass. He shows it now, though once we used

to think him a wise man. Do you know the cause of all his dudgeon? Once, at a conference of some kind, he proposed a course of action, and Talaat laughed at the proposal. And Mahmud Shevket and the others vetoed it. That was sufficient. Arif Bey declared himself insulted, and declined all further dealings with a body which supported his insulter. Because they were unwilling to espouse his private quarrel, he became the voluntary exile we have just now seen.'

'In sha'llah, in this pleasant air he will regain his wit,' said Camruddin.

'Unlikely,' answered Mustafa, with a contemptuous smile. 'Conspiracy is the vocation of some men. Our Arif Hikmet is a born conspirator. As such, he did good service in the time of need. But having helped to make the cause triumphant, he must still conspire. And to obtain the proper spirit and incentive, he must feel oppressed. And as there is now no one to oppress him, he must oppress himself, and then imagine it the work of an ungrateful party. He is not yet a danger, but he may become one. I liked not his insistence on religious grounds.'

'In what particular?'

'He spoke with horror of some men from Paris, who have been given commissions in the army, laughing at the soldiers' prayers as something foolish and old-fashioned. It may have happened once. Such beasts exist. But they have been well rated and most of them have fled already back to Paris, there to speak evil of our new régime. To imply, as he did, that their conduct was approved by the Committee, is abominable.'

The soldiers, who talked freely as they marched at ease, were still more frank in disapproval of the grumbling bey.

'If some young pimps are irreligious we do not regard their sneers, and if they interfered with us in practice, we could deal with them,' said one.

'You cannot be a man without first being a child,' remarked another; 'and we have yet to learn to walk in liberty. That grumbling bey is rotten. May he shortly burst!'

And yet another cried: 'The seat of his complaint is easy to discern. His mind is poisonous with jealousy. The man who once becomes a prey to that disease is like a horse that has a maggot in the brain. He should be shot, for he is dangerous as well as useless.'

A sergeant who had known the bey in Macedonia murmured sadly,

'He was a good man once. May Allah heal his mind!'

Thus chatting, with occasional attempts at song, the little force marched downward to the sea, and then along the shore until it reached a town, where Camruddin and Mustafa, reporting at the barracks, were informed that they were ordered off to Macedonia, and for preparation had been granted a month's leave, of which ten days were spent already. That very evening, having sent off telegrams to their respective wives, they set sail in a small boat for the nearest port which had a station on the Anatolian railway.

Chapter XXXIV

F<small>ERID</small> <small>BEY</small> was absent in the south of Europe; his
children and their tutor were at Yalova; so Camruddin
and Gul-raaneh had the whole vast pleasance to themselves in the long summer days, the baby in the arms of a
veiled country girl attending them. Basri Bey and Melek
Hânum came and spent two days with them, bringing
their child—a girl of ten months—to be inspected by her
uncle; and plans were formed for marrying Mukerrem
Bey, the son of Camruddin, to Nur Semá Hânum, still
dependent on her mother's breast.

From Basri Camruddin heard all the news. The
English would not help the Turks effectively; that was
now clear; as also that the Powers of Europe as a whole
were no more friendly to the new régime than to the old.
Indeed, it might be said that England was more friendly
than the others; but her idea of Turkish progress was still
typified in Kiamil Pasha and inert decrepitude. It could
not be accepted by men aiming at a great revival. And
so the watchful head of the Committee had begun to
think of Germany. They had had a fright, having been
informed on unimpeachable authority that the Entente
Powers were quite determined to destroy the Turkish
Empire, though the date of the destruction was not fixed,
and the portion of the spoil to be assigned to Germany
and her allies remained a subject of contention. In that

contention lay the only hope for Muslim progress. If Turkey could by hook or crook obtain ten years of peace, all might be well. But that, in the opinion of good judges, was improbable. In fact, the Revolution, far from changing enemies to friends, as had first been hoped, had made old foes impatient with the thought that in a few years Turkey, by her own exertions, might escape their greed.

'The threat, though cunningly disguised, is now quite plain to all of us,' said Basri in conclusion. 'It forces us to give our chief attention to defence when, Allah knows, we wish to give it to improvement. It forces us to take strong measures, which seem tyrannous, instead of a slow course of education and persuasion. That is why Mahmud Shevket Pasha is working day and night at the War Office; and that is why you and a host of others are being sent to Macedonia to enforce disarmament. We cannot have armed bands so near the frontier. There are measures being taken which I do not like—for instance, to impose our Ottoman Turkish as the sole official language for all nationalities. But they are intended to produce a closer union hastily. Their authors own that they are hasty measures, but say that we must move in haste, since no one knows how short may be the time allowed to us. We need protection and we need financial help, and since the English, whom we like, will not encourage us, we have to turn towards people whom we rather hate.'

'Allahu akbar!' exclaimed Camruddin, who could not take a gloomy outlook in his month of leave. Going to Stamboul one day to pay his respects to Sâdik Pasha, who had been appointed Commandant of the city, he saw Dikran Efendi, his old teacher, who dinned into his ear the same misgivings, but declared that the Armenians and the Turks, together, could yet defeat the fiendish purpose of the Powers, if Mahmud Shevket Pasha were but made dictator. His confidence in Mahmud Shevket Pasha was unbounded, and it was shared by his community—so he averred—because His Excellency took a firm tone with the Armenian revolutionaries. Sâdik Pasha also shared the views of Basri Bey, expecting treachery from all the Powers. He spoke his mind to Camruddin without disguises, saying: 'I am for the Revolution now, and for this reason: that it has given a new spirit to our Muslim folk. The Franks are all against the New Turks as they were against the old. It is now evident that nothing we can do can change their enmity. Old and New Turk are therefore in the same position. It is a question of the last resistance of the Turkish race. Yet many of my former colleagues fail to see it. They blame the Committee for antagonising the Franks, although they knew well that in Sultan Hamid's reign they were no less our enemies. In those days we all thought the country doomed, and only laboured to postpone the end as long as possible. What reason have they, therefore, for supposing, as they now declare, that if they were in power again the Franks would help us? "In what way are we better for the Revolution?" they demand to know. I answer: "Hope. The Muslim peoples cannot now be crushed by conquest. They could have been in Sultan Hamid's time."'

'Allahu akbar!' murmured Camruddin.

As the conclusion of his leave drew near, the thought of parting from Gul-raaneh weighed on him. He would have liked to take her with him to his mother's house, where he could visit her more easily, but did not dare to mention the idea to her, because the village life was homely and her friends were in Stamboul. It was a glad surprise to him when she herself proposed it, saying,—

'I have never seen your mother nor your brethren, nor yet the orchard and the house of which you have so often told me. May I not go and visit your relations now that you duty takes you to your neighbourhood?'

'I may be there for years,' objected Camruddin.

'And would you leave me here alone for years?' replied Gul-raaneh.

Reshideh Hânum happened to be present when they broached the subject. This beautiful and wayward creature, Sâdik Pasha's eldest daughter, accorded Camruddin the status of a brother and unveiled for him because, she, laughing, said: 'Gul-raaneh was, in all save fact, her sister, and Camruddin might, in a sense, be called her father's son.' Seeing his surprise at this petition of Gul-raaneh, she exclaimed,—

'Camruddin Bey imagines you are loath to part from me, your sister, and the rest of those who love you … Indeed, you do not know this creature, Bey efendim! She cares for none of us in these days; she is a contentious Unionist, and argues with us till we cry out, for the sake of peace, that the Committee of Union and Progress is composed of hero-saints, unspotted by the world. And since she has her baby she is unassailable, retires behind that little Muslim as into a tower … O foolish man, can you not see that she is mad for you—would follow you to battle if she could?'

Gul-raaneh hung her head at this exposure, but when she showed her face again to Camruddin it wore a look of faith which quite transported him.

It was arranged that she should travel as far as Saloniki with the wife of Mustafa, for the sake of the attendance which that lady's wealth commanded; and Camruddin would afterwards secure a carriage in which she should pursue the journey to his native place.

These plans were carried out without a hitch; and it was a constant solace to the mind of Camruddin, engaged in arduous, distasteful work, to know her near at hand. The disarming of the Macedonians was not so pleasant an employment as had been the hunting of the brigands in the Khodavendkiar Hills; for here the population, if not hostile to the soldiers, felt aggrieved by their relentless search for weapons. The Bulgars raised the loudest protests and at times resisted, saying they had not joined the revolution to be thus rewarded; but the Greeks were infinitely worse to deal with, being sly. The troops were not enraptured with their task, but they performed it thoroughly, in spite of pitiful appeals from fellow-Muslims, who, declaring that a number of the Christians had concealed their weapons, implored to be allowed to keep some rifles for defence; and they had the consolation, if it could be called one, of knowing that their task was easy compared with that of Jâvid Pasha's army, which was forcing the Albanians to disarm by actual warfare.

Then suddenly there came the news that Italy, without excuse of any kind, had raided Tripoli, a Turkish province. Tremendous was the wave of indignation. In Macedonia there were hosts of volunteers—Christian no less than Muslim—eager to go and fight in Africa. The Italians might have overpowered the local garrison. They could not for a minute face the Turkish army. The presence of their fleet forbade sea-transport of the troops, but, praise to Allah, they could march by land through Turkish territory. Italy was now outside the law of nations. She had broken solemn pledges, and the Berlin treaty made by England. There was no doubt in anybody's mind but that at this juncture England, even if she remained neutral, would befriend the Turks. When it was known that England had forbidden Turkish troops to pass through Egypt, still a Turkish province, it was seen that she connived at the Italian crime, and there were cries of 'Treachery!' since but for that injustice Turkey would have won the war.

Chapter XXXV

CAMRUDDIN SAT in the orchard on a sunny afternoon, a book, which he had finished reading, in his hand, in council with his mother and Gul-raaneh. His brothers were about their work upon the farm. His younger child was in Gul-raaneh's lap; the elder played about under the trees chasing the bright-winged butterflies which came and went. He had been two years in Macedonia, yet Gul-raaneh had not once expressed a wish to leave that house. Now at last he was obliged to make new plans, for his career was broken.

As a result of the Parliamentary elections, the nominees of the Committee, who were blamed for the Italian War and for the hostile attitude of England, fell from power, which passed into the hands of the reactionary party. And one of the first acts of the new Government was to cashier all officers who were known to be strong partisans of the Committee, because, forsooth, they were concerned with politics, and replace them with men well affected to the old régime without regard to military fitness. The troops resented such an edict, and waited for a word from the Committee. But that word, when it came, enjoined submission for the public good. The men of the new Government were England's partisans; British intrigue had helped them to ascendancy; and therefore it was hoped that England would befriend the country while they were in power. England's protection was so great a benefit that, to secure it, party sentiment should be suppressed. Camruddin experienced the feelings of an eager rider thrown in mid-career. His comrade, Mustafa, was in the same predicament, having refused the favour offered to him by the new command. They had arranged to go together to Stamboul, where life was likely to be safer than in a provincial town for men suspected of dislike for the new Government; and where it might be possible for them to find employment.

The question now before the little council in the orchard was: should Gul-raaneh and the children go with Camruddin, or wait awhile? His mother, though averse to parting with them, held strongly that a wife should be obedient to her husband's will, and was amazed that Camruddin should leave it to Gul-raaneh's judgement. If she desired to travel to Stamboul at once, Selimeh Hânum would be glad for her companionship. If, on the other hand, she chose to wait awhile, himself might possibly return to fetch her in the autumn.

'I cannot think. I will obey your order,' sighed Gul-raaneh.

'I give no order. I desire your pleasure. Think and choose.'

'Gul-raaneh Hânum could take little Ali, leaving Mukerrem here with me and with his uncles,' the grandmother suggested. 'He would be a hostage to us for another sight of you.'

Gul-raaneh did not welcome the suggestion.

While they were debating, Lefteri, their Christian neighbour, came in sight and shouted for permission to approach. He came to warn them that some people in the village—shameless time-servers—had formed a plan to capture and imprison Camruddin.

'That settles it,' exclaimed Gul-raaneh. 'You must go without me, and this very night.'

She had drawn her veil at Lefteri's approach. She now rose up and moved towards the house, signing to Camruddin to follow her. Lefteri remained with the old woman, explaining the position in excited tones.

'I like not that old man, nor yet his warnings,' said Gul-raaneh, when she had her husband in the house. 'I heard from Melek how he plotted against Basri Bey, and I have seen the eyes of greed which he and his ill-mannered sons cast on this property. He is no friendly neighbour, as your mother thinks him. He, himself, is the inventor of this plot to harm you. He has come on in advance to watch you till the others come. Those others are already on the road. If I had led you towards the fields he would have made some protest. I led you to the house, which has no other door, that he might think you safe as in a trap. I also said that you would start to-night.'

'How can you know?' cried Camruddin, incredulous.

'I know: let that suffice! I feel it in my flesh. It is like that when one loathes a person as I loathe that Greek. Be guided by that instinct in me, soul of mine! Climb through this window where he cannot see you; I will follow. Then down the terraces as far as we can go, to shelter of the forest. I will see you safe upon your road, and then return. Oppose me not, beloved, for your life!'

After climbing through the window they stood still a moment, listening. There was a sound of many voices on the road which led up to the house.

'I knew it!' breathed Gul-raaneh. 'Oh make haste!' They ran together down the steep hill-side, till they were hidden in the brushwood far below.

'What of yourself?' asked Camruddin, when he had got his breath. 'How can I let you go and face those wolves, who will be sure that you have helped me to escape their villainy?'

'Fear not for me!' she answered, with a shrug. 'There are among them Muslims of a kind, which means they dare not touch a Muslim woman. And now, go on, my love, in Allah's keeping.'

When, having gone a little way, he turned for a last look, she waved her hand and cried: 'Long live the Constitution!'

It made him glad, remembering her old opinions. He had gone a long way ere he noticed that he still held, in his hand, the book he had been reading in the orchard. It was the poems of Namik Kemâl, a new edition from Stamboul, which Mustafa, who was himself a poet, had bestowed on him.

Chapter XXXVI

A FORTNIGHT LATER Camruddin was in Stamboul, surprised to find the city quite unaltered in appearance. Having sought for certain of his friends in vain in their accustomed haunts, he took the boat to Haïdar Pasha, and repaired to Ferid Bey's kiosk. That rich eccentric was at home and made him welcome, crying: 'Kerata! This is the day of resurrection. I had thought you dead.'

His talk was more satirical than ever. If, of old, he had been mildly sceptical of the perfections of the New Turk Party, he now was pitiless in his contempt for the reactionaries.

'Their work so far,' he told his friend with gusto, 'consists of persecuting Unionists and congratulating one another. They offer governments to every one they meet who is considered not averse to their opinions—though Allah alone knows what their opinions are beyond their jealous hatred of the Unionists. They offered *me* the government of Adana! They have formed a ministry which seems designed to furnish laughter to all future time. No minister is less than ninety years of age. They get entangled in each other's beards, and are too weak to extricate themselves. They weep till some one comes to put them right. Not one of them retains the use of all his faculties … Great names, they say, inspiring confidence in Europe! … I call them the Government of the Seven Sleepers.'

'They say that England will support them,' put in Camruddin.

'Well, some one must support them, for they cannot move alone.'

Camruddin asked for news of Basri Bey: he was in prison. Of the leaders, some had been arrested, some were hiding; none had yet been killed, so far as Ferid knew; but their acceptance of defeat had not preserved them from indignity and all the petty persecutions that weak malice can invent.

'They annoyed me often when in power, but now I side with them; for their successors are such wretched mountebanks,' said Deyli Ferid. Can a flea be the successor to a lion, or a gadfly to a hawk? … Words fail me to describe their dire inadequacy. But you shall see. There is a gathering to-morrow in one-eyed Zekki Pasha's garden. I am invited: you shall go with me. There you shall see their naked folly —may they all go blind!'

'What of your respected uncle, Sâdik Pasha?'

'My uncle holds aloof. He still performs his duty, but refuses to be drawn into their scramble for appointments. He calls himself a Unionist.'

'And what of Arif Hikmet Bey, the bimbashi?'

'Oh, he is now a General. I used to have respect for that poor man's intelligence; and when he turned against the Unionists, it swayed my judgement for a time. But now I see him joining hands with these impostors, acclaiming them as noble heroes fit to save the country. I can discern his weakness plainly: he is all conceit. Still, I consider him about the best of them.'

Camruddin now knew the speaker well enough to understand that his descriptions were not meant to be accepted literally. He thought it probable that those whom he depicted as so ludicrous were men of ordinary parts and fair behaviour. When he went with him to Zekki Pasha's garden party, it was not in expectation of a comical display. He was utterly amazed by what he saw and heard there.

These people had thrown decency aside. They triumphed openly, and spoke of the division of the spoils, laughing 'Ha, ha!' at the defeated Unionists. They bragged of the support of England, France, and Russia, and joked upon the low intrigues by which they had attained to power. They shouted, laughed, and clapped each other on the back, aping the manners of the Franks for the behoof of certain Frankish guests who were in company. All this amid the most appalling din that human ears had ever been obliged to tolerate; for Zekki Pasha, wishing to be in the fashion, had hired a Frankish band from Pera to make noises for his guests, and, for his own delight, a band of Turkish music, and both now played against each other in the great reception-room of the selamlik; while Zekki Pasha and his lady moved among the crowd explaining with complacent smiles: 'We have no prejudices. We are modern. We wish everybody to be pleased.' They encouraged Turkish ladies to come out unveiled among the men, crying in French repeatedly: 'nous sommes en famille—quoi?' But few women took the liberty, and those who did appeared so brazen in attempts to hide embarrassment that Camruddin was sore ashamed for them.

Bewildered and dismayed by that indecent spectacle, he went as far off as he could from it, and waited by the garden gate for Ferid Bey. While he stood there, a lady neatly veiled in black, with long white gloves, paused in her way out and said: 'How is Gul-raaneh Hânum?'

'Well, in sha'llah! I left her at the village, in my mother's care, efendim.'

'And the children?'

'Both quite well, in sha'llah.'

'What is the baby's name? She never told me in her letters.'

'His name is Ali Haïdar, efendim.'

'You have not yet recognised me, efendim. Yet you have seen my face unveiled. I call Gul-raaneh sister.'

'Now I know, efendim; you are Reshideh Hânum.'

I am Reshideh Hânum , and I really stopped to tell you that I am a Unionist.'

'Praise be to Allah! And since when, efendim?'

'Since I came inside this gate this afternoon.'

'I understand, efendim,' chuckled Camruddin.

'You do not understand, or you would hardly laugh. I am in deadly earnest,' said the lady.

She glided out as Ferid Bey approached, murmuring softly: 'Au revoir, monsieur!'

The little talk with her had gladdened Camruddin, abating something of the sense of banishment which had oppressed him since his parting from Gul-raaneh.

'Well, now, what think you of our present rulers?' inquired Ferid Bey. Without waiting for an answer he proceeded to describe in detail, with appropriate action, the various conversations he had held, or overheard, compelling Camruddin to laugh against his will. For Camruddin, the state of things which he had seen in that assembly was anything but laughable. He thought it tragic; and so indeed it proved for the unlucky Turkish Empire.

The wonderful success achieved by the New Turks

in their high-handed 'pacification' of Macedonia and
Albania had caused ill-feeling in the Balkan States, which
saw their long-watched prey escaping them. The danger
was appreciated in Stamboul, and for the past two years
a force sufficient to deter assailants had been kept manoeuvring in Thrace and Northern Macedonia through
the summer months. This year, before the New Turks fell
from power, sure word had been received of an alliance
of Serbs and Greeks and Bulgars under Russian patronage, made with the object of attacking Turkey ere she
grew too strong. Therefore, a somewhat stronger force
than usual had been brought to Thrace, and happened
to be there engaged in innocent manoeuvres when the
reactionaries came into office.

In the early summer the Russian Foreign Minister had
visited France and England, and held conversations with
the Foreign Ministers of both those countries. It seemed
hardly possible to Turkish statesmen that, in those conversations, he could fail to mention the Balkan alliance
made by Russia against Turkey. The Powers of Europe,
after that, presented a collective note to the Porte, pointing out that the large Turkish army, then manoeuvring
in Thrace, might be regarded as a menace by Bulgaria,
and assuring the Sultan's Government that no attack on
Turkey was intended or would be permitted. The new
Turkish Government accepted this assurance, and at
once dispersed the said army, most of its units being
sent to distant provinces. And even Unionists approved
that action of the Government, for England was among
the signatories of the diplomatic Note, and England
had intrigued, as everybody knew, to bring the present
Ministry (including the old fetish, Kiamil Pasha) into
power. 'England will protect her slaves assuredly,' said

Ferid Bey. 'I think it is likely the Entente meant mischief
to us in the spring, but, having got their own way here
meanwhile, they have decided to forgo their onslaught,
or at least postpone it. Russia, no doubt, deferred for
once to England, since the Turkish Empire had become
the latter's protégé and docile to the will of the Entente.'

The troops dispersed from Thrace had just had time
to make their way to distant provinces when the posture
of the Balkan States became plainly threatening that war
was seen to be inevitable. Camruddin wrote a letter to
Gul-raaneh, entreating her to join him in Stamboul at
once.

And then the idiocy of the men in power became apparent. Only the Unionists were conscious of the real
position of affairs. Only from them was heard the cry:
'We are betrayed!' The Government and its supporters
were enraptured with the thought of war. They bragged
beforehand of an easy victory. Their favourite General,
Nazim Pasha, whose bad habits were notorious and were
treated as a pleasant joke by all the party, was depicted
in a comic paper as a tourist, with a whisky-bottle in his
ulster pocket, asking at a railway booking-office for a cir-
cular ticket to Sofia, Belgrade, Cettinje, and Athens. And
except for all the foolish boasting, and some shouting in
the streets, nothing was done until the actual declaration
of war. The usual garrisons, comparatively strong towards
the Bulgarian frontier, and weak towards the Serbian
and the Greek, but slightly reinforced, were left to bear
the furious onslaught of the enemy. The news came from
Vienna that the Bulgars were in Kirk Kilisseh. Then there
was frantic energy and wild confusion. Troops, many of
them new recruits, were brought from anywhere, hastily armed and sent off to the front. The transport and

the commissariat broke down completely owing to the Government's expulsion of the New Turk officers, who knew the work and understood the men. Yet the reactionaries, in a frenzy at their own incompetence, blamed the New Turks for everything that was amiss. They had demoralised the men and wrecked the fabric of the army. The wildest and most contradictory charges were preferred against them. Mahmud Shevket Pasha was accused of having hidden his own plans for the defence of European Turkey, of having stolen them from the War Office. He was called a traitor to the country. As a proof of treason, his failure to come forward now and help the rulers out of their disgraceful muddle was adduced. Yet in the same breath the same men would deride him, dubbing him the merest smatterer, inferior to everybody you could mention in the art of war.

Camruddin returning from Stamboul upon the evening of the day of Kirk Kilisseh, said to Ferid Bey,—

'I cannot bear it any longer. I must volunteer. Three of us Unionist officers chanced to be together in the café when recruits were passing. We all rose up, with one accord, and swore to go and fight as private soldiers. Efendim, may the Lord of Right reward your kindness to me. When Gul-raaneh Hânum and my children come, I beg you to explain the reason of my absence, and direct them to the house of Shukri Bey. Reshideh Hânum offers hospitality.'

'No, that I will not! They shall come in here. My house is no less hospitable than my cousin Reshideh. I wish that I could go with you; but I have not the feeling. Am I a coward? It is not a pleasant thought.'

Upon a cloudless morning Camruddin, with Mustafa and Basri, went to Sultan Eyub to take the vow of holy warfare. The waters of the Golden Horn were sparkling in the sun. The mosques along the ridge of old Stamboul seemed each a diadem. In the precincts of a mosque with old trees shadowing its pretty courts and pigeons strutting on its pavements with soft music, they stood in prayer before the mausoleum of the Prophet's standard-bearer, and afterwards strolled up the hill among the crowd of tombs beneath the cypress-trees to take a long look from its summit at the sovereign city—the city of Islâm with all its domes and minarets, and all its cypress forests shading Muslim dead. And Camruddin was sad to think that he would miss Gul-raaneh and the children; for he was starting for the front that very day, and even if he saw them now they were forbidden to him by his vow.

Chapter XXXVII

AN UNDULATING plain, of which the surface seemed to have been cracked and split across in places, forming strange winding gullies, underneath a lowering sky from which the rain had but that minute ceased to fall; with puffs of whitish smoke appearing and disappearing everywhere and smoke in all the creases of the land; a splattering sound which seemed quite unconnected with the smoke-bursts, and now and then a thud which shook the ground; a wagon with dead horses stranded in the foreground, and all about the distance little squads of men dispersing and assembling aimlessly, stooping to run and lying down for no apparent reason: that was the battlefield of Luleh Burgas as Camruddin and his companions first beheld it.

Told off to join the Kastamûni régiment, they had been packed into a train full of recruits, who had little of the soldier in appearance or behaviour beyond their rifles and equipment and such bits of uniform as had been thrust on them in haste before they started for the front. The train had travelled with them slowly for three hours, when they were all turned out and told to march for the remainder of the way. The officer who gave the order pointed the direction but stayed by the train. And so that herd of inexperienced men, bewildered, heartsick, set off without a properly appointed leader. But they were dutiful and anxious to do right. When those around him found that Camruddin knew more than they did, they said: 'He knows his business. Follow him!' and from that time obeyed his orders without question. It was the same with Basri and Mustafa. More leaderless recruits in the villages upon the road adhered to them, and it was with the human material from a battalion that they came at length in sight of Luleh Burgas, on the morning of the third day of the battle. The three ex-officers had been at pains to make a list of all the various units to which the men they brought with them were posted, and this they offered to the first high officer they met. He answered,—

'Empty words! Allah alone knows where to find these units, if they still exist. My advice to you is, stay together, and go down there. The General Staff should be in that direction somewhere.'

'By Allah! Let us keep together,' sighed the men contentedly. 'We are happy as we are, and we now know each other.'

Suddenly, in a sheltered dell, they came upon field-kitchens smoking, and a store of food in charge of a small guard of commissariat men. With praise to Allah, they ran forward. But the men in charge of the encampment waved them off, inquiring,—

'Are you the Trebizond brigade?'

They answered: 'No.'

'Then you have no right here. This food is for the Trebizond brigade. It is our painful duty to preserve it for them. We grieve the more because we have been here for some time and cannot hear of them, and some part of the food is spoilt already, Yet all day long we have to send away poor hungry fellow-creatures such as you.'

'Give us the spoilt food. It is good enough.'

'No, that we cannot either, for we must account for all of it. Our officer is strict, and it is all predestined for the men of Trebizond and no one else.'

'Suppose that you are overpowered and robbed of some of it!' suggested Mustafa.

'Ah, that would make a difference. It would be from Allah. But we should require a paper from the robbers as certificate.'

'Well, we are forty to one. We overpower you. And I myself will write you the certificate.'

The guardians of the food accepted the idea in theory, but in practice would concede but spoilt or broken victuals. The starving, mud-bespattered men, however, accepted the concession as a mighty boon, and gave much thanks to Mustafa who had secured it for them. While they were eating, a shell exploded near them, and a man exclaimed: 'The heathen envy us!' arousing general laughter.

Proceeding on their way with due precautions, for there was death on every yard of open ground, they saw in a depression of the land a mounted officer careering madly, who reigned in his horse at sight of them and shouted: 'Up and line that brow! And hold it! Hold it! For the love of Allah!'

The men ran forward to the rise in question, and lay down. And all that day, in spite of inexperience, in spite of losses, hunger and fatigue, they held that ground against the enemy. And when at last the order reached them to retire because they were already more than half-surrounded, they performed a very difficult manoeuvre perfectly. Handling them in action Camruddin could scarce believe them the same men, who, on the march, had seemed deficient both in spirit and initiative.

At night they came by chance to a divisional head-quarters, where they were given one day's rations and were told to march towards Cherken-keuy.

'But we are men of different regiments,' protested Mustafa.

'We have no properly appointed officers,' protested Basri.

'What matter?' said the aide-de-camp who was concerned with them. 'Since you have formed a fighting unit which can hold together. The regiments are not much better; they seem all mixed up. The Government has ruined everything with its accursed politics, dismissing from the service hundreds of our finest officers. If some of those dismissed had not turned up again disguised as private volunteers, the army's case would be much worse to-night.' The aide-de-camp bestowed a knowing smile on Mustafa.

The retirement of the Turks upon Chatalja has been represented by those who witnessed the return of bands like that of Camruddin, composed of raw recruits, imperfectly equipped, hungry, and splashed with mud, who but the day before had come to join their regiments but had failed to find them. In fact, the three days stand at Luleh Burgas and the subsequent withdrawal to the line of forts across the isthmus, were part of a considered plan made long before by von der Golz against the very circumstances which were now occurring. The Turkish force which fought at Luleh Burgas consisted of the framework of an army, only half filled in; and all the time the battle was in progress fresh drafts to dill the frame kept pouring up. Failing to find at once their proper units, they joined the first encountered, or formed new fighting bands like that of Camruddin. But all, when they arrived upon the scene and found a battle raging, bore their part in it. The army, though thus incomplete, succeeded in its purpose, which was to check the Bulgars for a time sufficient for the next step in the programme, the concentration on the isthmus by Constantinople, where the Bulgarian army broke on the Chatalja lines. The step to follow that—advance in strength—was never made, because the Turkish Government, deriving all its war news from the press of Europe, believed the story of a rout; and, being feeble, and by then demoralised, sued for an armistice. And after the New Turks returned to power, in January, the condition of the country, under water, made advance impossible.

Camruddin's men, upon the march back to Chatalja, were good children. In a Christian village where they begged for food the doors were shut against them with foul words. They only shrugged and murmured: 'It is our appointed lot,' with no idea of taking vengeance for such churlishness. Only when the Chatalja guns began to roar at the approaching Bulgars did they recover their energy and warlike spirit; and by that time they were scattered, having joined their own battalions. Camruddin, Mustafa and Basri fought side by side as private soldiers of the Kastamûni régiment throughout the series of Bulgarian assaults, until the enemy had learnt his lesson and held off at last. Then Camruddin was past the knowledge of events. His friends conveyed him to 'the house of groans,' as it was called; and when they left him, said: 'Allah have mercy on him!' They believed him dying.

When he regained his senses he was being carried on a stretcher—one of a long procession of such cases— over barren land on which the sun shone fitfully through driving clouds. Beside the muddy road, at intervals, lay writhing human forms, and human corpses horribly contorted. He turned inquiringly to one beside him, who, seeing the direction of his gaze, made answer with a shrug and smile,—

'It is the cholera. But Allah is just. The Bulgars, too, have got it. It is all quite fair.'

Then Camruddin lost consciousness again.

Chapter XXXVIII

THE NEXT scene Camruddin perceived was a large shadowy room, with beds upon the floor, on one of which he lay. A voice beside him said,—

'You are awake at last, I see, praise to Allah. Do you remember me?'

The speaker was the tenant of the nearest bed. His voice was weak.

Camruddin could not remember anything except that there was something wrong with his left side and arm.

His neighbour mentioned who he was—a leading light of the Committee and a former Minister, wounded while fighting as a private soldier at Chatalja. The tale aroused no wonder in the mind of Camruddin.

'My left arm feels peculiar,' he observed at length.

'Ay,' said the other with compassion, 'so it must. May Allah compensate you for the loss of it!'

'Then they have amputated?'

'Before yesterday.'

'Allah is merciful!'

Camruddin closed his eyes and lay a moment silent, getting used to the idea. At length he sighed: 'It was written that this, too, should come upon my head. Better the left arm than the right. Praise be to Allah!'

After that he exchanged occasional remarks with his illustrious neighbour, but it was long before he was sufficiently alive to ask for tidings of the war. Then he was told how Macedonia had been overrun by Greeks and Serbs, and the vision of the little farm beside the orchard in the pleasant valley came to haunt him, with cruel apprehensions for his family. He thought: 'Praise be to Allah that I wrote in time to save Gul-raaneh and the children from so fierce a trial.'

When the old army doctor came his rounds that night, he begged him of his kindness to ask Ferid Bey to pay a visit to the hospital. The doctor's answer was uncertain; he was very busy; and Camruddin was still too listless to insist. It was, therefore, a surprise to him when in the morning he heard the voice of Deyli Ferid in the room.

A minute later he lay stiff and gasped for breath. It was as if he had been bashed upon the head and stabbed in the same moment. Gul-raaneh and the children had not come. No letter had arrived. There was no news of them.

'But that is nothing wonderful,' said Ferid Bey consolingly, 'for no news, whatsoever, comes from the lost provinces. Nor is it a matter for despair, for it is known that a vast crowd of Muslim refugees is now encamped at Saloniki under supervision of the Powers. Some whom their relations had counted dead have turned up safe and sound here in Stamboul already. Take comfort, O my soul, for there is room for hope!'

Camruddin said nothing for a space, then in a voice half-choked, he cried: 'Those filthy Greeks!' His brain was throbbing painfully; he saw and tasted blood. He feared that he was going to have a fit of some kind and, by a mighty effort, kept quite still and fixed his thoughts on Allah till his rage subsided, when he murmured,—

'But they will be turned out again. The English said so. Their statement said that neither side would be allowed to keep its conquests.'

'Ah, that was while they still imagined we might win,' said Ferid, with a bitter laugh. 'To-day the case is altogether different. "Our Christian brothers must on no consideration be deprived of lands they have so nobly liberated." You can guess the jargon.'

'How many unarmed Muslims slaughtered?' inquired Camruddin.

'Allah best knows! They say five hundred thousand,' answered Ferid, with another shrug and laugh.

'And they have taken all our splendid roads, new schools, and public works of all kinds,' said a voice from the next bed. 'All built with Turkish money, Turkish thought, and energy, within the last four years. We began our work with Macedonia that the Powers might see. And now they take it all, yet they will go on saying: "The Turk does not make roads; he has no care for education. The Young Turks talk, but they do nothing"—all the usual lies.'

'Oh are *you* there, efendim? I did not see your Excellency,' exclaimed Deyli Ferid rather dryly. 'It seems that you have fallen a long way since we last met.'

'Nearly beneath the ground, and yet not quite, efendim. I still may live to make another fight, in sha'llah!'

The ex-Minister and Ferid fell into the half-satiric conversation of enemies who meet by chance on peaceful ground; but Camruddin could give no thought to what they said. His mind was full of poor Gul-raaneh and the children, his mother, and his brethren, and the havoc of his native land. When Ferid Bey had gone he lay consumed with grief, rejecting food and half resolved to die. It was two years before he could regain his equanimity, and say without a vestige of rebellious impulse,—

'It was written that this, too, should come upon my head.'

When at last he was discharged from hospital—a one-armed man who hobbled in his gait—and once more took up his abode at Ferid Bey's kiosk, his first thought was to seek for tidings of Gul-raaneh. Wherever in the city and its suburbs there were refugees from the lost provinces, he went and chatted with the men, listening to their tales of horror and of ruin; while his sister Melek, in the same anxiety, sought among the women for some clue which he might follow up. But very few if those with whom they spoke were from their province, and none of them from the immediate region of their native place.

At length, one evening, he was told that refugees from Macedonia had arrived, and were being sheltered in the mosque of Aya Sofia; whither he betook himself without delay. The pavement of the great porch, dimly lighted, was covered with a crowd of wretched people, and their few belongings wrapped in bundles. Most of them lay asleep, or sat in weary attitudes with faces hidden in their hands. Here and there a mother rocked a squalling baby, or a man endeavoured to amuse some restless child. Camruddin passed among them, speaking words of comfort, and distributing the gift of food which he had brought with him. Suddenly he gave a gasp and hurried forward. He had caught sight of a face familiar to him. It was that of an old man whom he had known from child-hood, the muleteer of his own village, by name Ahmed. He went and touched him on the shoulder. The old man looked up.

'What news for me?' Camruddin whispered eagerly.

'For whom, efendim?' inquired Ahmed, staring hard at him. Then, seeing it was Camruddin, the son of

Mehmed, a compatriot shorn of an arm, he dropped his eyes and hung his head—the picture of despair. 'May Allah comfort you my soul!' was all he said.

Camruddin gave a groan, then murmured 'Allah! Allah!' After a moment he sat down on the pavement close to the old man, and both kept silence. Camruddin was first to speak.

'Vouchsafe the story, brother,' he said huskily.

'It is short as death,' the other answered, raising both his hands and letting them fall slowly to his knees again. 'While yet we knew not whether to believe or disbelieve the talk of an invasion, a band of Greek marauders came into our village, and told us that the Greek king was triumphant and we were conquered dogs, and other insults. They bade us, if we wished to save our lives, hand over all our money, arms, and valuables. And when we had done that, then they began to torture us, the Greeks of our own neighbourhood directing them, the treacherous swine! Omar Ayha, whom you know, was done to death by torture, after they had ravished his wife and daughters in his sight, and killed them and their children, one by one, disgustingly … Alas, the day! But we are Muslims and resign our cause to Allah … The wicked sons of Lefteri it was who led the evil-doers to your honoured house, which else might have escaped, for it is off the road. Those scoundrels coveted the property. Only poor landless men like me were left alive—after they had heaped indignities upon us. I do not know exactly what befell, but we, who fled, could hear the shrieking down the valley; and Izzuddin, the smith, who joined us afterwards, said that they were all slain, your venerable mother and your brothers and the gracious Hânum and the little ones. He told me he had overheard some Greeks complaining that the pretty Hânum killed herself before they got to her. They tore her baby from her arms, and when she saw that she could no longer save him, then she killed herself.'

'Praise be to Allah!' exclaimed Camruddin, on a deep breath.

'She stabbed herself with a poniard, so he heard them say.'

'That poniard was a gift from me,' said Camruddin.

'As for the children, they made sport with them, then cut them into bits.'

'Allah! Allah!'

'Your aged mother and brothers struggled, so were slain the first. That is what I have been told, efendim, by Izzuddin, the smith, the man you know … Vâh! Vâh! All the best and noblest of our people were destroyed thus cruelly. Only old, worthless creatures like myself survive. I have been wondering why I should be kept alive, who have no longer any pleasure in the world; but now I think I know: it was that I might tell your honour that the lady killed herself.'

'Allah have mercy upon her and us, and on all true believers!' murmured Camruddin.

Chapter XXXIX

THE REACTIONARIES, though discredited and hated by the people, were still in power, only because the Committee of Union and Progress, which remained as strong as ever, wanted a good excuse to cast them out. But they were so little conscious that their tenure had become precarious that they still behaved with the extreme of arrogance to their opponents. One day, a number of distinguished Unionists, who for weeks past had been living under vexatious surveillance, were summoned to the Porte in order to comply with some new rule regarding registration of suspected persons. They were bidden wait outside the building until summoned. The place was windy, and the day was cold. Wrapping their cloaks about them, they walked up and down, stamping their feet and striking their hands together to keep warm. At length one, looking at his watch, exclaimed: 'We have been waiting here an hour. It is too much. Are we then dogs, to be thus disregarded?'

They were all men well and honourably known, who held power and still could boast of influence. They looked at one another and observed their goodly number.

'Suppose we go in and demand an audience!' some one suggested. 'They can do nothing to so large a company.'

No sooner said than done: they all trooped forward. A sentry challenged them, and when they took no notice lowered his bayonet. One of them bared his breast and walked straight up to it, daring him to kill a true defender of Islâm. The sentry recognised the speaker as a hero of the Revolution, and brought his rifle up to the 'Present' instinctively.

Inside the building the attendants tried to stop them, but they still advanced, the scandalised ushers followed them in remonstrance. The Government had sent for them, they said, and they had come. The clamour of this altercation, near the room in which the Cabinet was sitting, brought Nazim Pasha out into the passage in a towering rage. He was a cavalry officer, and had a cavalry officer's command of language when infuriated. Fixing his eyes upon a young man, whom he knew by sight, he called him a foul name, made an obscene remark about his mother, and bade him stop his noise or it should be the worse for him. In the twinkling of an eye the young man thus insulted drew out a pistol from beneath his cloak, and fired. The Minister of War collapsed upon the door mat.

That accident, which cut off their retreat, decided them. A few rushed off to bear the tidings that the revolution was in progress to the adjacent mosques and to the University, while the remainder strode into the room and faced the Ministers, who strove to hide as best they could behind the furniture. There was an anxious interval, which seemed an age to everybody in that room but in reality did not exceed a quarter of an hour, before the noise of popular rejoicing informed them that the revolution was secure. One of the demonstrators opened a window in the passage and looked out. Khôjas and theological students were chanting praise to Allah, and haranguing a delighted crowd which every minute grew more dense and numerous. He closed the window and reported to his comrades, who, having locked up the ex-Ministers for the time being, were gathered round the corpse of Nazim Pasha with sad faces, for the man, though a gross liver, had not been disliked. There were sighs of 'Allah have mercy on him!' One exclaimed: 'A bad day's work.' This futile sympathy attacked the nerves of the young man who had performed the deed in vengeance for a foul and deadly insult. When one said: 'It is not seemly he should be left lying here,' that young man seized the body roughly, and had dragged it some way down the corridor before the others realised what he was doing, and enjoined due reverence. Soon after that, having appointed certain of their number to keep going the machinery of government, most of the demonstrators went to their respective homes. The revolution was accomplished. The next step, the choosing of a Ministry, concerned not them, but certain thoughtful men who sought no office, the Committee of Control.

It was no longer possible for the Young Turks to work with extinct luminaries of the old régime like Kiamil Pasha, who had shown themselves opposed to the ideals of the Revolution. For the first time they had to form a Government from their own ranks. They had but one great man whom Europe recognised, and he, as usual, was averse to taking office. It is said that the Committee had to threaten him with violence before they could persuade him to accept the post of Grand Vizier, or even to admit their claim that he was eminently fitted for it. However that may be, it is quite certain that he accepted the supreme position most reluctantly, begging to be allowed to serve in one less prominent. But accept he did at last; and when the name of Mahmud Shevket Pasha was published as the head of the new Ministry, the country breathed once more with hope and confidence.

The State was bankrupt. The whole Civil Service had been unpaid for months. Yet somehow public credit was restored; nor only that, but something of the first enthusiasm of the revolution thrilled the people once again. The change, if gradual, was rapid. In a very few weeks' time the chaos and confusion in the army and the public service disappeared. Rules which had weighed too heavily upon the people were relaxed judiciously, and edicts were promulgated, pending the consent of Parliament, which relieved the suffering classes of the population of such grievances. Instead of crowds of ragamuffin conscripts, troops, well-equipped and drilled, poured steadily into the capital and on to Chatalja, while large, well-ordered camps were formed at Scutari, San Stefano, and other points upon the coasts of Asia and of Europe. Ministers agreed to take but one-third of their salaries. The civil service made no fuss about the arrears of pay; the very poor subscribed a portion of their wages to the cause of national defence; the people did not count its sacrifices, now that hope returned. Again there was the eager thirst for education and improvement, of public works and purity in the administration which had marked the birth of the new order. And the Young Turks were for the first time able to support this movement by effective legislation. After the revolution of June, 1908, reform on certain lines became a popular ideal; after the revolution of January, 1913, it became law. And all these orderly and hopeful currents emanated from one man, but seldom seen, a quiet, anxious man, who worked both day and night, spending his time between his office at the Sublime Porte and his office at the Ministry of War.

And Turkey looked once more to England, not with confident devotion, as at first, but with some expectation of purchasing effective help from that Power by great concessions. In order to secure ten years of peace, and expedite the vast reforms they had in view, the New Turks were willing to accept a British dictator and British instructors in every department of the State. It was considered that their recent turn to Germany had been the cause of England's evident displeasure of the last few months. Germany had failed to ward off from them the disasters of the Tripolitan and Balkan Wars. And Germany was no disinterested friend, as England might be. She had designs, which every one could see. So even after the first overture had been rebuffed, they went on making offers to the British Government.

There were critics of this policy who said that England had become no more than a fat tail to Russia, but even they agreed that it was wise to try it, though they deemed it sure to fail. These held that the Entente was pledged to destroy Turkey, and therefore Germany was now their only hope. When it was known that England had consented to provide inspectors to supervise the new reforms in Eastern Anatolia, the British party triumphed, and the German shrugged.

'They say that England is to-day a third-class Power immovably attached to Russia,' explained Basri Bey, in Ferid Bey's selamlik, referring to the cavillings of the pro-Germans. 'I cannot think it so bad as that. With all her wealth and territory, and her navy, she is surely strong enough to take an independent line of policy, and we can make it worth her while to do so.'

'I put no trust in any Christian Power,' sneered Deyli Ferid. 'They hate us so that they would see us all exterminated, or why should they let loose their savages upon us, and be always deaf when we cry out to them for justice? Do they not know that every Christian rising in our country means horrible extermination of the Muslim folk? If their intention was to rob us of our land and not our lives, they would set about the work with Western armies under discipline, and not suborn their bloody Greeks and Serbs and Bulgars. England is not better than the other Powers. All Christian peoples are, I think, at heart, mere murderous fanatics, spurred by greed of gain. Their civilisation is but that of wealthy rogues who hire another man to do their killing for them.'

There was a good deal more of passion in this speech than usually seasoned the remarks of Ferid Bey. Under his cynic's robe there was a tender heart, and the sad fate of Camruddin's relations had distressed him greatly.

'They are not all so bad as that, in sha'llah!' chuckled Basri, regarding the denunciation of the Christians as a joke, since no one could imagine Ferid as fanatical.

It would have been, of course, impossible for any nation to undergo the treatment which the Turks had met with since the Revolution with temper altogether unimpaired. There were some men, by nature purely imitative—the same who at first had wished to imitate the manners of the Franks too closely—who now, perceiving that unbridled nationalism was beloved of Europe, turned from the Muslim aim at universal brotherhood and remembered that they, too, possessed a nationality. They were members of a nation numbering some fifty million souls, whose lands extended from the Chinese frontier to the Mediterranean. Having seen how kindly treason, armed conspiracy, massacre and mutilation, rape and wholesale plunder were winked at by the

Powers when perpetrated in the name of nationality and independence by the Balkan Christians, they talked complacently of using the same methods to assert and advertise the human rights of Muslim Turks wherever found, and so retaliating upon Russia.

'For the Christians we do not exist,' they argued. 'because our nationality is merged in El Islâm. But let us only say we act as Turks upon behalf of fellow-Turks who are oppressed and sorrowing, and then at once they will be interested in our undertaking and allow our claims.'

But people who talked thus were few, and were regarded by the general public as insane.

'We have outgrown all that iniquity,' said Basri, who liked to talk of all these things at Ferid Bey's kiosk, where he found ready listeners. 'The Prophet himself abolished nationality, and denounced their narrow patriotism as a crime against mankind at large. And so it is, for see the misery that it has caused. Ah, the Christians boast of their mechanical improvements. But we are thirteen hundred years ahead of them in honest thought.'

Chapter XL

CAMRUDDIN spoke little in those days, nor did he always seem to hear when others spoke to him. With the return of spring the grief, which he had scarcely felt before in the benumbed condition of his brain, came on him overwhelmingly. Maimed though he was, he wanted to rejoin the army at the front, but leave to do so was refused him till his health improved. The distant roar of the Chatalja guns, heard in the peace of Deyli Ferid's garden, tormented him with longing for the hard routine, the nervous strain, the great fatigue which bring forgetfulness. But he was still too weak for much exertion, though no longer lame. Borrowing a heavy sporting gun of Ferid Bey's, he practised firing with the drawback of his mutilated arm and for the first time, since his great bereavement, really smile when he was able to inform his host that he had overcome the difficulty.

On a fine spring morning he was taken out in Ferid's carriage to a meadow bordering a brook well fringed with willows, which at that season was a place of popular resort for Turkish people, idyllic in their love of running water, flowers, and greenery. A shanty tent for the sale of home-made sweets and sherbet had been set up in a corner of the field, where there were chairs and stools for the repose of customers, and two large squares of gaily covered carpet for the women and old-fashioned people who sit cross-legged.

Camruddin was lying on the bank beside the stream, watching the ripples where a hanging branch opposed the rush of water, when a lady, elegantly veiled, drew near and said,—

'Tell me the truth about Gul-raaneh, Bey efendim.'

'Efendim, I would rather not,' he answered huskily.

The sunshine through the young leaves of the willows made green fire.

'Nay, tell me; it will ease your soul and mine,' she said, 'for I am Reshideh, her comrade, and I loved her dearly.'

Her manner was so sweet and winning, and her tone so kind that the hard edge of sorrow melted as ice melts beneath the sun. His tears fell freely as he told her all he knew. At the conclusion she said simply: 'She died well. Allah have mercy on her!'

She stood with one hand resting on a trunk of willow, at a distance of five feet from where he sat. After a space of silence she resumed in accents of compassion: 'And you have lost an arm, efendim, and your face is pale and thin. Great though your cause of grief, it is not well that you should pine in recollection when Islâm and our unhappy country need you, and every single-hearted Muslim like you, for defence. We now enjoy a little respite, for that cannonade will not destroy us.' She pointed towards the west, in which direction a dull, booming sound was heard at intervals. 'But I am certain there is worse to come. The enmity of Europe towards us has been plainly shown.

'Now, hear my story. Shukri Bey was killed at Luleh Burgas. I am now a widow—no longer the wild, forward creature that I was of old, when dear Gul-raaneh used to be my confidante. I know the grief which stops the breath and stills the heart. Efendim, it is in my mind that if I wed again, I shall not choose a gallant youth like Shukri Bey, whose memory is with me always in my heart, but some poor stricken hero of my country, whom my beauty perhaps may console a little and my wealth relieve, while he can guide my children and be my protector. Efendim, I am making a proposal to you; are you listening? It is a proposal that I would not make to any other man. I know no other men, but you I know, from the report of dear Gul-raaneh, to be trustworthy. And I have always from my girlhood had an admiration for you because of the heroic stories that my father used to tell us of your conduct in his regiment in the Arab wars. I do not look upon you as a stranger. Think the matter over. I have three children whose light-hearted talk will be good medicine for a mind oppressed with memories.'

There was a pause ere Camruddin replied: 'I offer thanks, efendim,' too much surprised to think at all connectedly.

'I ask not for an answer now,' she murmured, as she moved away: 'but think of it, and if the offer proves acceptable upon reflection, write to me.'

'Efendim, I am highly honoured!'

She was gone. The daylight had acquired new lustre in his eyes; the colours of the scene were brighter and more definite; the forms and voices of the pleasure-seekers had grown sympathetic. He had seen nothing clearly since his great affliction until now. It seemed a miracle that Reshideh Hânum—the daughter of the man he most respected, the delicate and lovely creature whose refinement awed him; the lady whom Gul-raaneh had admired above all others —should think of him, the son of Macedonian peasants, a one-armed man, no longer in the flush of youth. He rendered thanks to Allah.

But before he wrote to her, accepting her proposal, he felt in duty bound to call on Sâdik Pasha, and submit the matter to his judgement. He feared lest his old General should be angry at his daughter's whim; but he was quite unshaken by the news which Camruddin revealed with trepidation. He clapped his former chaûsh upon the shoulder, saying kindly,—

'In Yemen I did promise thee a daughter of my house in marriage, and at the moment of the promise I believe I meant a daughter of my body, so great was my delight with thy behaviour on that day. But when I saw thee there at Saloniki, in so poor a guise, I thought a girl attendant much more suitable, knowing that my inner meaning at the time was hid from thee, and knowing also that my daughter would have scorned thee wrongly, even if the only one remaining in my house had been of marriage-able age, which she was not. Now by thy conduct thou hast earned the greater favour and I would give it were it mine to give. My daughter Reshideh has chosen wisely: tell her that.'

Thenceforward Camruddin improved in health so rapidly that Ferid Bey and all his friends remarked upon the change, with praise to Allah. He once more took an interest in conversations.

Arif Hikmet was for weeks the guest of Ferid Bey, who quarrelled with him daily over politics. He had become a deadly enemy of the Committee, prayed for the overthrow of the Young Turks, and spoke of Nazim Pasha as a holy martyr whose death should be avenged a thousandfold. Ferid Bey opposed him in those views; and arguments between them always ended in the question which was madder of them two, which they debated hotly. Then Arif Hikmet disappeared one day. There was a plot on foot to reinstate old Kiamil Pasha; the police were active; and Arif Hikmet was suspected of a leading part in the conspiracy.

'He is a born conspirator,' said Ferid Bey, 'and Allah knows it would be better if they put an end to him. And yet I cannot wish it; he amuses me. Now he is hiding somewhere —in disguise, no doubt. He always had a passion for most strange disguises. I wish that I could see him but a minute. He is as funny as a Kara-gyuz, though he does not suspect it. Of one thing be assured: if this plot is exploded, he is at work upon another, more terrific. What I do not like is his recourse to foreign Powers. I know that he frequents the Russian embassy, like the worst of our old gang of public malefactors. He even dared to tell me that the Russians are to-day our friends—an insult to my common sense which I cannot forgive.'

Another old acquaintance came to talk with Camruddin in the person of Dikran Efendi, his old teacher, whom he met one noonday in a bookshop in Stamboul and asked to visit him. The Armenian was now hopeful for the empire—what remained of it. All the Franks, he said, were cunning villains; all the Greeks and Serbs and Bulgars fiends incarnate. But the Armenians and the Turks were still together; and they had a MAN.

'It all depends upon that man,' said Dikran with excited gestures. 'He is a marvel, the chief glory of the age. Only see what he has done in these few months and with no money. In sha'llah, he will save us from the greed of Russia. He protects our people both against Armenian revolutionaries —all in the pay of Russia—and against the stupid Muslims who, embittered by the crimes of a small section, confound the righteous with the wicked and curse all Armenians. In Eastern Anatolia he is working wonders by his influence, as I hear through my community. The Russian malefactors are all closely shadowed, and he has got his hand on all the threads of their intrigue. A mighty man! The Lord preserve him to us!'

One day he travelled out to Ferid Bey's kiosk, on purpose to tell Camruddin a piece of news which he had heard 'through his community.' The Russians had suborned some lawless Kurds to make a massacre. They gathered in a certain town, in various disguises, for that purpose. But Mahmud Shevket Pasha, through his agents on the Russian side had wind of their intention. He warned the governor and the police by telegram, with the result that, at the very moment of beginning their atrocious work, they found themselves surrounded by the Sultan's troops. Most of them were captured; but a few escaped, and these fled straight for refuge to the Russian consulate—'a slight embarrassment for Holy Russia,' chuckled the narrator. 'Now hear the cream of the whole incident. The Tiflis newspapers, which are the organ of Armenian traitors in the pay of Russia, not knowing that the project has miscarried, publish an account of with the horrid details of the massacre which had been planned but which did not take place. And Mahmud Shevket Pasha receives copies of those papers. He now has them in his hands. I myself have the honour to be chosen in the Ministry to make translations of their contents into French and Turkish. He has now sufficient evidence to make what he has long been contemplating: an appeal to the whole civilised world against the crimes of Russia. My friend, I hope as I have never hoped before. He is a great man. He will save us all, in sha'llah!'

Ferid was so much pleased with the enthusiasm of the fat Armenian that he made him stay to supper at the house, and afterwards conveyed to him in his carriage as far as to the landing-stage at Cadi-keuy.

'He might be right,' he said to Camruddin, when they discussed him afterwards; 'but I should be afraid if I were Mahmud Shevket Pasha. That evidence of which he speaks is a live bomb, extremely dangerous to handle.'

Chapter XLI

THE WEDDING of Camruddin and Reshideh Hânum was to be private, as became the widowed state of both of them, and quite without festivities of any kind. Upon the day appointed for the solemnising of the marriage contract he went to mosque as usual to perform the noonday act of worship. He was returning down the avenue of spreading mulberry trees which scattered shade upon the road which led to Ferid Bey's kiosk when, at a corner, he collided with an officer in uniform. This officer was in a hurry—an unusual case. Both had embarked upon a torrent of apologies and the officer was hurrying on, ere, recovering from the shock, perceived that it was Basri Bey, his brother-in-law. His cry of recognition brought the other back, without the air of haste which had till then disfigured him.

'I was on the way to visit you, my soul,' he said dejectedly. 'You cannot yet have heard the news … An awful tragedy! Mahmud Shevket Pasha has just been assassinated. He was on his way as usual, at the fifth hour of the day, from the Ministry of War to the Sublime Porte, in his motor-car, when, in the square before the mosque of Sultan Bayazid, just by the fountain, his car was forced to stop by some obstruction of the road. At once, as at a signal, five men rushed out from behind the fountain, sprang on to the step on either side and fired point-blank at him. It is said that they fired fifty bullets. The aide-de-camp who flung himself across His Highness to protect him was killed at once. The Grand Vizier expired some twenty minutes later in the lobby of the Ministry of War. The murderers, who had another motor-car in waiting, jumped into it and drove off like the wind … They say there is a plot to slaughter all our men. Allah forbid! We have already lost the flower of them —Niazi, Hasan Riza, and now Mahmud Shevket.'

'Allah have mercy on him!' murmured Camruddin, in deep concern.

They went together to the house of Ferid Bey, who, having heard the tiding just before they entered, smote his thigh, exclaiming,—

'Kerata! I am henceforth a Unionist. May every foreign diplomat go blind! May Russia burst!'

'The deed was done by Turks, efendim,' murmured Basri sadly.

'Of course, it always is. But who incites them? Say, have we ever had a man of real power whom they allowed to live? The Russian embassy is but an agency for organising murder and sedition in this luckless country. May Arif Hikmet rot, and all men of his kidney. It is now seen what they are. I wash my hands of them.'

'It is the beginning of the end, I fear,' sighed Basri Bey. 'Allah has turned His face from us,' exclaimed a servant of the house.

The khôja who gave lessons to the sons of Ferid Bey and kept watch on their conduct, rebuked their tone of conversation mildly, saying,—

'We see but the externals of this mortal life, and for a little while. What can we comprehend of Allah's purpose? But this at least is manifest in Scripture: that misfortune is a state more hopeful than prosperity, if men be staunch and persevere in righteous action.'

'Or do you think that you shall enter Paradise ere that, which came to those before you, has befallen you? Misfortune and calamity assailed them, they were shaken, as by an earthquake, so that the apostle and those with him questioned: "When comes Allah's help? Now truly Allah's help is very nigh." Allah's help comes in the hour of man's despair, to men who, notwithstanding persevere. My brothers, we have suffered much, but much remains to us. Our state can nowise be compared to that of the Messenger of Allah (may God bless and keep him) in those days at Mecca when old friends derided him, and all the happiness and the success, which he had found in life, seemed past. He looked back to the former portion of his life as to a period of happiness, light which never could return, for he was nearing fifty. His sole support was in the inspiration Allah sent to him; and for a time that also was withdrawn. He was disconsolate. The heathen, his opponents there in Mecca, mocked him, saying: "Allah, of whom he talked to us so much, has forsaken poor Muhammad, it is seen, and now abhors him." In that, the darkest hour, this word of Allah came to him,—

'"By the early hours and by the night when it is darkest, thy Lord has not forsaken thee nor does He hate thee. And verily the latter portion shall be better for thee than the former.

'"And verily thy Lord shall give to thee and thou shalt know His favour."

'Was not that prophecy fulfilled? Yet who could have foreseen, in that dark hour, the splendour of the latter portion of the Prophet's life? That word is spoken to Islâm to-day. We may not—Allah knows!—have reached the darkest hour. But this is plain for every man to see, who looks beyond the mere externals of this mortal life: five years ago was born a new, more fervent spirit in Islâm, drawing men nearer to the Prophet (Allah bless and keep him), and his fortunate companions, away from dead traditions. From that we may reasonably date a new beginning. My brethren, it is once again the early hours. And that new, faithful spirit which we cherish and defend will not be lost, for it is good; it cannot die, for it is part of Allah's mercy. Here, or elsewhere among the Muslim peoples it will be triumph, and in triumph flourish and become a blessing to the world—if Allah wills! Not all the might of all the Christian powers can extinguish it. What matter then though we all suffer, though we die a cruel death, so long as we are servants of the Heavenly will against the Powers of Evil which must pass away.

"'Say not of those who are slain in Allah's way that they are dead; nay, they are living, only you do not perceive,

"'And assuredly We shall try you with something of fear and hunger, and lack of men and fruits; but give glad tiding to the persevering.

"'Those who when calamity befalls them say: 'We are Allah's, and unto him we are returning.' These are they on whom are blessings from Allah and mercy. These are the rightly guided.'"

He ceased speaking. There was silence until Camruddin exclaimed,—

'Allah reward you for that sermon, khôja efendi, for it is truth, and it has healed my soul of pain.'

Nobody else had time to speak, for at that moment Dikran Efendi, the Armenian, rushed into the room, weeping, dishevelled, and gestulating wildly.

'Efendilarim, pardon! But the news—the awful news!
It is the end for my unhappy race. His noble Highness,
most enlightened and benign of men, riddled with bullets like a savage beast. May the murderers be crucified
and hewn in pieces! May those who urged them to the
deed rot painfully, and taste the pangs of hell while yet
alive! May lepers spit upon their deathbed, and dogs de-
file their graves both morn and evening! … Efendilarim,
pardon! I am deeply moved. What will become of us
Armenians now? I ask you! Now that we have no strong,
sincere, enlightened Highness to protect us from those
malefactors of our race who are the hounds of Russia:
may they all be flayed alive and disembowelled! … Allah,
pity! It is seen now that the Russians are too strong for
us. They will conquer all the country and enslave us.' He
collapsed, with sobs, on the divan.

'Never, while there remains a Turkish State and Turkish
army,' exclaimed Basri bey in reassuring tones. 'Things are
not yet so desperate, in sha'llah. Be comforted, efendim.
Allah is merciful. He gives the victory to whom He will.
Our simple duty is to fight against injustice, every man,
to the last gasp. And if we perish in the struggle, we are
sure of our reward.'

'Vâh! I am not a fighter, Bey efendim. Such noble sentiments are not for me, or such as me. I thrill to them;
they stir the marrow in my bones; but I cannot espouse
them. They are the glory of the Turks; for that we love
them as we love all virtues inherent in the splendour of
your noble race. To see that race condemned, its splendour dimmed by foul aspirations, the menace of extinc-
tion hanging over it, is hell's torment for us. That is chief
among the causes of my grief to-day …

'Efendilarim, pardon! I am deeply moved, Our hope

was in His Highness Mahmud Shevket Pasha, that he would shame the wicked Russians, and overcome, by reason, the objections of the Western Powers. To-day that hope is dead. The Russians are too strong and clever for us, that is evident. They are going to conquer—may they all be crucified! What is to become of us Armenians now? We shall be forced to listen to the words, the harsh commands of those of our own nation who are slaves of Russia. What else in reason can we do, since they are going to win? That is my trouble. It afflicts me horribly. It breaks my heart—a lover of the Turks, a friend of liberty and progress—to witness the approach of this most dire fatality … Efendilarim, pardon! You will understand, for you are generous, that fear alone could drive us to adopt a course so hateful, so totally opposed to all our inclinations—our hearts are all Osmanli, faithful to the only friends we have on earth. But they, the malefactors— may they all be blown to bits—will threaten us with death and loss of property …What can we do? O Allah, slay me quite! O Jesus, help me, for I writhe in torment. O Holy Ghost, give comfort to my soul! … Vâh! Vâh! the world is cruel and most vile!'

The well-bred, quiet Turks surveyed the speaker with amazement, supposing that the shock of evil news had turned his brain. The substance of his speech, when they collected it, seemed passing strange to their intelligence, and such as no man worthy of the name would utter in his sober senses. There was a space of silence broken only by the sobbing of the stout Armenian, who sat now with face hidden in his hands. At length the khôja said in an indignant tone,—

'Efendim, deign to answer me one question! Would you rather be the victim of injustice, or would you rather commit injustice, supposing that the choice were put before you.'

The Armenian raised his head and eyed the questioner a shade distrustfully. His sobs had ceased. He hesitated for a moment ere he answered with a smile, half knowing and half deprecating: '"The victim of injustice" is the right religious answer, that is known. But as the world goes it is better to be on the top. No one would choose to be the victim of injustice if he could by any means escape that fate. A man must live. His natural aim is to preserve himself ... Efendilarim, pardon! Have I answered right?'

The Turks said nothing, but Dikran Efendi did not seek to know the meaning of their silence. Remembrance of his bitter grief recurring to him, he hid his face again and sobbed anew, till Ferid Bey, moved to compassion by his state, gave orders for a room to be prepared for him where he might rest until his manhood was restored; whither he soon afterwards repaired, supported by two servants of the house, exhausting thanks for such unheard-of kindness.

Directly he was gone Ferid turned towards the khôja and asked curiously,—

'Why did you put that question to the wretched man?'

'Because it is a test by which to tell infallibly a true believer from an infidel.'

'Then I am a believer,' exclaimed Ferid gravely, as if in awe of the most strange discovery. Every one laughed, but the mad bey continued seriously,—

'Camruddin, my friend, at last I can partake of your sublime enthusiasm. Henceforth I am a Muslim and a Yeni Turk. The feeling came to me when I first heard the tale of Mahmud Shevket's martyrdom. I longed to lead an army against Russia. And the khôja efendi deigned to speak s feelingly—I wonder why he never spoke to me like that before—the feeling became fixed. Praise be to Allah, I am something now.'

'Praise be to Allah!' said the khôja, smiling gravely. 'If it is Allah's will, you are reformed, efendim. But conduct only is the test. We have your Honour's bare assertion, but no proof as yet.'

'Cuckold!' roared Deyli Ferid. 'Do you doubt my word?'

Chapter XLII

IT WAS CLEAR moonlight. Camruddin sat out with Reshideh Hânum upon a balcony of her kiosk which overlooked the garden. Both were too anxious and too sad to sleep, for thought of what might be occurring in the sovereign city towards which they listened for the sound of firing. The death of Mahmud Shevket Pasha, people said, was intended as a prelude to a general massacre of the Progressive party. If that were so, there might be danger for a man like Camruddin. He was not thinking of himself, however, nor was the woman whose hand rested on his arm concerned for him. Their fear was for the Turkish realm and Muslim progress.

But as the hours wore on towards the dawn, the beauty of the night possessed them more and more. The task of listening, indeed, was hopeless, for the night was full of noises. Four nightingales were singing in the very garden underneath their balcony. The frogs were quacking hoarsely in the lily-pond. Cocks kept crowing, dogs kept howling afar off, and a watchman in the distance raised from time to time the cry of 'Yanghîn Vâr!' (There is a fire.)

'It is a midnight of old Turkish poets,' murmured Reshideh, clasping the arm of Camruddin. 'The light imprisoning those trees is like a milky gem. And hear the bulbul, how he pipes in clear Osmanli: "Rose, Rose,

Rose, Rose! Open, open, open!" Surely he must under-stand. The frogs, too, speak good Turkish, so the chil-dren say. All harmless creatures choose our language as a compliment because we are not proud and cruel towards them like the other nations … Hear that faint sighing of the trees! How exquisite! Man's lordship over other creatures seems an empty boast. The other creatures are to-night in full command. They make their voices loud and beautiful, to calm our grief. It is as if they took us in their arms. Poor, poor Osmanlis! Efendim, I have always been in love with night. It seems to understand the feel-ings of a tragic race. Its very sadness used to fill me with wild pleasure when I was a child. And all the creatures of the night are kind, I think, since it is theirs, and yet they welcome us.'

Camruddin quoted the Coran, declaiming,—

'And not an animal in the earth, nor a bird flying with wings, but is a people like unto yourselves. We have omit-ted nothing in the book of Our decrees. Unto their Lord they will be gathered.'

'True,' she whispered; and after that sat silent a long while, inhaling gusts of perfume from the garden, until Camruddin inquired what she was pondering so deeply.

'Pardon, efendim! I was thinking there would be no bitterness if we should perish and resign our sovereignty to all those "peoples like unto ourselves"—peoples who act as Allah has decreed that they should act, without reflection, so without injustice. I think of Nature as our friend, for we have never wronged her. It is the thought of greedy, cruel and unnatural men as our supplanters, and not the thought of death, which maddens us.'

'The thought of death is dear to us Osmanlis,' an-swered Camruddin, with pride. 'That is Allah's mercy to us, since the menace of a cruel death is always on us from the Christian hordes. The Christians, as I gather from their literature, are afraid of death, esteeming it the greatest evil in the world.'

'You are now thinking of our dear Gul-raaneh. So am I.'

'Gul-raaneh, Mahmud Shevket, Hasan Riza, Niazi— not one of them but met death as a friend. The grief is not for them, but their survivors. Efendim, I am not considering my private woes. My thought is of Islâm and of our country. I ask myself whom have we left, and I see no one who is able to replace the great ones lost to us. I see a number of good men, but none of that high virtue which marked Niazi Bey and Mahmud Shevket Pasha. The Pera Palace and Tokatlian's appeal to some of them more than the mosques of Aya Sofia and Sultan Ahmed. And Europeans, meeting them, misjudge us all, for as my comrade, Handsome Mustafa, has often told me, an Osmanli is not an Osmanli while in their surroundings, and they, for their part, cannot see him in his home. I fear that now we may lose sight of high ideals and, with no great man to guide us, may indulge in quarrels and ambitions dear to lesser men.'

'Then what will happen to us?' faltered Reshideh, 'surrounded as we are by none but enemies? I feel to-night that we are doomed, and yet I am not downcast.'

'Why should you be downcast, for we are not the end, though we shall serve the end if Allah wills. If we are doomed, it may well be that our destruction by injustice will be the signal for the great revival of Islâm. These are the early hours; for light and darkness, good and evil, life and death, succeed each other always by Divine decree. Each has its usefulness towards Allah's purpose. But evil will not triumph ultimately, that is sure. "It is a promise of Allah, who never breaks His promise, but the majority of men do not perceive." Allah is greater!'

'Allah is greater!' cried his wife with fervour. 'Then let them kill us! We are His and shall return to Him.' ~

Glossary

Aferîn	Congratulations!
Arabaji	Driver
Bashibazouk	Turkish irregular soldier
Bimbashi	Major
Caïmmacâm	Governor
Chaûsh	Sergeant
Charshaf	Islamic headscarf
Cavass	Policeman or courier
Efendim	*Sir*
Efendilarim	*Sirs*
Eyvet	Yes
Fedaï	Someone prepared to sacrifice himself in war.
Ghiaours	Unbelievers
Gyuzel	Handsome
Hânum	Lady
Hâzir	At once!
Istaghferu'llah	God forgive me!
Jehennum	Hell
Kaïk	caique, Turkish rowing-boat
Kalfa	craftsman, journeyman
Kara-gyuz	Turkish shadow-puppet
Khalifa	Caliph
Khôja	Muslim religious leader

Kismet	Fate
Mekteb	School
Mujahidlar	Men engaged upon Jihad.
Mukhtâr	Village headman
Mulâzim	Lieutenant
Mushîr	Field Marshal
Ombashi	Corporal
Osmanlilik	Ottomanism
Selamlik	Men's reception area of a house
Sultan Eyub	The holiest shrine of Istanbul
Takbîr	Cry of 'Allahu Akbar' (God is Greater)
Tokatlian's	Hotel and Restaurant on the Grand Rue de Pera, disliked by Pickthall.
Padishah	Emperor
Ulema	Muslim scholars
Von der Golz	Colmar Freiherr von der Goltz (1843-1916). Prussian general in Turkish service.
Yeni Turk	'New Turk'; Young Turk
Yuzbashi	Captain